June 1995

To Margaret —

With much love and special Thanks for making our 50th the "best".

# WHERE THE WIND BLOWS FREE
# A STORY OF THE CHEROKEE INDIANS

*Lyle Rishell*

GEORGE MASON UNIVERSITY PRESS
Fairfax, Virginia

Copyright © 1994 by
**George Mason University Press**
4400 University Drive
Fairfax, VA 22030

All rights reserved
Printed in the United States of America
British Cataloging in Publication Information Available

Distributed by arrangement with
National Book Network

4720 Boston Way
Lanham, MD 20706

3 Henrietta Street
London WC2E 8LU England

**Library of Congress Cataloging-in-Publication Data**

Rishell, Lyle.
Where the wind blows free : a story of the
Cherokee Indians / Lyle Rishell.
p.    cm.
1. Cherokee Indians—Fiction.  I.  Title.
PS3568.I66W58     1994
813'.54—dc20     93–37083 CIP

ISBN 0–913969–63–X (cloth : alk. paper)

 The paper used in this publication meets the minimum requirements of
American National Standard for Information Sciences—Permanence
of Paper for Printed Library Materials, ANSI Z39.48–1984.

# Cherokee Trail

To the big tree
walked the Indian
tears falling
spirit broken.

A new day
beginning
you can
only go up
expressing
a proud heritage
take someone
with you
you cannot
reach the top alone.

Indian walk
upright this way
may he continue
ascending forever.

# TABLE OF CONTENTS

# *A*CKNOWLEDGEMENTS

I wish to thank several people for their assistance in the preparation of this novel without whom my efforts would have been much more difficult. Many gave of their time and offered help when needed, and I am indebted to them for their patience.

Special thanks are offered to Ms. Marcia Rishell for permission to use the poem, "Cherokee Trail," written by her late husband and my brother, Les, who shared with me a warm affinity for the Cherokee Nation.

To Mr. Jonathan A. Taylor, Principal Chief, and Mr. Dan McCoy, Tribal Council Chairman of the Eastern Band of Cherokee Indians for their assistance;

To Dr. William Anderson, Professor of History and Cherokee historian, Western Carolina University, who reviewed the manuscript for historical accuracy, and who provided valuable insight and detailed suggestions that were incorporated into the story;

To Ms. Joan W. Greene, Archivist, Museum of the Cherokee Indians, who generously spent hours with me researching and reviewing historical documents and writings of the Cherokee Nation;

And finally, to my dear wife, Marilyn, who continues to be my severest critic and greatest supporter in everything I attempt to do.

# *Author's Note*

This is a story about Native Americans, or more specifically, the Cherokee Nation. I have attempted to describe the historical events that affected the tribe as well as their day-to-day activities, and have taken the liberty to change two significant happenings. The first is the earthquake.

A major earthquake rocked the Ohio-Mississippi Valleys in 1811. The epicenter was near New Madrid, Missouri. It was of such intensity that tremors covered an area of 300,000 square miles and reportedly was felt on both the East and West coasts. It was conceivable that earlier quakes would have impacted the Cherokee land area, one of which I created as happening in 1790.

The second event occurred in 1796. The dissension within the tribe caused by the broken treaties led to various Cherokee factions going into battle against the whites. Although some had limited success locally, the pressure of the white regular and militia forces signified the end of an era for the Cherokee Nation. During this time the tribe was dispersed and a small group of Indians escaped into the mountains. Grandfather Mountain is the second-highest topographic feature in North Carolina and is situated in the northwestern corner of the state near Tennessee, a part of the Great Smokies. I have portrayed Grandfather Mountain as a refuge or stronghold used by a small band of Indians as they tried to escape the migration of white settlers. Artifacts found there provide evidence that Indians lived on the mountain at one time. It may well have been a stopping place for Cherokees before moving into the Oconoluftee River region. I have used these actions as a basis for the search for a new homeland and the events that followed. All other dates are consistent with the historic era.

To paint an accurate picture of the Cherokee Nation during a very complex period of time, I have created a single village as the backdrop of the story. Some Cherokee villages, while integrated in many ways, remained isolated and retained the cultural traits, customs and habits of an earlier time. Descriptions of the primary characters—the Peace chiefs and the War chiefs, shamans or medicine men, white traders, as well as the political, judicial, social and religious systems that formed the basis of Cherokee life and society—have been constructed carefully.

For the most part, the major characters have been created to lend substance to the novel. However, several of the Indian and white personae played a significant and historical role in the Cherokee fight for independence. I have changed the names of certain tribal members to conform to the story, but the actions in which they were involved are authentic.

When one reconstructs the enveloping pressures on the Native Americans, it appears a certainty that white settlers would roll into the heartland of the country and force the Indians to give way. One wonders what might have happened to the Cherokee Nation if the revolt by the American colonists had not succeeded. The fact is that as large numbers of French and English immigrants arrived in the colonies, there was a continuing demand for more land to support a burgeoning population. With the English pushing from the coastal regions, the French from the North, and the Spanish in the south, major clashes were inevitable and the Indians were doomed. The white man's manifest destiny was to acquire land whenever and however he could. In that acquisition, he excelled.

Lyle Rishell
Potomac, Maryland
1992

The wind blows where it will and you hear the sound of it, but do not know whence it comes or whither it goes; so is everyone who is born of the Spirit.

John 3:8

# PROLOGUE

The man lay motionless in the tall, wet grass, face pressed to the ground, trying to gather strength ebbing from his battered body. He had been hit three times, and his right leg was nearly useless from the large bullet that had entered and torn apart as it slashed through. He had managed to stay on his feet until the second round smacked into his arm, but still he refused to give up the fight. The last bullet was the mortal wound. As he swung around and sank his hatchet blade into the blue-clad soldier ending his life, the heavy slug struck the man's chest and knocked him backwards, and he screamed in frustration knowing he was finished. Only the adrenaline coursing through his body kept him moving forward.

The end was near, that much he knew, but some inexorable force urged him on as he inched his way over the ground toward the rocks jumbled together at the edge of the clearing. He turned his head and licked droplets of water from the grass as the soft rain continued. Only dimly could he hear the occasional sound of firing or yelling as he faded in and out of consciousness. The pain in his torn bloodied leg and arm was unlike any hurt he had ever experienced, and his chest heaved at each breath he sucked, but he pressed on determined to reach the rocks. His eyes focused on them laying directly ahead, and then glazed over and he could barely discern their shape. He slumped in place and gulped the sweet air that tore at his lungs.

The warrior was like a dying animal seeking some place to die. He moved, a few inches at a time, using his good leg and arm to pull himself forward. His body was on fire, each severed nerve-ending sending impulses to his mind, telling him it was nearly over. He was on the knife's edge of semi-consciousness, but he willed his tortured body to move again, and then again, over-and-over levering his body, sliding it forward, until he reached the pile of rocks and pulled himself into the shadow of the largest one where he lay quietly, waiting for the end.

He lay there in his sanctuary. "Oh God," he cried aloud, as he suffered his wounds before he lost consciousness again, and then there was no pain. When he came to again, dark had fallen and the night sounds intruded on him. He thought of the battle just fought, and knew the tribe had won the day and that made him happy. His thoughts turned to his wife waiting on the mountain for him to return, and he grew sad at the thought of not seeing her or his young son again. Then, as he lay there, he realized that he was beyond pain now and a serenity enveloped him, wrapped him in its arms, lifted him from the depth of despair, and he knew peace as he had never known peace before. Sweet, blessed peace. And he surrendered to it.

# 1

# LAND OF DREAMS

The howling winds of sleet and snow that had slashed across the open valley and iced-over streams were fast disappearing. Winter was ending for the tribe gathered under the branches of the woods. Four long moons had brought sickness and despair across the lands of the Cherokees. The trees had shed their clothing of ice, the snow patches in the forests had melted, and the streams ran with icy waters drained from the hills above. Spring was now upon the tribe. Those who had died during the harsh season had been placed upon the death-posts, and the warming sun hurried the healing of the rest.

Spring came. It came after the freezing, leaden skies of yesterday. Wild flowers, yellow as bear fat, and the red blossoms of the crabapple trees, heralded the way. The sun rose slowly, as if rising too fast would spoil the breaking day. It brought beauty to all who looked for it, and it took nothing away, except the gloom of the winter days just past.

It was a time of joy, of anticipation, of hope. Trees exploded with buds, grasses and flowers came alive with vivid colors, birds sang and mated, and the tribe celebrated the bursting season. The Great Chief held council with the young braves, telling them of the hiding places of the black bear and scores of other animals. In spite of a depletion of game the Cherokees were still successful in their hunt. The women cleaned the animals and prepared the cooking fires, and when they were lit and the coals ready went about their work, happy to see and feel the sun's warmth. Peace was in the land and all was well again. It was the beginning of a new season.

The Cherokee Nation held these lands of the Eastern forests as their territory, while on their northern boundary lay the Shawnees. To the northeast the Powhatan occupied the rolling hills and valleys of the James River. For the most part the Cherokees and Powhatan kept friendly council and did not treat each other as enemies or 'count coup'. Their most bitter foes were the Creeks, and the two tribes waged war frequently. The Creeks and the Cherokees were well-matched. They were powerful warrior tribes who delighted in warfare against each other, and raiding parties were dispatched constantly to harass or attack and revenge a previous fight.

The Cherokees knew the Tuscarora of the coast who lived among the swamps and along the Great Water and considered them enemies as well. At some point in their history the whites had suggested the two nations sign a peace accord, but the Cherokees demurred. They loved to fight, and giving up war was completely unacceptable.

Near their camp site was the Nantahala, where the river waters raced and plunged hundreds of feet into a beautiful, deep canyon, which the tribe believed was haunted with spirits from the past, called the Little People. Here the Cherokee lived, for the mountains were home to deer and bear, quail and squirrels and rabbits, and even an occasional mountain cat. Their skins and meat provided shelter and food, containers for storage, and clothing to protect them against the elements. The forests gave them wood for their fires and weapons, bark for their canoes and boughs for their beds. As long as the tribe held this land it could weather the seasons, live and die in harmony, and pay homage to the Great Spirit for supplying its needs.

The young girl, like all the other members of the clan, welcomed the Spring weather. She sensed the freshness of the changing season and was aware that all around her, family and friends were shedding the indolence and lethargy of winter and slipping easily into the joy and excitement of Spring.

As the sun rose higher in the sky, broken by a few gentle clouds of fluff, she yearned for the tranquility of another place. She felt some inner need to gain her freedom from all the activity around her. Rising from the pile of new furs which lay at her feet, she picked up her staff, and without fully comprehending why, started toward the river far beyond the camp. The sun, one-quarter of its way across the heavens, was warm, and she savored it on her shoulders. As she gained the river's edge she was surprised to notice ice fragments along the shore where the rays of the sun had not yet reached.

She walked slowly, completely attuned to the birth of the season, lost in her thoughts, pausing now and again to enjoy the sight and sound of the running waters. Upon reaching the Nantahala, she marveled at how her stream joined the larger river near the gorge, and just as quickly shuddered, as she remembered the legend of the Little People, or the Nunnehi, other creatures rarely seen, who lived in this place.

The Little People were tiny humans, so the legends told, who lived in the forests and caves and other inaccessible places, and were known to have special powers. The tribe accepted these spirits, called on them for certain needs, and left food and water for them as an act of kindness. Some of the children had seen them, had even talked to them. They said the Little People sang songs and danced among the trees and rocks. But whatever and wherever they hid, Snow Deer wanted no part of them.

Hurrying away from the confluence of the rivers, she climbed along the larger stream, wanting to get away from the deep darkness of the canyon. As she walked higher and farther, her confidence and joy returned.

She wondered aloud who might live here in this lovely place, where the waters tumbled over and around the rocks below, where birds gathered at a quiet pool to drink, and where no other sign of human life existed. She saw three deer, a doe and her twin fawns eating the tender buds from a wild cherry tree, but they did not flash their white tails as she passed them by. Starting to tire, she decided to rest beside the stream where she could watch the waters far below. Too absorbed in the beauty around her, she failed to notice the hairline crack on the stone ahead. As she stopped, placing her weight upon it, the rock split and moved beneath her foot.

She tried to catch herself, but the soft ground on which the stone lay yielded to the thawed earth, and as she scrabbled frantically to catch her balance, fell toward the rushing waters below. Falling, she had time to utter one scream, and then she hit the water.


The man had been startled by a flock of geese winging up the river. He lifted his head slowly, as if to smell the wind. Then he lowered the trap he was holding into the water, picked up his rifle, and withdrew from the river's edge. He climbed carefully up the steep slope and paused briefly at the crest before slipping effortlessly into the forest. He stopped when he reached some large stones surrounded by trees, a perfect place from where he could watch the path along the river. He was nearly six-feet in height and broad-chested. His hair was thick and long and light, pulled back from his brow and tied with a rawhide thong. His eyes, a brilliant blue, sparkled from beneath his long brows, and he was tanned from the sun and the wind and the weather. He wore buckskin pants and an overblouse made of rabbit fur.

Standing in the shadows, he withdrew some pemmican from his waistbag and slowly nibbled on the cake as he carefully scanned the path. Then he saw her. He was relieved to see that it was a woman, for she would cause him no harm. He watched her as she slowly approached, head held high, dark hair, proud legacy of an ancient race. Never glancing to her right or left, she looked ahead, seemingly oblivious of the deer around her as she moved among them. There was no sense of awkwardness about her movements, but only grace and beauty, like the young doe and the fawns grazing, untouched or spoiled by the stag waiting nearby.

As she came closer he studied her, not wanting to reveal his presence because he did not want to frighten her. She was small, perhaps five feet tall, and slim of body. She was wearing a knee-length tunic, nearly white from bleaching, with small rosettes of beads or colored bones outlining the bodice which clung to her body. Her hair, as black as a raven's wing, flowed down and over her shoulders. A white headband held her hair in place, and moccasins covered her feet. She was exquisite.

Snow Deer moved slowly, not wanting to break the magic of her adventure. As she moved he continued to watch her. Who was she? From what tribe? From where had she come? Was there a camp nearby? There was something about her which captured his attention. What was it? And then, in his mind, he saw in her womanhood an admixture of innocence and maturity, fashioned together in perfect form, and he wanted to call out to her, but refrained from doing so. Nathaniel Tennyson, a newcomer to America, could not remember having seen anyone quite as lovely or as graceful since leaving Jenny.

He had arrived in Jamestown four years earlier in 1779, expecting to find his fortune and a new life in this new nation. But it was a time of revolution. The American colonists had decided they no longer wished to be vassals of King George, and the drums of war beat stronger after a series of tax and trade laws were pressed upon them. The King, out of ignorance, poor advice, or lack of charity, expressed little sympathy for the colonists. The Crown maintained the colonists had representation in England, and indeed wanted the benefits of the relationship without the obligation of taxation. The enmity between the motherland and the colonies surfaced, and the seeds of independence planted by Patrick Henry and others in the Colonial Capital of Williamsburg commenced to sprout.

The Crown's position on the colonial issues leading to the revolt had been publicized daily in the English papers. Every Englishman was expected to put country before the colonies and support the King and the British army in America. A formidable force had been assembled to put down the insurrection, but as he read between the lines Nathaniel discovered that the irregular troops of the Continental Army were fast becoming proficient in the art of war. The militia and volunteer groups were bloodying the British, and additional Redcoats, hired German soldiers, even convicted prisoners were being shipped to fight the American "rabble in arms."

The colonists were not to be taken lightly. First there was Lexington, and then Concord and Bunker Hill, and a series of battles that culminated in the Declaration of Independence. Three long years before, the thirteen colonies had signed and adopted the charter which established the association of the various states. Never again would the colonies be subservient to the Crown. The British army continued to fight, but the losses at Boston, Trenton, Valley Forge, and the extraordinary defeat of the British at Saratoga signaled the revolt was far from being over. A year earlier the French had become America's ally, and surely this move would change the outcome of the war.

There was something about these colonists that ignited Nathaniel's interest. And so it happened that he found a berth on a merchant ship carrying war supplies to the British forces still hanging on in America. He was certain that as a British subject he would be compelled to join the army once he arrived in the colonies. But when he disembarked there was such disorder during the unloading that he quietly slipped away and disappeared.

For him there was no doubt about the future. Eventually, the British would be defeated and the colonies would get on with their task of recovery from the war. Now he was glad that he had come, for he had found an excitement and sense of vibrancy in this new land, and this was where he intended to remain.

Nathaniel was born in Sussex, England in 1758. His parents were God-fearing people who instilled in Nathaniel at an early age that whatever he set out to accomplish in life, he should pursue it to the end. They were strict disciplinarians who often used the rod on the rebellious boy, but they tempered the punishment with fairness. Although they allowed Nathaniel more freedom of expression than the other boys of the village, he wanted more than they were willing to give. Shortly before his eighth birthday, they sent him away to school. They believed, and certainly hoped, that the headmaster would take Nathaniel under his guidance, and with determined tutelage (and blows, if he so needed), he would return to them a model child.

This was not to be. Nathaniel loved every facet of the school away from home. He enjoyed the camaraderie of the other students, the learning experience, and he even tolerated the rod when he got out of line for some infraction of the rules. The boarding school sparked his imagination, and it soared as he learned what the Crown was doing around the world. He loved reading about the unfolding events, and he devoured every morsel that was thrown his way. His awakened passion soon focused on the colonies and the hardships and disappointments the English settlers were experiencing. He listened attentively to his teachers who spoke of great events happening abroad, and of the men and women who were making a home in the savage land.

Above all, he became excited most about the native Americans. He read everything he could obtain about them. These "Red men," who had come out of the forests and saved the early English pioneers, who had taught his fellow countrymen how to plant and harvest grain, and had helped them preserve their foods and hunt game in the dark forests. He thought they must be magnificent people. He allowed his imagination to soar. He observed the natives were teachers, in every sense of the word, and while they were heathen peoples, or so the books said, they must also have been generous to come to the aid of the English.

He was not content to just read about the Indians; he made himself a nuisance to the teachers. He asked questions endlessly, and spent hours waiting for the proctor so that he could pounce on him, to hear the stories told again, and he never tired of reading and learning about the natives.

"Tell me more," he pleaded, "for you say the Indians are savage creatures. Why? What have they done to the English?"

The proctor erupted. "They are less than human! They fight for the love of war. They cannot be trusted; they pretend to be friends but are quick to change loyalties."

"Have we not taken their land? Are the English any better?"

"Of course we are better. We have a great country, and our system is based on laws that protect our society. What do they possess? They live like wild animals, never caring about themselves. All they know is war. What do they know about social justice, the right and responsibility of government? Nathaniel, you are young and idealistic, and you see only what you want to see."

"You said earlier that when our first settlers arrived the Indians helped them. What made them change? Why do you think they are inferior?"

"We cannot educate them or convert them to our religion. We want them to be farmers and take up our ways, but they refuse. Now all they want from us is our strong drink and guns which they then turn on us. No, Nathaniel, they will never be like us. Forget your ideas that the Indians are good people. They will always be savages."

Nathaniel could not accept what the procter had told him. His quest for knowledge was the beginning of his belief that only if he could see them himself, and have the chance to live among them, would he be totally satisfied.

His interest in their way of life continued to grow. When he sat for his history boards, during which he wrote an impassioned plea for the native Americans, his teachers were so impressed that he was recommended to the university. There he would have gone, but for an incident that occurred the last summer before he was to start. He fell head-over-heels in love.

When Nathaniel returned home, his parents realized how he had changed, intellectually and physically. They could hardly believe their good fortune. No longer was he wantonly rebellious or dissatisfied with life (or so they believed), but he had matured into a fine young man. He talked with them about the English settlements and the Indians in America, but their world had not expanded as his had, and he found them less than interested in what he said. They were pleased when he told them he was going on to university, and his folks insisted that he spend the summer with them relaxing and having fun; school would be time enough to get serious. They thought that a party would be just the thing to get the young man's attention away from America.

The homecoming party was arranged for the following week. As he had anticipated, it was good to see neighbors and old friends as well as new ones. Then he met Jenny Howard. She appeared late in the party, and he was so taken by her physical beauty and excitement that he quickly forgot about Indians and America, or even about going off to the university.

He was standing with an old school chum when he saw her for the first time. "Where did she come from, Peter?" he exclaimed, drinking in the sight of her.

"Oh, she's a new neighbor of yours, Nate. The family moved in several months ago. From what I've heard, the beauty is untouchable. Her name is Jenny Howard."

"Do you know her, Peter?"

"Sure, but not as well as I would like. I met her at the Stans' party about a month ago, but she hardly gave me time to introduce myself. She's very smug and sure of herself. The Swains hereabouts have tried to break through her shell, but none have made it. I'm frankly surprised she is here tonight."

"Do me a favor. Introduce me."

They pushed their way across the room to meet her. She was standing apart from the rest of the guests, surveying the crowd. She smiled toward him, and his heart melted as they came closer.

"Hello, Jenny," Peter said, but before he could make the introduction, her eyes met Nathaniel's. She ignored Peter.

"It's Nathaniel Tennyson, isn't it?" she asked.

He smiled. "That's right."

"I'm Jenny Howard." The lass before him was beautiful. He guessed her age to be around twenty. But what fascinated him most was her long, black hair that framed her face in curls. She was wearing a black and white gown, cut low in front, and he was instantly aware of her loveliness.

"So Peter has told me," Nathaniel smiled. "He says we are neighbors, and that he met you at another party." As soon as he said this, Peter coughed, "Excuse me. I've caught sight of someone arriving. I'll leave you two alone. You can get acquainted."

As soon as Peter turned away, she said, "I understand you're home on holiday. Mother said you sat for your boards and will be going to university this fall."

"That is the plan right now, but since I've been home and announced my intentions, I've had second thoughts."

"And what is that, Nathaniel?"

"It is just an idea that I'm thinking about. It may be an alternative to school. But enough of this. Let's go get a drink and escape somewhere. Parties bore me dreadfully." She put her hand on his arm. "Only if you tell me what the alternative is," she threatened playfully.

Taking her arm he guided her to the food and refreshments and eventually, they were able to escape the guests and go off to the garden. When they had found a bench and sat down, she said, "I'm glad I came tonight. I felt I wanted to meet you. After all, we are neighbors."

"What have you seen since moving in? Have you been to the old ruins? I love it here, and I've never grown tired of it. People say that it is stifling but I've always found peace here. I would like very much to show you around."

"That would be lovely, Nathaniel. If you are going to be home for awhile, I would like that. But tell me, kind Sir," she said impishly, "what did you mean earlier when you mentioned 'having second thoughts'?"

"Jenny." It was the first time he had used her name, and he liked the sound as it rolled off his tongue. "Jenny, if you promise not to think me foolish, I'm interested in the New World. I think I want to go to the colonies."

"That's splendid," she said, "but for whatever reason? Surely you must have something in mind. And what would you do there?"

"If I decided to go before I finished university, I would have to learn some trade. I don't think that would be much of a problem, however," he added.

"But what is your real interest, Nathaniel?" she asked.

He did not answer her immediately, afraid she would not understand. He had heard much about America and how rich the lands were, and the opportunities for anyone who wanted to work. There were many trades to choose from, and the people were friendly, and he would make it on his own. He knew from all the tales told at home that America's frontiers were being pushed further West, and he wished to be a part of the movement. The study of the Indians had been his primary and consuming effort.

Finally, he replied. "I'm interested in the American Indians . . . no, Jenny, it is more than interest. I want to see them for myself. I've read everything I could find about them and I want to see them before they are gone."

"Gone where?"

"I don't know. Just gone, I guess. The colonists keep moving into their lands, and I suspect that soon they will be forced into the wilderness even more. I want to see them before that happens."

"A noble thought, Nathaniel, but not very realistic. Shouldn't you finish your studies first? Then you will not have to learn a trade."

"That is true, but let's forget it for now. It is good to talk with you, especially since I have not gotten through to my folks. Thank you for listening."

"My pleasure," she said flippantly. "So what do you want to show me?" She leaned toward him and said, "Nathaniel, I came tonight because my mother and your mother thought we might have something in common. She talked you up a bit and I was curious. Now that I've met you, I'm a little confused. I don't know what it is that we have in common." She squeezed his hand. "I think you have already decided to go to America. But then again," she laughed, "I still want to see everything hereabouts . . . you did promise to show me, you know?"

In the dim light he looked down on her. "Jenny, I haven't decided anything. Of one thing I am certain though . . . I like you very much, and I do hope we can spend some time together. I'm glad you decided to come tonight. You are a good listener."

"Nonsense, Nathaniel, if I didn't like to listen I would not be here with you. Look, why don't you come by tomorrow and show me your kingdom," she teased. "Now we should return to the party, don't you think? You're the guest of honor, you know."

Walking back across the lawn toward the house, he thought, "She ought to love her mirror." She was small and lovely and there was an expectancy about her, as if life had just handed her a special gift. From the shape of her ears to her clear, sparkling eyes, to her pleasing lips and endearing smile, she was complete. God had made in her an original and she needed no re-touching, no change, and no improvement.

The following morning he saddled two horses and rode over to meet her. She came out carrying a small wicker basket and swung easily into the saddle without his help. Jenny was dressed in a dark riding suit, and Nathaniel flushed when he saw her figure. He watched her closely as she tied the basket in place and started down the trail.

"Do you know where we're going?" he shouted.

"Of course not! You take the lead. 'Shouldn't waste any time, should we?"

He laughed. "I thought we would ride along the river to the ruins and show you one of the trails through the forest. Did you bring something to eat?"

"I did. You did not say how long we might be gone, and I guessed you would not remember," she replied. "How far is it?"

"Several miles, I suppose . . . at least, several hours. But when you get tired we can stop."

It was a beautiful day, and when they got to the river Jenny suggested they stop and rest the horses. They sat beside the flowing stream while the horses grazed nearby. "It is peaceful here, Nathaniel, just like you said last night, and so lovely. Do you think you will find anything half as pretty in America?"

"Probably not. Certainly I will not find a lass as pretty as you there."

"You say all the right things, kind Sir, but how much is true?" she asked.

Now he turned to her and looked into her eyes. "Jenny, do not think unkindly of me, but you're lovely. I said so last night when I first saw you. Peter agreed, but he also thought you were untouchable. I think we get along well, but I'm afraid for you as well as myself. I didn't know you existed until yesterday and already I'm under your spell."

Jenny took his hand. "Please don't be, Nathaniel. I feel much the same. Last night, as we sat and talked in the garden, my emotions were very tangled. I did not know quite how to react. I liked you from the moment I first saw you, but after we talked I suspected that you had already decided to leave, and there was little chance that I could say anything to change your mind. Like you, I too am afraid."

They were silent then, until Nathaniel pulled her and she came into his arms. "Hold me, Nathaniel, just for a bit. And give me time to think this through." He held her close, lost in the magic spell she had cast upon him, and she succumbed to his embrace and lay in his arms quietly.

From that moment on, Jenny and Nathaniel were inseparable. For the next several months they were together every day. He showed her all his childhood haunts, escorted her to the never-ending round of parties, introduced her to pleasures neither had previously experienced, and fell hopelessly in love with her. He was consumed by her, intoxicated by the very sight of her, and there was none other who equalled her promised love. For her part, Jenny believed in this man who had brought so much happiness into her life. He was all she desired or would ever want, and yet, there was a part of her which she withheld from him. But she could never say why.

There was much more to her than met his eyes that first time. Within her mind, hidden away from most, underlying her most secret ambitions, was a changing soul. Its composition was much more complex, more difficult to perceive, and more easily camouflaged. How did he know? Her eyes gave her away. They spoke volumes, but one had to look into them to glean their mysteries. They shed light on whatever she said, even the way she said it. Her eyes sparkled and danced when she became excited about something, but they quickly lost their lustre when she lost interest or sought some escape from the problem at hand.

Nathaniel could not escape her look or her smile or her physical beauty. She shared her thoughts with him, opened the hidden part of her a bit, and he was grateful for the few moments she gave him. When she talked he remembered the way she had of pushing her hair away from her face, opening her countenance as well as her confidences. There was a special grace in her acceptance of his sympathy and understanding, but when she talked about unhappy experiences or the memories of another time and place, her features changed, and sadness washed across her face as the innocence and wonders of the youth she remembered were gone.

There had been no other women in his life. She was lovely and every sense he mustered amplified this simple fact: when he looked at her, he saw beauty; when he looked on her he saw indefinable goodness; and when he looked into her, he saw someone he wanted to love. He knew she would be easy to love, and that her love in return would be totally open and complete.


Jenny Howard. How long had it been since she had crossed his mind? Now he remembered, and his thoughts turned to her even as the Indian girl approached. Jenny had come into his life without pretense or promise, and when he first saw her he was certain she would leave it just as easily. There was an independency about her which unsettled him, but still one of the first thoughts that hit him when they met was that she was someone worth knowing.

He remembered the first time he saw her. She was dressed in black and white, and her coal-black hair was teased by the wind and fell to her shoulders, and he was captivated by her smile. She had grace and culture, but somehow her clothes did not fit the image she projected; they did not match the colors of her mind. She should be wearing red, he remembered thinking, for red is passion and excitement and joy of life and intensity and pride, and he saw each of these in her.

Looking back at that innocent period, he recognized how she had been able to insinuate herself into his life and his world, even though she was unaware of doing so. There were times when he could sense a "oneness" in their thinking; there were other times when she was so far away that he could not reach her, or break down the fences she had erected. He knew that he had presumed on their friendship, seeking much more than she was willing to share, and he also knew that he had desired her time and attention more than she was willing to give.

Now he attempted to rationalize it all away. He could pretend it never happened, that his love for her was nothing else but an illusive game of imagination. But he knew better, for what his eyes saw and what his heart felt was real. And that was certainly not his imagination.

He saw her one last time before he departed. She had made her decision to leave him, and he suspected it would be the last time he saw her. "Mother and I are going away for awhile too, Nathaniel," she said quietly.

"Oh. Where?"

"London. She thinks that I'm getting too wrapped up over you. She thinks I need a change of scenery."

"Do you? What do you think about it?" Nathaniel asked.

"She's probably right. I've been trying to sort out my feelings for a long time. I've guessed for some time that you had made up your mind about America. As much as I've tried to push the idea aside, hoping that you will stay, I know it won't happen. I love you, Nathaniel, but I can't go with you, so . . ."

"I'm sorry, Jenny. I really am." He reached for her hand but she pulled it away. "Like you, I have tried to figure it out myself. I want to stay, but something stronger than my love for you is pulling me away. And I do love you, Jenny. Very much. I wish I could explain it better, but I can't. Please don't think badly of me. Maybe, if I get it out of my system, I'll be back."

"I don't believe it, Nathaniel. There will be too much excitement and challenge for you there. But I'll miss you, my dearest friend, very much."

"I too, my love. Perhaps, more than you." He held her then, crushing her to his chest, as she sobbed her heart out over the ending of their love and the beginning of his new adventure.

Of their final meeting a few days later, he wished she had reached for him, or touched his hand, and told him that she understood the emotions that swirled around him, but that she resolutely refused to do. Yes, it was time to make an irreversible break, to shut out the inconsolable knowledge which all his experience had taught him, that the physical and emotional pleasure of knowing her was pure torture. Yet he knew that when they parted, they would remember nothing but good of each other, and they would never think badly of what might have been.

Before he left, Nathaniel penned one last note to her. Now he recalled the words he had written. "Stay sweet, and think of me with kindness. Remember also that I wished for you, as I shall do again as I leave. You are real to me, and whatever my faults, it is no fault of mine that I met you and fell in love with you. That is a very precious memory I take with me."

# 2

# *W*HITE *H*ORSE

Nathaniel had found many things he liked about America. But there was much that he did not enjoy or which he could accept. He longed for the open space of this great country, and during the time he worked in the settlement he envied the Indian tribes and the freedom they had, or what he thought they had. After nearly a year, he left the town and gravitated farther west to a new settlement. The town was located about a mile from a small Indian village. It was there that he started work as a trapper.

Nathaniel had become good at his trade. He knew the habits and the habitats of the otter, muskrat, and beaver, learned how and where to set traps, skin the animals, and preserve the furs. The land offered unlimited opportunities; animals were plentiful, and there was great demand for the furs. During his first year in America, surrounded by the Powhatan tribe of Virginia, he studied and learned Iroquoian, the mother language of the Cherokees. He was happy in the new village and its proximity to the Indian village located nearby.

On his daily excursions to check his traplines, he passed close to the small village, and over a period of time met some of the Indians who were trapping or hunting in the forest. Each time he came upon them in his wanderings, he stopped and talked. He asked them for advice about trapping and hunting and listened carefully to their words. He tried to get them to open up to him and share something of themselves; but while they were courteous to him, they kept their distance. The Indians paid little attention to the trapper whom they knew as

"Na-tan," but they respected his knowledge of the land and liked him for his interest in them.

As the months passed, Nathaniel became increasingly restless, and he decided to move on. The lives of the people were changing. The Indian village had become the crossroads for the traders moving east and west, and as they came and went, the Indians started to lose their identity. Traders were taking Indian wives, family structures were disintegrating, and the males of the tribe were taking up the same habits and customs of the whites.

It was a time of transition for those Indians living in the settlements. The whites wanted the Indians to raise cattle and hogs, to till the soil with a plow, to ride in a wagon, to wear white man's clothing, and to trade or sell something they owned for the goods they found in the trading stores. Rarely did they meet in Council, and they lost their desire to fight. The Indians of the village were being assimilated in the white man's culture without being aware of what was happening. Step-by-step, month-by- month, they became more dependent upon the white man and began sharing his ways and using his goods.

No longer was the Indian in control of his destiny. The white settlers quickly became the power and authority in the village and commenced establishing laws and imposing restrictions on the Indians. Their festivals and dances were banned; their religious ceremonies could no longer be conducted; and their land further subdivided to allow more settlers to come in. The whites continued to want even more space and there was little the Indians could do about it. The settlers were becoming a law unto themselves, and resented what they believed to be intrusions by the Indians into the life the whites had created on tribal lands.

It was at this point that White Horse came into Nathaniel's life. One day, as Nathaniel was returning from checking his trapline, he heard English voices yelling in the woods ahead. His first thought was that an Indian raid was in progress. Then the firing started, and he was certain that the whites were defending themselves from a war party. From the sounds of the guns he guessed there were two, but he had no way of estimating the number of Indians in the attacking force. He moved quickly through the woods hoping to surprise the raiders from the rear. As he got closer he realized the screaming was coming from an Indian, crying in English interspersed with Indian words. He started crawling forward. When he got within sight of the clearing, he was stunned to the core of his heart!

He saw the Indian first, his feet tied to a limb, hanging head down and almost touching the ground. He was shouting at the white men as they fired wildly into the grass at his head. He had been stripped, and the indignity of his nakedness brought fury to Nathaniel's mind. It was more than that; he was enraged at the scene before him! Never had he seen anything to compare with the suffering and humiliation the two young men were inflicting upon the hanging man. He leaped to his feet and raced for the men who appeared to be in their late teens. As he roared out of the woods, he fired a shot into the air. They froze in place as they watched Nathaniel explode on them. Before they had a chance to react, he stripped them of their rifles and grabbed them and threw them to the ground.

He looked down at them and screamed, "What in the name of God are you doing? Who is this man? Why do you have him hanging there? Are you both crazy?"

The younger man looked up at him and his mouth opened and closed as he tried to find words, and finally he blurted out, "We caught him down by the creek. He was fishin' in our favorite place, so we jus' decided that we din't want him near that there hole."

"Yeah, we thought mebbe we'd teach him a lesson. He don't need to be at our place. 'Sides that, he jus' an ole Injun, and he don't own this land."

Nathaniel was furious at what he had seen. He wanted to lash out at them, but instead he kicked their rifles out of reach and went over to the tree. He turned to the boys. "Stay where you are; I'll settle with you after I see to the man."

He reached above the Indian and with a quick move slashed the rope. The Indian fell heavily to the ground. Now he saw they had tied his hands behind him. Leaning down, Nathaniel carefully cut the thongs. Then he reached out and pulled the man to his feet. "You alright, my friend? Have they hurt you?"

The Indian brushed the debris from his face and body where it had lodged from the firing, and pulled on his loin cloth. He looked to be in his forties, but Nathaniel could only guess at his age. The Indian said nothing but a tear slowly rolled down his face.

Nathaniel switched to Iroquoian. "What is your name, Oldtimer? Tell me, I mean no harm to you."

"I am White Horse. I am Cherokee."

"They call me Na-tan. Do you live around here?"

"Yes, I am from the village."

One of the lads started to say something, but Nathaniel cut him off. "You will speak when I want you to speak. Be quiet! I want to hear from this man what he was doing that made you act like crazy men. Tell me, White Horse, why did they do this to you?"

The older man glanced down at the boys. "As they said, I was fishing, and they came and asked me why I was at their place. I did not know the white man owned the waters or that he had places where only he could fish. This is our land, and I needed food for my family. Then they grabbed me and held me, and brought me here and tied me to the tree."

As White Horse spoke, he emphasized his speech with sign language, swift and complex, in order to get his message through to Nathaniel alone. In those brief words and signs Nathaniel felt great compassion for the Indian and utter scorn for the boys. He wanted to punish them some way, but his mind argued against it. He knew that White Horse could not say anything to the families of the boys; he would be laughed away. He, Nathaniel, could go to the families and tell them, but he was not sure what good would come of it. He decided to put the fear of God in them.

He lifted their weapons and made sure they were unloaded. Then with hatred in his face he leaned down and jerked the boys to their feet. "I should beat the devil out of you!"

One of them, trying to regain control of the situation, looked at Nathaniel and hissed, "What are you, an Indian lover?" Seeing the look of hatred that spread across Nathaniel's face, he knew he had overstepped himself. He said, "I'm sorry, Sir, we were just havin' some fun with him. We meant him no harm."

"Yeah, that's all we were doin'. We din't mean nothin', nothin' at all. We jus' wanted to scare him a little."

Nathaniel wasn't sure they were sorry but as he thought about it, he said, "You may go, but first, come over here and shake this man's hand and tell him you're sorry. I promise that if I ever hear of you doing something like this again, I'll hunt you down and make you wish that you were dead! Now come, and tell White Horse that you made a mistake."

They moved over and took the Indian's hand and mumbled an apology. They were embarrassed by what they had done and seemed genuinely sorry for the episode. Nathaniel handed them their rifles and told them to get home. They ran off as Nathaniel yelled after them.

He turned to White Horse, took his hand, and said, "I too am sorry for what the white man has done to your land and your people, and I am ashamed for what happened here today. Come home with me, White Horse. It has been a long time since I've met a man like you. Let's be friends and not enemies, that I might learn more about your people."

It was the beginning of a friendship that lasted until Nathaniel left the village and moved west. Following that first encounter, he spent many hours with White Horse and his Cherokee friends, learning more about the tribe and studying the language. With his knowledge of the Iroquoian language gained earlier, Nathaniel soon mastered the Cherokee language with the help of White Horse.

Nathaniel soon had many Indian friends, and he listened frequently to their tales around the fire, about their prowess in battle, the ways they meted out justice, including members of their own blood. They were vicious when they believed they had been dishonored. Blood feuds within and without the tribe were common, but for the most part, the Indians were dedicated warriors who rarely gave up a battle unless hopelessly outnumbered. But those days had ended for these Indians, their manhood threatened, and it was sad to see the dissolution of the tribe.

He listened to many of their legends, and understood for the first time why the philosophies of the two races would be difficult to reconcile. One day, White Horse put it all into perspective. "Na-tan, there is an old legend of Kanati and Selu, the man and the woman. It is hard for the whites to understand this. The man is endowed with the powers to hunt, to bring home meat for the cooking fires. The woman has the powers to plant the fields and grow things. The man would feel shamed and weak if he worked in the fields; the woman is not trained to stalk and hunt in the forests." It is not the same for you.

"I understand what you say, White Horse, but you must also try to understand the white man's needs. He wants to expand and clear the land so that he can plant and harvest the good things that come from the ground."

The old man shook his head slowly. "When the white man takes our land, he takes it forever. He thinks that if he works the land, it belongs to him. No, Na-tan, you do not understand me. The Great Spirit provided the land to all Ani'-yun'wiya for our needs. Our people share it together. It is for all, not for one."

White Horse looked at Nathaniel, sadness written across his weathered face. "When will it end, Na-tan? Will my brothers wander forever, never to see the sun and moon in the same place because of the white man's needs?"

"I don't know, my friend. But wherever I go, I hope you will be there."

When Nathaniel discovered what was happening around him, he made the decision that would forever affect his life, and from which there would be no turning back. He saw the Indians in the village change and witnessed a creeping, inexorable malaise overcoming them, destroying a once proud race of people. His thoughts turned to the Cherokee Nation beyond this simple village, and he decided it was time to leave and move farther west.

It was an easy decision for him to make. His mind, steeped in history of the Native Americans and how they had survived in this great land, refused to allow him to remain in the relative luxury of the village. He needed to make a break and move on. His deepest regret was saying goodbye to White Horse and his other Indian friends.

One evening, as they sat together, he decided he could no longer delay telling them what he planned to do. Gathering his courage, he said, "My dear friends, I have something to tell you. It is not easy for me to speak of this, but it is time for me to move on."

"You look sad tonight, Na-tan. Have we done something to make you sad?"

"You have been friends for many moons, and you have made my days brighter, but I will be leaving you soon."

White Horse knew that Nathaniel had made up his mind. They had talked about it earlier so it did not come as a shock to him. Nevertheless, he was saddened by the decision and he asked Nathaniel to share with the others the reason behind it.

"Na-tan, you have been like a son to me and we have talked before, but your friends do not understand what you are thinking. Please tell them why you feel this way."

Nathaniel rose from his seat. "It is time for me to see new places in the west. I know about your tribe and your early way of life, but before it is gone I want to be a part of it. We all know that your ways are changing. There is not much the Cherokee Nation can do about it. The whites will continue to force their ways upon you, and you will not be able to resist. Your brothers in the west have a bit more time, but in the end, they too will be changed. No one will be able to stop the movement of the whites; they are too strong! I am white and I believe this will happen soon."

An Indian stood, "If you have decided to go, how can we help?"

"Surely, there is something that we can do," another offered.

"I don't know this great land as you know it." He thought a moment before continuing. "Perhaps, you could tell me the safest way west . . . some way that offers me a safe passage. I might meet your people on a raid and they would not hesitate to kill me. Teach me something that is common to all of your people so that I can use it if necessary. A sign that I can make or words to speak. That will be more than sufficient."

Nathaniel could not remember later what else happened at that final meeting. White Horse cut his wrist. Then he did the same to Nathaniel. Pressing them together he made him swear to the Great Spirit that they would always know each other as friends and not enemies. They smoked the pipe one last time as each sorted out his emotions. Beyond that, Nathaniel had no recollection of the events of the evening. Before they went out White Horse took Nathaniel aside and removing a small metal disc from his pocket, placed it in Nathaniel's hand.

"Go with the Great Spirit, Na-tan, and when you need help, show this." Then, after putting his arm around Nathaniel, he slipped into the dark night.

The following morning, as dawn broke, Nathaniel left the village and headed west. He was sorry to be leaving his friends behind but it was a new, fresh day, and he knew that he had made the right decision.

# 3

# *F*ACE OF *F*EAR

Now, as he watched the girl, his voice failed him. As she came on, he suspected that she was Cherokee, but he still was not certain. He decided to wait until she was on the river opposite his hiding place. Then he saw her pause, reach out to catch her balance as the rock split wide, and she slid over the edge into the rushing waters below. She screamed as she fell, and then there was only the sound of the river below.

Nathaniel was moving even as she fell, ripping off his waist bag as he ran, leaving his rifle behind him, slashing through the brush to the spot where she had fallen. Looking down, he saw the rocks had divided the river, and a dead tree had formed a small dam across part of the channel where it lodged against some rocks. She was was draped across the branches and was being pelted by the water which had pushed her there. For a moment she reminded him of a rag doll, arms outflung, pinned by the tide.

He jumped feet first, hoping the water was deep in the pool. As he struck the surface, he was engulfed by the chilling flood. He swam even as he was pushed toward the girl, heedless of anything except the need to get to her before she drowned. The water pounded him and pulled him under. As he rose and gulped for air to feed his tortured lungs, he reached her and lifted her head above the water. Her eyes were closed, but her hands clutched at the branches of the tree, and when he touched her she opened her eyes and screamed and started to thrash about. He spoke to her then, yelling to be heard above the roar of the water, telling her that he would help her, and she stopped kicking but would not release her hold on the tree.

She was in shock as she stared at him and tried to speak, but her voice failed her. His body was getting numb and Nathaniel knew that he had to get her out of the water, and himself as well, or it would be too late for either of them. He grabbed at her hands, trying to pry her fingers from the branches, but she stubbornly held fast. Pulling all his failing strength together, he reached for her waist and wrestled her free and started swimming for shore, tugging her behind him. Kicking and thrashing, she was able to break loose. As she sank into the icy water, Nathaniel lifted her again. This time, she reached for him, her eyes wide with fright, and pulled herself into his arms. There she clung as he made his way to shallow water. She pressed her body into his, certain now that he meant her no harm. As he climbed the bank and dropped on the ground, she held tightly to him.

Utterly spent, they lay in the sun, hearts pounding and lungs gasping for air, as his arms encircled her and she would not let him go. As their bodies quieted, he spoke gently to her, trying to learn who she was, but she said nothing, nor did she move from him. For a few long minutes he held her, trying to sooth her fear and she was content to stay.

As he lay with his eyes closed, savoring his life, drinking in the smell and feel of this Indian maiden in his arms, she released one hand from his neck and shifted her weight on him. Slowly, she moved her arm away from his body until her hand found what she was seeking, and as she grasped the stone and lifted it above his head to strike him, her movement alerted him and he opened his eyes and, tossing her aside, rolled away.

The stone struck him a glancing blow, and for a few moments he felt faint. Then his mind cried out "why," before he realized that he was not of her race or tribe. They were not friends, this girl and him, but cautious enemies, and he had trespassed into her world.

The girl lay still, her dark eyes alert and fastened on him. Now there was fear again in her face as she contemplated his reaction. She had tried to kill him; it was as simple as that! She knew he would take her life—that was his right and duty. Another part of her was happy that she had not killed him, even though she would die. She wondered if she could have finished the job if he had not caught her in the attempt. He had saved her from the river, brought her to the shore, lay with her as they regained their strength, and even spoken her language. But she would have killed him, she knew for certain.

She sensed something else about him. He was rubbing the side of his head which the stone had grazed, making no move to hurt her, to cause her pain or death. She thought he must be crazy. Her father, who had killed many enemies, shared his stories over and over around the fires. She knew the immensity of her action and expected no mercy now. Why had he saved her? Where had he lay waiting along the path? Why was he so quick to act? He must have known she was coming and was ready to kill her first.

Still he did not move. The maiden became conscious of the burning pain in her leg. The shock was wearing off and she knew that her leg was broken. She must wait for him now, like a trapped animal awaits its slaughter. She knew she could not move from him. Inwardly, she grimaced from the hurt, trying to will him to act but he would not move.

Stoicly, she accepted her dying and death as part of the Great Spirit's plan for her. She was acutely aware of her situation, and she was not afraid to die. She hoped it would be quick, but she had seen many die a slow death after their capture, and she did not expect the end for her to be any different. She shuddered as a certain sadness crept over her and her thoughts turned to the tribe and the family left behind in the valley. What were they doing? Until evening approached they would not be very concerned for her.

She had left the tribe before many times. Her people would attribute her absence to something a young girl frequently did, as a chance to get away on her own, and would expect her when she chose to return. She had gotten away, but now she would never see them, never have the choice of sitting and listening and dreaming as they recounted the day's happenings. She knew that her clan would accept the fact that she was lost or had been killed by a wild beast. They would search for her, of course, for her father could not allow

her soul to wander forever in the forest. She had to be sent to the
Great Spirit with gifts and food so that He would take her in, and she
could share the hunting grounds which the legends told were filled
with game, and where it was always warm and the grasses sweet and
the waters cool.

Her thoughts turned to the tribe and a feeling of utter desolation
and loss permeated her being. Her body would never be found; she
was alone, except for the man, and could not move. He would kill her
and drag her into the forest, where the wild animals would tear at her
bones, and where her soul would travel aimlessly forever. With this
last thought she turned away from him and cried silently, not wanting the man to know her sorrow or her pain.

Nathaniel lay on his side for some time watching the young girl.
Realizing that she was not going to attack him again, he closed his
eyes and rested under the warm sun. He remained mute, his emotions boiling around him. The physical hurt she had inflicted was
subsiding, and the hurt of rejection by the girl bothered him. He had
saved her from certain death; yet, she had tried to kill him! Still, she
had not moved from where he had thrown her.

Nathaniel turned, trying to decide what he should do. Quietly
he said, "Why did you try to kill me, Little One? I meant no harm to
you."

The girl, her back turned to him, did not answer. She was surprised by his soft voice speaking in her language, but her thoughts of
dying had been interrupted by his words and for a long moment she
remained still.

"From where did you come? To what tribe do you belong? You
may go if you want. Do not be afraid of me."

She hesitated before replying, not wanting to talk to this man, or
to give him the chance to ask her more questions. Yet she knew that
she could not leave without his help. She could crawl to the camp,
perhaps, but then dismissed the thought abruptly. Of course, she
couldn't go far! If he left her alone, some one from the tribe would
find her. But how would she protect herself while she waited? Sensing that he truly did not wish to harm her, and would allow her to go,
she turned to him, trying to hide the pain which enveloped her body.

"I am Cherokee," she replied in her tongue. I am called Snow Deer. My father is Chief Oconostota." Her tone of voice was imperious.

Nathaniel saw her grimace as she moved and asked, "Do you hurt? Let me see."

"No! Stay away from me. I am fine."

"Of course you're not. You are hurt from the fall. At least, I can help. You would not be here now if I had failed to jump after you."

As he crawled over to her, she cringed away from him. Then realizing that she must trust him, must rely on his help, she looked pleadingly at him. For the first time she noticed his azure blue eyes looking steadily at her. They were gentle too; there was not a hint of meanness in his face. He would not harm her. His eyes held hers for a long minute as she tried to fathom whether he would hurt or help her.

Snow Deer made her decision then. This man, not of her tribe or race, would not hurt her. There was something about him she trusted. Perhaps it was his piercing eyes, or the face tanned nearly the color of her skin, or the gentle voice, but she knew. As she looked into his face and saw the red mark on his face where the stone had struck, she was instantly sorry for what she had done.

"It is my leg. It burns hot," she said, "I think it must be broken."

He reached for her. "Which leg? Show me where." She pointed and he saw swelling. He touched it. "I'll have to set your leg and make a splint. It will hurt for only a minute, but it has to be done."

Kneeling beside her, he grasped it above and below the break, and reset the bone with a sharp pull. She did not cry aloud, but tears welled in her eyes. "I am sorry, but I had to set it."

"Don't move. I must get something to hold it. I will be back in a minute."

He reached for his short knife, strapped to his right leg under his leggings, but sensing her eyes on him, he decided against using it for the task he had in mind. It was better to leave the knife hidden. He rubbed his hand over his leg and then stood up.

Taking his sheath knife, he stripped bark from a willow, and picking up a short stick and patches of moss, returned to the girl. He laid the fresh moss along the leg and fashioned a splint, winding the bark tightly in place. Satisfied with his work, he placed an arm under her back and lifted her into a sitting position. Then he offered her something to drink.

Sitting back on his haunches he again studied her. She sat with her eyes shut, but she was aware that he was watching her. "Perhaps, if I could find a broken branch for support I could find my way home. Would he allow me to go? Is he toying with me, as the mountain cat plays with its wounded prey? Why has he fixed my leg if he planned to kill me?" The thoughts swirled around in her mind in a never-ending spiral.

Nathaniel could not lift his eyes from her as he pondered their predicament. "She is a lovely girl," he thought, "fresh from the river's bath, and she is alone and afraid of me. But she tried to kill me!" He thrust the thought from his mind. "I would have done the same had I been in her place. What should I do now? Without stopping to think I rescued her, so she is in my charge. Perhaps her tribe is nearby and will soon be looking for her. They will finish the job for her, of that I am certain. If I left her now with some food and water, she will be fine for hours, until they come for her. By then I could be far away. But will they come? If I left her and some wild animal . . . no, that wouldn't happen, or could it? She might try to crawl to the camp, but will never make it, however short the distance. She will only fall again. No, I can not let that happen! I must stay with her no matter what. There is no other alternative, but to wait for someone to come for her."

He spoke to her, "Where is your camp, Snow Deer? Do you think someone will come for you?"

"Yes, as soon as the sun starts to drop."

He shook his head, "Do your people know where you are? How will they find you?"

"I told no one where I was going. I did not know myself." Summoning her strength, she said, "I can take care of myself. I do not need you. Please leave me alone!"

Nathaniel looked down at her, and then shrugged his shoulders. His head still ached, and he wanted to wash the hurt away. Gathering his water bag he rose and made his way to the river. When he finished washing his wound and drinking his fill, he filled the bag and returned to Snow Deer.

He said, "My mind is made up. You do not want me to stay, so I will go."

He reached into his pack and found a few strips of dried jerky and laid them on the grass beside her. "Eat this and don't move around too much. I'll go down the river and try to make contact with your clan; perhaps, I can lead them to you."

"There is no need to do that. Someone will come for me. I'm sure of it."

"How can you be so certain? You said yourself that no one knew where you were going."

"You do not know our ways. They will find me, so please go. It will be better for you."

He looked down at the defenseless girl lying on the ground. There is no arguing with this woman, he thought. He moved over to the large stones and picked up his rifle and an empty trap, and without a glance in her direction, turned away.

Nathaniel had walked only about a mile before meeting the Indians. He heard them before they came into view, and quickly jumped off the path and hid himself. His first inclination was to determine whether they were Cherokee or some other tribe. The Indians were laughing and yelping, enjoying themselves loudly. He could not imagine that it was a war party, but he did not want to chance it. Surely, he thought, if it were a raid, they would be moving quietly and not be making so much noise. If the Indians were from her tribe they would force him to guide them to her, but if they were not, he planned somehow to divert them until he could get away and find her village.

He had formulated this plan as soon as he left Snow Deer. Damn the girl! Why had she been so obstinate? If she had given him any encouragement at all he would have stayed with her. But no, she made it clear that she wanted him gone. How she expected to get to her camp he didn't know, nor at the moment, care! Or so he thought.

The men came on. They had stopped their yelling and appeared to be coming slowly up the trail. Nathaniel could hear them clearly now although they were talking in low voices. Then they stopped. He could detect no noise at all. The silence worried him; they must have discovered some sign or mark on the trail. Then it came to him. Snow Deer had traveled the same path less than an hour before, so they must have spotted her passage. Now they were moving slowly again, and then the first one came into view. The feathers he wore gave him away. Then two more appeared in trail behind him. As they paused and knelt down to examine the path, Nathaniel froze. They commenced talking again and he knew the tongue was Creek, enemies of the Cherokee. It was a war party. Nathaniel identified the face paint and the slashes on their bodies, and he knew they were looking for trouble.

His mind raced. He was sure that unless he did something fast, they would find the girl. His mind conjured images of what would happen if they got to her. They would make sport of her and then kill her, or they could take her as ransom. She had told him who she was, and he believed she would tell them too. A chief's daughter! Of course, they would carry her to their camp, but not before they had their fun. He could kill them quickly enough with his rifle, but he discarded the idea. The Indians might be scouts, and if the main party heard the shooting there would be no way to get back to Snow Deer.

His plan came together. First, he would try to divert and separate them, get them off the track and into the woods. He would have a better chance one-on-one than if they stayed together. One Indian started moving ahead while the other two remained where they had stopped, studying the trail. This might be the break he needed. "Keep coming," he begged under his breath, trying to will the first Indian to move. Nathaniel picked up a small stone and threw it behind the two kneeling on the trail. As it clattered to the ground, they looked up and started back down the trail to investigate. Now the party was split. Nathaniel had the steel trap in his hand and was moving toward the first one, swinging it by the chain. As the Indian saw him and opened his mouth to yell, the trap slashed into his face and he dropped without uttering a sound. He pitched forward, and Nathaniel fell on his back and sank his knife into the neck and gave it a final twist.

Leaping to his feet Nathaniel let out a yell and ran into the woods. The other Indians screamed something and then followed after the wild man ahead of them. They spread out and crashed through the woods, making no effort to move quietly. It was what Nathaniel had hoped for. Quickly spotting a large, fallen log he crept behind it and waited. He heard one of the Indians coming his way. He slowed, looking for the signs of Nathaniel's passing. When he got closer Nathaniel smelled his sweaty body, and abruptly hurled himself over the log and into the startled Indian. It was no contest. Nathaniel pushed his knife forward and skewered the Indian in the chest. The man howled once and then died.

The second Creek rose before Nathaniel. He had rushed forward when Nathaniel jumped, and was now yelling as he swung his tomahawk. Nathaniel sidestepped just in time. The hatchet sliced past his head and glanced off his upraised arm. As Nathaniel's knife again found its mark, the Creek tumbled. He roared again and came off the ground, spinning the axe toward Nathaniel. A few feet more and it would have caught him, but at the last moment it was deflected by a small sapling that twisted the handle, and the tomahawk smashed into his chest, knocking the air from his lungs. The Indian was on him, blood pouring from his chest, and Nathaniel made one last effort and sank the knife into the Creek's side. His black, hateful, gleaming eyes lost their fire, and he died with Nathaniel beneath him.

Nathaniel pushed the body aside and lay there, gasping for breath. His arm hurt dreadfully where the axe had struck. The skin was bruised but not broken, and his chest was on fire too. Slowly he got off the ground and wiped his long blade on the tall grasses. He opened his water pouch and took a long drink and tried to wash some of the blood from his shirt.

He glanced down at the Indians, trying to decide whether he should take their scalps or leave them intact. When he had been with White Horse, he had heard the stories of the barbarous custom. It was considered by the Indians to represent valor and strength in battle over their enemies, and to return from a raid carrying their gruesome cargo brought honor to the scalper. It was singularly a battle trophy, one that could be displayed on the body or lodge or hung on a spear. Nathaniel did not like the bloody tradition but he understood why it was used. He decided that he would not take the scalplocks; perhaps another time he would not hesitate to do it.

Then he picked up his rifle and started for the trail. He was going back to Snow Deer; there was no other way. She would have to come with him if she wanted to live this day. He moved cautiously, not knowing whether more Creeks were behind him or not, until he came to the place where he had left Snow Deer lying by the large stones.

# 4

# PRISONER OF THE CHEROKEES

His heart stopped; Snow Deer was nowhere in sight! His eyes swept the ground around the stones, looking for some sign that would tell him what had happened to her. Then he knew. She had been taken by another raiding party. The signs were very clear. Snow Deer had put up a fight despite her broken leg and must have suffered a lot of pain. There were pieces of the moss and some bits of bark that he had used on her leg laying on the ground. Searching further, he found what he had not wanted to find. The signs told him at once there were six Indians in the party. He could trace the ground where they formed a circle around the girl. The lingering scent of their bodies permeated the crushed grass where they had rested before moving on with her.

Now, Nathaniel faced a dilemma. She meant nothing to him. She had refused to go with him and did not want him to stay with her. He had saved her from drowning, and she had tried to kill him. If she had gone with him they would have reached the village by now. If they had been together they could have hidden from the Creeks. If that had happened he would not have killed them. Too many ifs! Well, he was sorry, but she should have listened to him. Yet, her father was the Great Chief, and he, Nathaniel, would be called into account when they found him. They would want to know why he left her, and his explanations would be worthless. Then what would they do to him? He knew the answer and that knowledge made the decision for him. He would have to go after her, it was as simple as that! Damn the girl, again!

Nathaniel was a trained trapper and tracker. He found the trail of the Creeks immediately and set out behind them. He moved swiftly for it would soon be dark, and he wanted to catch up with them before they stopped for the night. They couldn't move quickly; they had to carry the girl, and at least two of them would be slowed by their burden. He discovered that he was right. They had stopped to rest, and when he examined the ground he found a strip of bark that Snow Deer had slipped on a bush, close to the ground. She wanted someone to find it, to give them a direction of the move.

Farther on he came upon a dead white trader. There was little evidence of a fight. The Indians had simply surprised the white man, killed and scalped him, and stolen his pack horses. Nathaniel wanted to do something for the man, but time was running out. As he left the scene he silently promised the trader that he would avenge his death. The two Indians carrying Snow Deer had halted there also, and she had left another sign.

It was nearly dark when the war party stopped for the night. A small cooking fire was lit, casting a dim light on the circle of Creeks who sat before it. They had stripped the horses of the packs and were rummaging through each one as Nathaniel came upon the camp. Goods were flying in all directions; each Indian was showing the others the treasures they had stolen. Nathaniel crept closer, trying to see Snow Deer in the poor light. The war party had built no shelter for the night, but he knew she was there. Then she moved and he saw her, slumped against a dark tree. She was bound with vines wound across her chest to hold her upright. Her hands were tied in front of her, laying on her lap motionless. She was on the far side of the clearing. He would have to make a large circle around the camp and come in behind her. He backed away a short distance, and started crawling slowly through the woods.

Suddenly there was a yell, and the Indians started to jump up and down and around the fire. One of the Creeks had found a bottle of rum in the baggage. The yelling, now taken up by the rest of the Indians, covered the noise of Nathaniel's circuit. He crawled faster as they continued to howl and yelp and drink the liquor. Then another bottle was hauled from the trader's loot, and still a third appeared, and the Indians danced faster and yelled louder between drinks.

One of the Creeks danced over to Snow Deer and leaned down and offered the bottle to her. She spit at him and he jumped backwards and fell. This made him angry and he grabbed her about the neck and pushed the bottle toward her the second time. She tried to twist away from him, but her bonds held her tight. Then he straddled her body and again held her head as she screamed, loud and long. The rest of the Indians stopped howling, and the leader of the war party crossed over to the brave, grabbed him by the hair and threw him to the ground. His face twisted into a hideous grimace as he screamed drunkenly. Then he started laughing, and they all went back to drinking.

During the diversion, Nathaniel was able to move directly behind Snow Deer. He had not decided how to get her out of the camp until the Indians found the liquor. If they continued drinking he guessed that he could execute his plan. He waited and watched while they drank. When one bottle was emptied, they opened another. He thought the leader was beginning to get unsteady on his feet, but all of them were getting drunk fast, and he knew drunkenness would lead to sleep and he could then get to Snow Deer.

One by one, the Indians had their fill and laid down around the fire. One of the Creeks was given guard duty, but he was as sick with rum as the others. He staggered over to Snow Deer and sat at her feet but within minutes fell over on his side into a dead sleep. It was time to move. Nathaniel inched slowly toward the girl. When he got to the tree where she was tied, he whispered to her. Her head had fallen forward and he thought she must be asleep. Reaching around the tree he gently covered her mouth with his hand and whispered again. This time she acknowledged him and thrust her hands to the side so he could cut her thongs. Then he cut the vines holding her body. She stretched in place, trying to get circulation back, and at his motion, moved her body slightly and lay back beside the tree. Nathaniel squeezed her hands and after waiting a few moments, pulled her toward him and away from the camp.

Not one of the Indians moved. They lay in their drunken stupors, oblivious to the fact that their prized hostage was being dragged from their midst. Nathaniel had no doubt about their motives. They would have held Snow Deer for ransom because she was the daughter of a Chief, and the Creeks would have played the game for all it was worth.

As soon as they got into the forest, and out of the light of the fire, Nathaniel picked up Snow Deer and held her to him. "Are you all right?" he whispered.

"I think so, but my leg hurts much."

"We've got to get away from here quickly," he said, "but I can't drag you. Can you put weight on it?" He placed her on the ground and thrust his water bag at her. She drank deeply while he looked at her.

"No."

"Then I will carry you. Climb on my back. This is the only chance we have, Snow Deer," he said quietly as he turned his body to accommodate her.

Hoisting her onto his back, he turned his head and said, "Now hold on tight. We have a long way to go."

Snow Deer, exhausted from the ordeal she had just suffered, slung her arms around his neck and held him. No words were spoken, and she soon fell asleep on his back. Nathaniel was tired and his body ached for relief, but he knew that when the Creeks awakened and found their bounty gone, they would be after her. He plodded on through the night, stumbling from exhaustion, as they moved through the dark forest. Snow Deer slept on.

At first light, Nathaniel still carried the girl. He had not stopped to rest, and he was feeling the effects of his burden. He did not know how far they had traveled, but he guessed they must soon be near her village. Then, as they crossed another ridge and were descending, Nathaniel saw the fires of the camp.

It was dawn as they arrived in the village. Morning fires had been started, casting flickering light on the scene. Nathaniel remembered that fire to the Indians symbolized the sun, around which the home or dwelling of each family symbolized the universe. He saw many Indians moving around the area as they passed in front of the fires, and if each burning fire counted for a family, then by his reckoning perhaps as many as 200 families lived there. He had not expected the tribe to be so large. While he had read about their villages, he was surprised by the number of lodges and the way they were situated.

In the dim light the Council House stood out against the night sky. It was large, and it sat on a great circular mound of earth which appeared to overlook the village square. There were loghouses, each with pitched roofs, and some with small porches. Family lodges were scattered everywhere. They appeared to be covered with some kind of reed mats or grass, and for a moment, Nathaniel was reminded of the thatched cottages of his native land.

He did not receive the greeting that he expected. When he arrived at the first lodge, he handed Snow Deer to the women who were standing at the fire. Then he was surrounded immediately by several men of the tribe who grabbed him and pushed him to the ground.

"Wait! What are you doing?" he yelled. "Dammit, I just brought the girl home. Are you all crazy?"

An Indian kicked him. "We should kill you now. What happened to the girl's leg?"

"What did you do to our woman?" another screamed.

"I did nothing to her," Nathaniel replied. "I carried her all night. Let me go. I cannot fight you."

He looked for Snow Deer, hoping she would come to his defense, but she was no longer in sight. The women had taken her away.

He collapsed then, his mind confused, not understanding the screams that were hurled at him. He was tired and hungry and sore from the fighting. He needed rest more than anything. At the moment he could not understand why they were angry with him. He had returned the girl safely; what more could they want?

He was half-dragged to the side of the clearing. His captors, who had kept the gathering clan away from him as they entered the village, threw him into an empty lodge in which a small lamp was burning. When his guards closed the hole which served as a door, he started to explore the lodge to find an escape. The house was well constructed. Parallel rows of saplings were bent and tied together to form the shell of the house, and then covered with bark. The exterior was plastered over with clay or mud, and the only light was from a fire hole on the roof. Opposite the door, Nathaniel pushed hard on the wall to gauge its strength. He found that it hard and tough, and there was no resiliency whatsoever. For the moment he decided to wait for more light. He was exhausted and needed sleep. Along one side of the lodge was a curved bench on which a skin had been stretched. It was too short for his frame but it was off the cold ground. He slumped his body along the bench and fell asleep.


Nathaniel slept fitfully, falling briefly in and out of consciousness, as the sounds of the awakening village intruded his cell, and dreamed he had been captured by the Creeks. They were getting set to punish him for killing the war party and for helping Snow Deer escape. He was now in their hands and they would make him regret that he had ever ventured from the settlement. In his dream, he was being lashed to a pole in the village public square.

Everything he had ever learned or heard about the Creeks came to him in his dream. His captors, who had kept him tied and without food and water for several days, now took him to the 'Chunky Yard', the place where all prisoners who were sentenced to die were held. In the center of the yard was a low, circular mound, on which was placed the chunky-pole. Spaced around it, on the outer corners of the yard, four posts were embedded in the earth, each about ten feet in height. These were the slave posts. The victims to be burned alive were bound to the posts, and there they would suffer hideous death when the fires were set. On three of the posts, dry, white skulls of previous captives had been placed, and scalps fluttered from other rings set on the posts.

Nathaniel, dragged from the lodge that served as his prison, was now tied hand and foot to the vacant pole. As soon as he was bound the villagers started gathering in the square to take part in the torture games that would precede his death. A small fire was built near Nathaniel, and there was much laughing and yelling as the tribe waited to set upon the man.

It was just a game to them: men, women and children all taking a part in the event. The children were as cruel as the men and they were given first right to torture the victim. They jumped around Nathaniel, prodding him with sharp sticks, and when they tired of the game, threw rocks at him. His body was soon covered with welts and bruises from the sticks and stones. Then using their sticks as tongs, they plucked coals from the fire and thrust them against Nathaniel. They wanted him to cry out and beg for mercy, this white man whom they hated, but he stood defiantly before them not uttering a sound, challenging them to kill him and have it over.

This man was not humbled like most of their prisoners. They wanted him to suffer mightily before the Great Spirit took him to the sky above the stars, but since he was white, what could he know about the Great Spirit? That made them tease him more. The old women poked at his lower body trying to get a response from him, and though he was overwhelmed with pain, he refused to cry out. Then they brought the knives and threatened him anew. They jabbed and cut, and his blood spurted from the wounds, and it spurred them on to greater punishment.

Nathaniel felt himself weakening. His time was running out. Blood seeped from hundreds of cuts that had been inflicted on him. A numb feeling permeated his body and he guessed the end was near. His head sagged on his chest, his eyes closed, and he would have fallen if the ropes had not held fast. But he was not finished yet! He wanted them to know that he was stronger and braver than any of them. As they gathered the dry grass and the wood to light the fire, he lifted his head and summoned the last vestiges of his strength. Facing the crowd he laughed at them, telling them he too knew the Great Spirit, and they would know war and famine for killing him, that their sons and daughters would never grow old, that the wild animals would disappear, and that they would die and wander forever and never find peace.

They listened, and the crowd grew quiet as he spoke of these things, but only for a few minutes until a young Creek set the pile afire. As the grass smoked and the wood caught and the flames licked, and then leaped around his legs, Nathaniel called upon some hidden strength. Raising his head high, he screamed to the sky one last time, a dying animal howl, an interminable, blood-curdling cry of pain and terror, of outrage and of death.

His screaming brought the Indians running to the lodge and the guards threw back the covering and entered. Nathaniel, awakened from the most frightening dream he had ever experienced, was crouched on the crude bench keening to himself. The legends everafter would tell of this brave white man, turned Cherokee, who had killed many Creeks and rescued Snow Deer from death twice in the same day. But the tale never to be told was that the vision of death seen in his dreams was so horrible that he would never repeat it to anyone. They knew, and they were afraid.

The guards, who had never faced a similar scene before, stopped in mid-stride and stared at the man crouched on the bench. A chilling breeze raced over them. They were certain that evil spirits had consumed Nathaniel and for a long moment they tried to sort out what the tableau before them meant. They did not want to remain where they were. Without saying a word they turned and slipped through the opening. By now many Indians were converging on the lodge. The shaman, who by rights would be called on to exorcise the demon that had taken refuge in the prisoner, was among the villagers. There was something wild and frightening going on inside the lodge, something that conjured a scene of death and destruction. The scream had been so intense and fearful that most of the Indians felt some compassion for the animal that had emitted the obscene cry.

Suddenly, the crying stopped. Before the Indians could recover from the surprise and shock Nathaniel emerged slowly from the opening. He appeared to be disoriented, shaking his head back and forth, his eyes unseeing. As the Indians looked upon this apparition in their midst, his eyes opened wide and focused once again. The shaman, who had started forward when Nathaniel appeared, stopped short.

Wanting to keep them confused a bit longer, he spoke to them in the Cherokee tongue. "Why am I being held prisoner? I know you are Cherokee and are not as cowardly as the Creeks. When I came here of my own accord early this morning, you threw me into this pigsty! Why?"

For a minute, not one of the Indians replied. That the white man could speak to them in their language caught them by surprise, and they looked to one another, hoping that someone would answer. One of the guards stepped forward and threatened Nathaniel with his weapon.

"You are our prisoner. You will not go anywhere, except to die, if you do not go inside."

Nathaniel pulled himself straight. "My friend, you speak strong words for one so weak. I am Nathaniel Tennyson, and I come to you peacefully. I am not your enemy. Your tribe has no reason to fear me or to hold me like an animal."

"You are being held under the tribal laws. You will have the chance to speak to our great chief, but when he wants you to speak, he will call for you. Until that time, you will stay where you are!"

"That may be so, but I am hungry and I need food and water, and a blanket or skins. Do not treat me like an animal! I brought the chief's daughter to the village. I killed three Creeks who would have killed her. I rescued her from six more who would have held her for ransom. Ask her to come here. She will tell you that I speak the truth."

"It does not matter whether you speak the truth or not. She cannot come here. Her leg is broken and she needs rest." The guard was very emphatic, and his words had a ring of finality about them.

Nathaniel would not give up. "I know her leg is broken, but I carried her all night to bring her here. Certainly, someone can carry her from her lodge!"

"It is not your right to demand these things. We will bring water and food, but you will wait until our great chief wants you to speak, and will see no one. Now, you will stay here!"

Nathaniel realized there was no sense in arguing. The guards had been given their instructions and would keep him in the lodge as long as necessary. At least he would get some food and water, and perhaps before the day was over he would be taken to the Chief. He was disappointed in not being allowed to see Snow Deer. He was sure that she would confirm what he had done for her and he would be released. Then he realized that he needed more from her than mere confirmation. He wanted to see her again. There was something about this girl which had piqued his interest. He had a fleeting image of the rescue from the water, when she had clung to him before she tried to kill him, and he remembered the flight to the village with her arms entwined about his neck. He liked the feel of her in his arms, the first woman in many years that he had held. But it was more than this. He wanted to hear her voice and see her smile, and that was really the reason he had asked the guards to bring her.

* * *

It was late in the day when Nathaniel was marched to the Chief's lodge. Earlier, he had been taken to the river where he used sand to scrub some of the blood from his clothes and his body. After his bath he was allowed to lie in the sun while his clothes dried. He enjoyed his freedom from the dirty lodge and had no desire to return there. When they called for him to be taken to the chief, he was ready. He was anxious to see Snow Deer again, particularly to hear her confirm what he had told the Indians who had gathered at his lodge earlier.

Nathaniel was not prepared to meet Chief Oconostata. Snow Deer had told him she was the daughter of a chief, but not of the Great Chief. He had also expected to be welcomed with kindness and thanks for bringing her home. He thought that act alone would ingratiate him to, or at least win favor from, the Chief. He also believed that the two of them would speak man-to-man, but this was not going to happen.

Thus, Nathaniel was puzzled when he was taken directly to the Council House. He climbed the mound upon which it sat, and was shoved roughly through a serpentine passage that opened into the main building. He was surprised by its size and shape. The Council House was constructed with seven sides facing the center. He knew the significance immediately, for in the earlier days when he had sat with White Horse he had learned about the clans and their functions in the tribe. Seven large posts had been sunk into the ground, and on each a carved wooden mask stared down on the center where a small fire smoldered. A fire hole in the ceiling allowed the acrid smoke to escape. Its high, vaulted roof and circular shape was quite impressive, he thought, a tribute to the designer and builders of the house.

Opposite the entrance, the Principal Chief sat. On his right was a small bench on which several other chiefs waited. Seven sections, matching the sides of the Council House, had been laid out around the building. Crude benches had been constructed facing the center, and now were filled with the villagers who had come to the meeting. Of all the surprises experienced since arriving, none was as great as seeing women in the gathering, waiting to see this white man before Council. He quickly glanced around the room, but there was no sign of Snow Deer. His heart fell; he had expected her to be present and tell her story, but more than that, he wanted to see her again. He guessed at once that this was not to be an ordinary welcome.

As he entered, he was aware of the low murmuring voices that seemed to fill the immense space of the house. His attention riveted on Chief Oconostata. Seated on a low platform, covered with a blanket, the Chief appeared to be bigger than life. He was enormous! His dark red face was frozen. His greying hair, pushed back from his forehead, was covered with the headband supporting his badge of office—a brilliant plumage of feathers and beads. Nathaniel had not seen a headdress so magnificent. The Chief's cloak or mantle lay easily on his broad shoulders as he sat stiffly, looking at Nathaniel.

Then their eyes met, the blue and the black, the Chief's eyes boring into Nathaniel's soul. The dark orbs remained motionless in the weathered face, steady, no flickering of the eyelashes, as if he thought the white man before him could be cowed by the piercing stare. For some minutes the white man and the red man held each other's gaze, and there was neither movement nor change of expression in the other's eyes. The spectators grew quiet.

The Chief opened the meeting. "You have been called before this Council under tribal laws. The Council will hear what you have to say. It knows the white man came here with one of our women. The woman has a broken leg. The Council wants to know why this happened and what you want from us. Tell us who you are."

"I am Nathaniel Tennyson. I am a friend of the Cherokees and mean no harm to you. I came from across the Great Water two summers ago. I am a trapper and a hunter; I am nothing more than this."

The Chief continued, "You do not tell us why you come to our land. Were you a soldier? Have you fought us in battle? These are the things we want to know."

"I have never been a soldier and I have not fought the Cherokees. I came to your land because I wanted to see it for myself."

"Then perhaps you try to get knowledge about us so that you can tell your people and they can come against us as before," the Chief said derisively. "For many summers the white man has tried to take our land. The white man is not happy with what he has stolen from us. He wants more, always more! Why are you not happy with the land you have taken?"

"It is true what you say, but all white men do not want your land. I know the red man does not hold ownership of the land. In my country, across the Great Water, the white man does. It is different from your ways, but it gives the white man something that belongs to him, something that he can give to his sons when he is gone. If you cannot give your sons land, then what do you give?"

The Chief did not answer right away. He looked at the men in the council and then returned his eyes to Nathaniel. "The white people have said this before to us and sometimes we have followed your ways, but the Great Spirit has given us the land to use and that is what we do. The white man steals our land to get ownership and they push us deeper into our hunting grounds, and soon they will want these also. When will you stop? The land of the Ani'- yun'wiya is for all Indians; that is what we leave to our sons! We have no need of more."

Nathaniel wanted to lead the Council back to him. He wanted to know what they planned to do with him. "I am sorry that the white man comes upon your lands. But you know the white man does not understand this. All he can think about is getting more space for farms and new settlements."

Nathaniel had to change the thrust of the discussion. He sensed he was getting nowhere on the issue of land ownership. He said, "All white men are not like the ones who would force you off your hunting grounds. Some believe the Cherokees are their equal in many ways, If I did not believe that, I would not have returned here with with Snow Deer. Would you rather I left her with the Creeks?"

As Nathaniel mentioned the name, the Council members stiffened. There was a murmur in the Council House. Chief Oconostata raised his hand for silence and the voices died. "What about the Creeks? How do you know about them?"

"I know they are your enemies as well as mine. I told you that I was not a soldier, but while I searched for your village to get help for Snow Deer, I met three of their kind. I showed no mercy on any of them! They were stinking, filthy animals, and I killed them like I would kill any wild beast!"

Again, the members started talking. They were shaken by what Nathaniel had told them. The Chief waved them to silence. "Where did you kill them? We know nothing of this."

Nathaniel told them the story, starting with the rescue of Snow Deer from the raging river, how he had set her leg, and how he had left her behind while he tried to find her clan. They sat impassively while he recounted meeting and killing the Creeks and how, when he returned to find Snow Deer gone, he had picked up the trail of the raiding party and followed them until they made camp for the night. He told them of finding the trader scalped and his goods taken, and then the drunken orgy of the raiders which had allowed him to cut Snow Deer loose and pull her from the camp and return to the village.

When he had finished, he looked around the Council. The Indians did not move. He couldn't tell whether they believed him or not. There was only half-proof of what he had done. They would know only that he had gotten Snow Deer away from the raiding party. Then Nathaniel remembered that he had not told Snow Deer of his encounter with the Creeks. There had been no chance to tell her so she had not known.

The Chief spoke softly to the assembly, "The white man has told us a story and I think he speaks the truth. He may not be a soldier, but he seems to be a warrior. He has killed our enemies, the Creeks. We will find the bodies and know this to be true. We must send a party after the Creeks who continue to raid our lands. If we find them, they too will die. Snow Deer did not tell me of these things. I will ask what else she knows about this man. Then we will decide what to do with him."

Nathaniel knew that he would be taken from the Council House and that the Indians would debate him further. He had not embellished his story, and he felt relieved the Chief thought him truthful. What would happen now was anyone's guess, but he felt confident enough to raise one last question.

"Chief Oconostata, I know there are tribal laws that govern what should be done with me, and I am willing to accept the judgement of the Council, but I have one request to make." Then in a quiet voice, he said, "I would like to see Snow Deer again."

"That is possible, but first we have other things to look after. You will be told when it is time."

Then he called for the guards who had brought Nathaniel to the Council and gave them instructions. "Find a new lodge for the white man. Give him food and water and clean skins." Turning to Nathaniel, he continued. "You may move freely in the village and as far as the river, but do not try to escape. You would not get far." Then his dark eyes softened a bit. "Your weapons will be returned to you, but while you stay with us, use them on our enemies, not against us."

He dismissed the guards and Nathaniel curtly and waved them out. Nathaniel, who had listened carefully during the assembly, had the impression that the Chief was amenable to his request and that he was pleased with him. At least, he had gotten a fair hearing, Nathaniel thought; the Council could have voted, still might vote, to put him to death! He thanked the Chief as he turned and left the Council House.

# 5

# RELEASE FROM CAPTIVITY

Since the Council meeting, Nathaniel had been permitted his freedom, and he spent most of his time observing the village activities. He was known as the white man who brought Snow Deer home, and while he was not shunned, neither was he particularly welcomed. As he moved freely, he was aware that the Indians watched him, trying to understand this new person in their midst. He felt, rather than saw, members of the tribe casting glances at him, but when he tried to meet their eyes they looked away. Sometimes, he would catch a pretty maiden lowering her gaze as he strode by, but for the most part the villagers went about their work and play without inviting him to participate.

Except for the children! Unlike their parents who were reserved and taciturn, the young boys and girls followed him wherever he went. Nathaniel was a curiosity, but he quickly won them over with his good humor and horseplay, and they fought over their right to be first behind him or the closest to him, whatever he was doing. They jabbered interminably, not realizing at first that he understood their language, and their comments frequently brought a smile to his face. He showed them how to make whistles from a willow branch, and how to take a piece of grass and make it screech. He let them examine his traps and rifle and long knife, but he never revealed the smaller one strapped to his leg. They loved to watch him as he sharpened his knife, and his mock attack on them as he leaped out and slashed in every direction. When he showed them how to throw the knife expertly and hit a moving or stationary target, they let out feigned yelps of fear which brought the squaws running.

They followed his footsteps day and night, through the village, to the river, and into the woods. They rarely left him alone. From his early morning bath, until he closed the cover on his lodge, they stayed with him. But he enjoyed them as much as they liked him, and that was good. One of the boys was Snow Deer's younger brother, and Nathaniel asked him about her.

"So, my young friend, how is your sister?" he inquired. "I have not seen her in the village."

"That is true, Na-tan. Her leg is getting better, but still gives her pain. My father is grateful for what you did for her."

"If that is so, why have I not been allowed to see her? I have asked each day about her," he said. "I do not understand your father. He has not called me before the Council."

"He is very busy," the boy said simply.

"Has your father sent a party to look for the Creeks?" Nathaniel asked.

"I think he has done that. Soon you will know everything. And Snow Deer will see you, that I am sure."

He could not understand why he was not called by the Chief so that he could visit her. Surely by this time, he thought, they would have found the dead Creeks and know his story was true.

He passed by her lodge on many occasions, hoping to get a glimpse of her in the sun, but to no avail. He thought of her a lot. He remembered back to that first day and the tentativeness about her as she tried to sort out her emotions. She was lovely and easy to look at, and he had been drawn to her in some inexplicable way. But how? That was the question.

It was several days later before Nathaniel was summoned to the Chief's lodge. It was early evening and Nathaniel had been fishing to add some variety to his food. For days now, the former guards had brought him meals in a bowl or a basket, and he ate alone by his lodge surrounded by the children. It was the single occasion when they did not talk. Now he wished for adult talk. As he came to the lodge he noticed the fire was strong, and a large roast was cooking above it. His mouth watered as he stared at the meat dripping over the flames. Oconostata was sprawled on a skin before the lodge, waiting for his food to be served. Snow Deer was nowhere in sight.

"So, Tennyson," the Chief's voice boomed, "how do you like our village?"

It was the second time Nathaniel had been before the Chief. The first meeting was the formal tribal council when Oconostata had given him a measure of freedom to move around the village. He didn't know why he had been singled out to eat, but he would take advantage of the situation.

Studying the Chief, Nathaniel guessed he was getting old, perhaps fifty, give or take a few years, but strength and power emanated from the figure reclining before him, like a mountain cat ready to spring forward. Here was a man who had fought in the French and Indian War. Taking sides with the French, the Cherokees had fought the British Crown, and this man had been a part of it. Nathaniel had heard some of the stories: Chief Austenaco, who took one hundred men into battle; young warriors on the warpath, raiding white settlements; even this chief before him now, who had fought at Fort Prince George twenty-odd years before.

"I am happy here, Chief Oconostata, and I would like you to tell me what the Council has decided."

"That can wait. Now we will eat together and then talk." The Chief made some motion and his wife appeared and laid out the food boards before the fire. Snow Deer's older brother, Nanatola, came from behind the lodge, grinned at Nathaniel, and sat near his father.

"Where is Snow Deer?" Nathaniel asked. "It has been many suns since the Council met, and I would like to see her again."

"She will come soon. Now eat!" the Chief commanded.

Nathaniel knew there would be no further talk until the Chief was finished. He tore into the meat laid before him. It was excellent, every bit as good as any food he had eaten for a long time, and it felt good to be sitting there before the fire. When the meal was finished, the son spoke to his father and went into the lodge, returning seconds later with the Chief's pipe. Tamping the bowl with tobacco, he reached into the fire for a burning stick, and handed both to his father. The Chief pulled on the pipe a few times and passed it to Nathaniel. He smoked the pipe, but the tobacco sucked suddenly into his lungs made him cough and he handed the pipe back.

"Hai, the smoke is too strong for the strong warrior, huh?"

Embarrassed, Nathaniel replied, "No, it just went down the wrong way." The Chief grinned and Snow Deer's brother giggled.

"Tennyson, I want to talk to you about Snow Deer." As Nathaniel started to interrupt, the Chief held up his hand. "No, let me speak. I thank you for bringing her back. I know you want to see her," the old man paused, "and she wants to thank you too."

He looked away and did not speak for a minute. "When my daughter was lost, my heart was sad. We looked for her, but my people could not find her. I wanted to cry, for she is my only one. Then you carried her home. It was a brave thing for you to fight the Creeks. We found them where they died. If you were Cherokee there would be much celebration for what you did. But you are not one of us, and your ways are not our ways. I know it is hard for you to understand this.

"Tennyson, I have known your white brothers for many years. Many snows have fallen since I last fought against them. During the seige at Fort Prince George, many unarmed chiefs were being held captive there. During the battle, many were massacred but I was set free. I found it hard to forgive the English for what they had done to my brothers. Then I took my braves and went against Fort Loudoun. We laid seige to the fort and captured the garrison. We fought well, but the Red Coats were strong."

The Chief paused, and he closed his eyes and slumped, before continuing. "These things happened before you came across the Great Water. Hai! I was proud of my warriors. I was a great warrior then, Tennyson! What I tell you is true. After the snow fell, your countrymen came against us. They were angry because we took sides with the French. They said we killed white settlers and wanted to punish us. Yes, we killed some of your countrymen, but only after our warriors were slaughtered as they returned from the northern lands of Virginia. A great white army came upon our lands and set fire to our lodges and fields of corn. Our villages were destroyed and many people died and hundreds more were driven into the mountains. We had little to eat, and the disease of the English killed many more. Our hearts were sad."

Again, the Chief stopped .speaking and looked out across the village. "We made peace with our white brothers. For ten or eleven snows, our land was quiet. Then we lost land east of the great Kentucky River. More land, a few snows later. When will it end, Tennyson? Why do the whites want more of our lands? Now you can understand why it is hard for our tribe to welcome you."

Nathaniel wasn't sure what the Chief was saying. He reckoned that the Chief was thanking him for bringing the girl home, but at the same time he was trying to tell him that he would not be permitted to stay. Somehow, Nathaniel had to overcome the thought. This is where he wanted to remain, and he knew it at that moment that he could not let the Chief make a decision unfavorable to him.

"My heart tells me that you or the Council have already decided my fate. You say that I am not Cherokee, and yet I fight as a Cherokee warrior. Now you would have me leave the village, to give up what I have desired for a long time. If I am not one of you, then make me one of yours! You have the power to do that. I want nothing more from the tribe." Nathaniel continued his plea. "For two moons I have traveled to reach my brothers, the Cherokees, whom I hoped would welcome me into their life. I want the chance to prove myself—I have proven myself. Ask Snow Deer!"

"We do not ask you to prove anything. We accept what you say. But there are some things we cannot change, any more than you as a white man can change."

As Nathaniel started to speak, Snow Deer made her way from the lodge assisted by her brother, and sat on a bench outside the door. Dressed in the same simple tunic she was wearing when he first saw her, she was lovely. He stared at her, taking in her beauty, before he hastily summoned his voice and reached for her hand. Her father observed the maneuver.

"Snow Deer, it is good to see you again. I am Na-tan, remember me?"

She looked at her father, wanting permission to speak to this bold man. He waved his hand and she said, "Of course, I know who you are.

You saved me twice, and I too thank you for bringing me home. I have told my father this."

All his thoughts rushed to the surface as he listened to what she was saying, and then they poured out. "Were you sorry that you did not come with me? Where did you think I went? Did the Creeks hurt you?" Then wanting her to remember the first meeting, he asked, "Were you really trying to kill me?"

She looked at him kindly and said, "You ask many things, but as for the last, yes, I wanted to hurt you. I am sorry for that."

Nathaniel grinned. "I would have done the same. I must have frightened you a lot."

She smiled then. "Yes, I was scared, but I am happy that you are here with us."

Getting serious again, Nathaniel said, "There are others in the tribe who are not so happy. I have spoken to your father about this, but he says I cannot change and the tribe cannot change. What can I do, Snow Deer? What can I say that will make them hear?"

The Chief had listened to the exchange between them. He detected in Nathaniel a sincere desire to remain with the tribe, and his father's eyes also told him that Snow Deer would not mind having him stay. He was torn between his love for her and her happiness and his respect for the tribal laws. He looked at Nathaniel, whom he was beginning to like.

"I heard you call yourself Na-tan. So Na-tan, you believed the Council had met and decided your fate. I waited because I wanted to hear what you had to say. Now you have told me. We will discuss it in Council and then give you our answer. That is what we must do!"

Nathaniel knew he was being summarily dismissed, but he wanted to stay a little longer with Snow Deer. He asked permission of the Chief.

"You say that I cannot change, but I am changed from being here today. When I was in the settlements, I heard some of the stories and I understand what you have spoken. But I cannot go back now to live with the whites. You must try and make the Council understand that." Then he glanced at Snow Deer before speaking. "I know that it may not be your way, but I want to see Snow Deer again. Would you ask her if I can return tomorrow?"

* * *

As he waited for the Council to convene, Nathaniel continued to observe and learn more about the tribe. He had the sense that Chief Oconostata was delaying the meeting, and each day he remained with the tribe, the better his chance seemed to be that he could stay. It took only a short time to discover that some of his perceptions of the Cherokees were wrong. He found the men of the tribe spent a lot of time hunting and playing games, while the women of the village were the farmers, furriers, and the family head. This notion was completely foreign to Nathaniel. The women wielded tremendous influence and power in the tribe. Their rights exceeded those in his own country. They decided whom to marry, where and when, and what was acceptable as a dowry. He learned something more: they had an inalienable right of authority and they practiced it at all times.

Women participated in Council. The 'Beloved Woman', or 'War Woman', was surrounded by her own assemblage. This sisterhood consisted of seven women, one chosen from each clan by the Beloved Woman, who kept company and assisted her whenever she desired. The Beloved Woman sat in Council and her position was such that she, like the men, had a vote on making war.

The Cherokees had adopted a matrilinear system, and the Principal People traced their descent through the woman, who established the clan kinship or blood ties. The clan was comprised of a group descending from a common ancestor. The Cherokees had seven clans: Long Hair, Deer, Wolf, Red Paint, Bird, Blue, and Wild Potato. As he began to learn more about the clan system, Nathaniel thought it likely that each clan had specific hereditary duties and privileges. Relatives were traced on the mother's side, and the extended family consisted of the grandmother, mother, sisters, sister's children, and brothers. The mother's clan was predominant and the children were considered the mother's progeny. The clan organization intrigued Nathaniel; it also dominated the society.

Marriage was forbidden between persons of the same clan. Nathaniel found that when a man married, he moved into a house built for the couple by the man's clan. If the man decided to separate from his wife, he moved back into the house of his mother and sisters. Many of the lodges were built to house the extended family, however large it might be. The woman's role was so established that she could institute the divorce, and the husband would be ejected from the marriage couch. The children remained with the mother. The Cherokees never considered the child to be related to the father or the father's family.

Nathaniel discovered that in Cherokee society, the mother's brother assumed responsibility for teaching young boys about the clan and tribal traditions. Consequently, rather than the natural father, "uncle" gained usage as a term of respect even when the person being addressed was not of the blood line or related in any way.

Nathaniel spent as much time as possible with Snow Deer. She wanted to know more about him, and he told her about his life before meeting her. Somehow in his sharing they became closer. She told him about her kinship, the Deer Clan, and that clan loyalty was the basis for life, for teaching, and for the retaliatory wars aimed at seeking revenge for the death of a clan member.

"Tell me about your clan, Snow Deer. I know there are seven clans, but why are you of the Deer Clan?"

"Na-tan," she tried out the sound of his name for the first time, "Is it important for you to know?"

"Yes, I want to know more about you and how you think and what you are. The more I learn, the better I can understand the tribe."

Snow Deer thought for a minute before answering. "The legend tells the story, Na-tan, of many people wandering in the land, scattered to the four winds. Then the Wind Clan, the first to see through the surrounding fog, found the people and gave them our names. That is all I know."

"But why seven clans? Why not five or six?"

"Because to us the number seven is what the Great Spirit decided was best for the tribe. I cannot tell you more."

As he grew to know her better, he found it easy to talk to her. She was much more sophisticated than he expected. Her understanding of the world around her was reassuring. He found in her a kind person, one who was family-oriented, one who expressed a willingness to help others. Soon he found that his initial fascination for her was changing.

He anticipated seeing her, and he sensed that she was becoming an important part of his life.

He discovered something else: she was strongly influenced by her cultural heritage, and because of this she built fences around her emotions. When he tried to explain that he understood her feelings, she was not ready to listen. Yet, for all of this, she possessed a strength of character and understanding not often found in one so young. As she talked with him about many common areas, she had the unintended ability to make him stand a bit taller, to walk with a lighter step, and to know that in her presence, he was a better person for it. She brought an exciting dimension into his life, but he did not believe she knew it nor thought about it.

# 6

# CHEROKEE SUMMER

The Indians knew the land intimately: its boundaries, its forests and fields, its mountains and valleys. They recognized the interrelationship of the land and its bountifulness to the sun and the moon and the cycles of change. They understood the meaning of the changes of seasons, the fire and the cold, the rain and the drought, and attributed it all to the Great Spirit, the provider of everything they needed.

The sacred fire, normally kept burning in the Council House, was revered for its purity and life sustenance. It was also used for setting the lodge cooking fires and for the purpose of providing heat and light. Fire was considered to be the representative of the sun, and anyone who profaned it was subject to swift retribution.

The Cherokees could never understand the concept of land ownership and why the white man wanted to possess it. To their way of thinking they were tenants-in-common; the land was to use only and to share with one another. That is why the Great Spirit had given them a land filled with high mountains and lush, fertile valleys, a place of great beauty. Wild animals and game birds of great variety provided the Cherokees with abundant meat, and the cleared spaces were planted in many crops to add to their menu. It suited their nature and lifestyle [more than adequately].

This place, this land, offered the nation something more, and that was harmony. The Ani'-yun'wiya, above all else, desired harmony in their lives. Harmony meant that sometimes they were forced to fight to correct a perceived wrong or to control their boundaries. They performed rituals when the corn ripened, when they killed a deer, or when they appealed to the Great Spirit, and by doing so maintained harmony. By nature they were not acquirers—that would have upset the harmony in their lives. The few possessions obtained, whether gained in battle or as gifts, were just as likely to be given away or wagered at any time. They used the land to sustain the balance, and they believed it pleased the Great Spirit as nothing else would.

The lifestyle of the Cherokees was simple. Its simplicity centered on the land. Early in the morning, when the households were awakening, the women stirred the ashes and added wood to the fires. Food was then prepared for the family. When the meal was over, the children were assigned tasks. They might be sent to the forest for wood or to pick berries, air the animal skins, or sweep the floor of the hut. There was much to do and the children helped, however they could, even at an age of four or five.

There was a daily search for food in the woods around the camp. Numerous plants and roots had to be gathered and stored. Of the root vegetables there were wild onions and potatoes, arrowroot tubers and lily bulbs, and a vast assortment of greens. In season, nuts were gathered: hickory, walnut, pecan and acorns. Some were crushed in the shell, dropped into boiling water and the oil skimmed from the top to be used later for cooking. Others were roasted and shelled and ground between stones to make into meal. Acorns had to be washed repeatedly to remove the bitter taste before being made into cakes or gruel.

The growing fields had to be tended, and these tasks were relegated to the women. They collected wild berries, sassafras and ginseng, and other plants used in medicines for the clans. Corn, squash, and beans were planted, harvested and dried, and these, when added to the wild foods collected, provided an immense and rich variety of edibles. Fish were caught using traps, hooks and nets, and even poison that temporarily paralyzed the fish. But the Cherokees were mainly meat users, and adult males consumed several pounds daily when it was available.

It appeared to Nathaniel that these activities consumed most of the Indians' waking hours, so it was a few days later before he met Snow Deer outside the lodge. He sensed immediately a change in her acceptance of him. He did not know that she was becoming comfortable with him and enjoyed his company. But in her own way there was still much to learn about him, and she needed to know his true reasons for staying with the tribe.

As they sat together, she smiled, "Na-tan, you have told us that you want to stay here, but you haven't said why. You know so little about us and our way of life. How do you know this is the place for you?"

"Snow Deer, you know I came here because of your accident. If I had not seen you fall, I would have continued on. When I was back in the settlements, even before that in my own country, I learned a lot about your people. I guess I would have been happy with other tribes, but then I met an old Indian back east, and he told me a lot about your tribe. He and his friends took me in and made me a part of their life."

She looked at him, still stunned by his blue eyes and asked, "But were those friends of yours of my tribe . . . were they Cherokee?"

"Yes," he nodded. "I spent many hours with them. They knew I was getting restless and wanted to leave."

His mind slipped back to that time when they were together. Many of his friends told him of the legends of the tribe, passed down from father to son. They regaled him with stories of great battles, and their way of life. He found them to be a proud people, totally consumed by their love for the land and tribe. The legends fascinated him. The Indians were consummate story-tellers, weaving together the threads of a story, giving it fabric and color. Whenever he found time on his hands, he searched them out, trying to learn more of their way of life.

He returned to the present. He said, "My closest friend was White Horse. He . . . "

Nathaniel glanced up sharply as he saw Snow Deer raise her hand. She spoke excitedly, "I know of a man called White Horse—he was my uncle, but it can't be the same one for he died in the Great War. Anyway," she said as she stared past Nathaniel, "go on with your story."

"Are you all right?" Nathaniel asked. She nodded her head and her eyes returned to him.

"Yes," she smiled, "but when you said 'White Horse', you startled me."

Nathaniel continued. "Yes, well, he told me many stories about the Cherokees. We spent much time together. White Horse and I are blood brothers." He held out his wrist to show her a slight pink scar. "I would die for him as he would for me!"

Snow Deer was quiet for a few moments, and then said, "I believe what you say, Na-tan, but you have much to learn about us. The Cherokees have been in this land for many years, far longer than you may believe, and our ancestors were here even before us." Then she abruptly announced, "Do not think of us as savages. Our people established a system of government long before the white man came to our land. So you have much to learn still."

"I know that. I learned that a long time ago." Nathaniel moved to take her hand, but she drew back. "I know far more than you believe I do."

Snow Deer did not argue the point. She sensed that he had told the truth, but he was the first 'Long Hair' she knew, and it was hard for her to give in. He reached for the disc which White Horse had given him. "Show this to your father. It will be easier for him to decide about me, and to call the Council."

Snow Deer looked down at the small silver disc in his palm and froze, for at that instant she recognized it as the talisman carried by members of the tribe, and she shook with the knowledge that Nathaniel had one too. "Where did you get this? Who did you take if from?" she demanded.

"White Horse gave it to me. But why are you upset? Here, take it as a sign of friendship. I want to know you more. White Horse told me that if I needed help, to show it—and I need all the help I can get!"

His petition for help touched her deeply. She reached for his hand, pressed it to her chest, looked into his deep blue eyes and smiled, "Na-tan, you bring me great happiness, and I do like you. Perhaps soon my heart will open more to you. For now, it would be wise to learn as much as you can about us. When you have found this knowledge, tell my father so that he too understands what I have learned today from you." Then she stood, released his hand and turned to enter the lodge. "Hold on to the gift from White Horse. You do not need to prove anything to me."

He sat and thought about what she had said. Nathaniel, in fact, knew quite a lot about the Cherokees and their ancestors, the Iroquois. He had discovered that when the early settlers had arrived, the Iroquois had an established political and social order. They had rules governing the conduct of the members of the family and protocols for dealing with all other tribes. He was aware that for a century-and-a-half the colonists, who lived tenuously on the scrap of the land running along the eastern coast of a much greater land, failed to grasp the fact that the Iroquois were governed by strict and complex constitutional laws.

It was suggested that originally the Cherokees had been a part of the Iroquois Nation, that they had crossed the Mississippi River, perhaps from some western tribe, to explore new lands in the east. There may have been truth that the Iroquois were related from long ago, for Nathaniel frequently heard them called "uncle." Moving into the eastern mountain range they had battled and swept the Algonquins aside, and found the mountains to be overflowing with game and fowl. They staked out their claim. Because they struck regularly at the Algonquins, the tribe referred to them as "Iriakiow," or rattlesnakes, from which their name derived.

Legend told that the Delawares moved into the picture, extending their power and control along the range of mountains, and forced the tribe to split north and south. The Delawares pushed hard, and it was said the southern tribe became the Cherokee Nation. They were good fighters, always willing to take to the warpath, and they believed personal bravery and death in battle to be the highest honor a man could achieve.

It occurred to Nathaniel that Snow Deer was suggesting that he meet with her father again before he called the Council together. In a subtle way, she had hinted that his visit would give Chief Oconostato grounds for supporting Nathaniel's request to stay. He chuckled to himself and started for his lodge, smiling happily at what she had told him.

Suddenly, he was drawn up short as the medicine man jumped from behind a tree and stood before him. Nathaniel had seen the apparition the first time when he had suffered the dream of death shortly after being taken prisoner. Small, compared to the other braves, the shaman looked as if he had just emerged from a dirty fur bag. The man was a bit like a ruffled ferret, Nathaniel thought. His clothes, tied together with sticks and thongs, draped the slight frame. On his belt he carried the tools of his trade: small, woven baskets and bags hung everywhere. Nathaniel wondered what magic potions and useless implements the conjurer had squirreled away. A dried, dirty cap made of a crow's feathered body, perched crazily on his head. He was, without a doubt, a thoroughly disreputable and obnoxious-looking specimen. His name was Black Crow.

The shaman, who had spoken against Nathaniel's acceptance into the tribe, had not liked the white man from the beginning, and a mutual dislike had sprung up between them.

Black Crow, black eyes glittering and arms askew, screamed. "Why do you talk to the Chief's daughter, Long Hair? We do not want you here! Why do you stay?"

Nathaniel was stunned momentarily by the outburst. He had been happy talking to Snow Deer, and the shaman had disrupted his thoughts. "Get out of my way, Black Crow. I have no time to talk to you, nor do I want to."

"Hai, but I will talk to you—you are not one of us, and there are many who think you have brought poison to the village. They do not like the way you play with Snow Deer. She is not for you, Long Hair! Soon she will marry another of the tribe—one of her own kind. We will have harmony again if you go."

"Look, Black Crow, I am not going anywhere. I will stay until the Council meets and decides, and whether you like it or not, so it is. Now stand aside—I do not want to fight you."

"I do not like you, Long Hair," the shaman sneered. "You are nothing to us. Go before there is more trouble."

Nathaniel attempted to placate the man. "Black Crow, we think differently, that is plain. I bear you no grudge, but I do not respect you as a man. You take advantage of the people, what with your mutterings and incantations. You are allowed to remain the shaman, I think, because sometimes you are able to help one of us when we are sick. But most of the time you are a begger who grovels and complains. If you are to be respected, then act like a man! Help the sick and the hurt. Work with the rest of us. You have something which the people need, but don't pretend you are something that you are not! That is all I want to say. Now I am going to my lodge."

He pushed past the man and walked briskly away. The shaman, who had failed in his mission, screamed after him. "Long Hair, you will be sorry for this day. You have made the Great Spirit angry—and I place my mark on you—and curse the day you came here."

Nathaniel stopped and turned, and looked back at the wild man. "No, my friend, it is you who has angered the Great Spirit. I hope He forgives you, Black Crow."

Nathaniel had a hunger for fish, so early one morning he went to the river to try his luck. He enjoyed the solitude of the place, especially in the early hours before the tribe was up and about. It gave him time to reflect on his life, which he felt had been placed in a state of limbo for too long.

As he sat by the running water, basking in the warmth of the spring day, an older man approached. By now many of the tribe knew him and while few were effusive, they seemed to tolerate him. The man standing before him appeared to be in his forties, although Nathaniel knew it was hard to determine an Indian's real age unless he was very young. He was of medium build and rugged looking, and his long hair was pulled back from his face and tied in a single braid. But his distinguishing feature was a long scar that started at his left eye and ran down his face into his neck. Nathaniel thought it looked rather dashing. There was something else about him that piqued Nathaniel's interest. The Indian reminded him of White Horse, and for a moment in his mind his old friend was standing there before him. The thought made Nathaniel happy. Unlike so many of the tribe who were reticent, this man started talking as soon as he got into range.

"Hai, Tennyson, I know you from the Council. I am Bear Claw. As you can see from my face, the bear was very fast. He grinned as he spoke the words. You may call me this." Then he looked at the flowing water. "How is the fishing today? Are the fish many?"

Nathaniel was caught off-guard for a moment, but quickly collecting his wits, he smiled, "Yes I have caught some. Why don't you call me Na-tan?"

"I was in the Council when you spoke. You made a good impression on us."

"If that is so, why doesn't the Council tell me what they want me to do? It has been nearly a moon since I stood before you," Nathaniel reminded him.

Bear Claw looked at Nathaniel for a moment before replying. "Do you think that we want to make a decision quickly? When the Great Chief decides to call the Council, then we will listen. You must not be so impatient, Na-tan. Perhaps, the Chief has reasons to delay the meeting."

"That may be so, but Snow Deer has not told me what is in the Chief's heart. We have talked together, but she said nothing!"

Bear Claw threw his line into the water, and smiled. "That is good, She should not know what is decided before the Council is called."

"Bear Claw, Is there something you want to tell me? Say it openly. I want to know what the tribe intends to do."

"I have heard that you want to stay here with us, and that you are willing to accept our ways. Is this true, Na-tan?"

With resignation in his heart, he said, "It's true, but I am afraid you have already decided my fate. I do not wish to leave here. I am a white man, but I think I could serve you well. Also, I want to stay for Snow Deer."

"Hai, it is for Snow Deer more than anything else! Do you like this woman, Na-tan?"

"I will tell you a secret, Bear Claw. Do you know that Snow Deer tried to kill me? Can I like someone who would do that?"

Bear Claw looked at him in surprise. Nathaniel continued, "The Chief did not know until I told him. But my heart tells me that yes, I do like this woman very much."

"Now I must tell you a secret. Snow Deer is my niece. She is of my blood and my clan's blood, and as her uncle I have much to say about what she wants or doesn't want. If she wants you, and you hurt her, I will kill you easily. Remember that, Na-tan!"

Out of respect for the older man, Nathaniel said, "I thank you, Uncle, for giving me eyes to see and ears to hear. I mean no harm to Snow Deer or any other member of the tribe. I want to stay. I hope the Council allows this."

Nathaniel felt very comfortable with Bear Claw, and unlike most of the Indians, Bear Claw seemed to be genuinely interested in him. Bear Claw thought he liked this man standing before him. He sensed the man's sincerity, and there was something about him that was almost Indian. He knew many of the villagers would rather see Nathaniel go, but he hesitated to tell him. He too wondered why the Chief had not called a meeting. Many of his own clan had discussed Nathaniel and his request to remain with the tribe, but nothing had been decided. He looked at Nathaniel and wondered how he would feel if it were he waiting for the Council to decide.

He smiled, "Be patient, Na-tan. You will soon know what has been decided. And in the meantime, you and I will have more time to fish together—and for others to get to know you."

When Nathaniel had fallen in with the Cherokees, his long rifle had been taken from him. While some of the Indians possessed guns, ammunition was also in short supply so many members of the tribe continued to use the bow for hunting and killing. The few rounds available for the old rifles used during a raid were kept hidden away. The Indians could not make gunpowder nor ammunition, and thus relied on the traders or the occasional traveler to replenish the small amount they had. As a result of the shortage, they could not practice firing, and they were less than accurate when they shot at anything.

Nathaniel's rifle had been returned, but he rarely took it with him when he left the village. He decided that he had to learn the traditional weapons of the tribe. The principal ones were the bow and arrows, blowguns and poisoned darts, spears, axes and slings. The blowguns and slings were for the smaller animals, while the others were used in the hunt and for fighting. He planned to become proficient with them all.

One day, he sat watching Bear Claw make a bow and some arrows. The Indian had found in the mulberry tree the limb from which he would fashion the bow. When first squatting together on the ground, Bear Claw looked at Nathaniel for a long moment. He seemed to be studying the white man, and it made Nathaniel a bit uneasy. He could not imagine why the old Indian stared at him for so long. After a few minutes Bear Claw dropped his eyes and began stripping the bark from the wood. His hand moved deftly along the wood, turning and shaping the bow. Then he cut it into the desired length.

Using the hot ashes of the fire, he commenced bending and molding the bow. Nathaniel was fascinated with the procedure. The wood was thrust into the fire, held there for a moment, and then withdrawn. This went on for some time. Bear Claw thrust, withdrew, and applied pressure on the wood. After he had gotten the required shape he used a piece of sandstone to smooth the bow. There was still another step, and he quickly wrapped the middle and ends of the bow with thin strips of rawhide to add strength. Finally he took a long piece of sinew, formed the bowstring, and popped it into place.

During the entire time neither man spoke. Nathaniel found this to be the custom whenever an Indian was working on anything. He devoted his attention to the task at hand and rarely allowed speech to divert him from his concentration. When he had finished the bow, he extended it before him and examined it carefully. It seemed to meet his standard. The bow was gleaming as he handed it to Nathaniel for approval.

"How do you like it, Na-tan?" He asked.

Nathaniel took the bow, turned it over several times, and announced, "It is beautiful work, Bear Claw." Wanting to joke with him a bit he added, "But I think you should polish it some. Maybe that will make it shoot straighter!"

Bear Claw's face, which beamed when Nathaniel had first replied, now dissolved into a frown and then darkened. "What do you mean, Na-tan? Why does it need more polishing?"

Nathaniel grinned. "Much fun, Bear Claw, to see your face. It really is good work."

Bear Claw reached out and pushed Nathaniel to the ground. "Na-tan, some day you will say the wrong thing to someone and get hurt."

"But not from you, my friend! You'll be there to help me if I do. Now give me your hand."

Bear Claw then showed Nathaniel how the arrows were made. The shafts, arrowheads, and feathers had already been selected, so it was a rather simple matter to put them all together. Bear Claw wasted little energy as he took the shaft, cut it to the right length, placed and tied the chipped arrowheads, and added the flights. Nathaniel was intrigued by the way the old Indian's hands flew up and down the shaft. It was like a pantomime, telling the story of the ancient process underway.

Again, Bear Claw worked without words, only a grunt or two coming from his throat. He completed the work quickly. Gathering his tools and the bow and arrows, he got to his feet before turning to Nathaniel.

He thrust them forward. "These are for you, Na-tan," as he held them before him. "Now, you have your own bow for the hunt. I hope it fits."

The offer caught Nathaniel completely unaware. For a moment he stood there, looking at Bear Claw. He wasn't sure what he should do. Then Bear Claw pushed them again toward Nathaniel. "My brother, I want you to have them. It is a gift from Bear Claw. I know my brother will shoot straight with them." He smiled, and added, ". . . without too much rubbing."

Now Nathaniel smiled, "You make me proud, Bear Claw. I will hunt well with them. The bow is shaped right and the arrows are straight, and I thank you for this gift." Responding to Bear Claw's teasing, he said, "And I'll try not to wear them out with rubbing."

Then both men started laughing, and flinging their arms around the other's shoulder, they turned and walked toward the lodge.

Nathaniel was overwhelmed by the gifts of the bow and quiver of arrows. But it was not until the two men separated and Nathaniel had returned to his lodge, that he began to fully appreciate the beauty of Bear Claw's workmanship. For the moment he hung the bow on a peg in the lodge and went out to see what food had been left on the fire for his supper.

It was a good stew of meat and vegetables. As he ate he wondered what woman had brought it to his lodge. Could it have been Snow Deer? If so, she was a good cook! Since she could not get around too well and stayed near her lodge, she might have had time to prepare the meal for him. Then he realized that it could have been any one of a number of squaws. Oh well, he shrugged, it was the perfect way to end a good day, and maybe tomorrow the Council would meet and he would know more about his status. In the meantime, why not take advantage of the situation and learn how to use the bow.

Taking it from the lodge he examined it carefully. He gripped the bow in the middle and turned it back and forth as he looked at the tapered ends and saw how the twisted deer gut was attached. He flexed the bow, testing its strength, and was surprised at how hard it was to draw back the string. Nathaniel was impressed by the way it seemed to fit his arm, and he remembered how Bear Claw had studied him before he commenced working on the bow. "That man! All the time he was at work, Bear Claw was making the bow for me! I owe Uncle something," he mused, "but what do I have to give him?"

He picked up an arrow. It was as straight as a gun barrel, and Nathaniel was more impressed as he took each arrow in turn and sighted along the wood. He saw that they were identical and nearly flawless. The flights were made from trimmed turkey feathers, evenly proportioned, one to another.

He fit an arrow to the string, and holding it in place, aimed it at an imaginary animal. Then he decided to try it out. He pulled on the string, but the arrow slipped from his fingers and fell to the ground. He tried a second time, but when he attempted to pull back on the bow-string with the arrow, he failed. He blamed it on his clumsiness and promised himself that in the morning he would ask Bear Claw to teach him how to use the thing. Nathaniel was determined to learn as quickly as possible. The lance and the blowgun would have to wait! This was what he would master first.

The day following was sunny and warm. When he had eaten he hurried over to Bear Claw's lodge. He wanted to catch him before he left for the day. He was in luck and his friend agreed to teach him. They went off into the woods to use it, and they remained there until the sun cast long shadows around them. Bear Claw told Nathaniel they had practiced enough, that it was time to stop.

"You have done well, Na-tan, but it is late and I am tired."

Thank you, Uncle. For the time you have spent with me, and for giving me good teaching. I owe you for that!"

"You owe me nothing, Na-tan. It makes my heart happy to see you using the bow. I think you will be a good hunter very quickly. Whether you will do as well on a raid, we must wait and see."

"I will make you proud, Uncle. And I will tell all in the village that you taught me." Nathaniel grinned, "Now I had better shine my bow— my teacher knows it must be rubbed often!"

# 7

## *Raiders in the Dark*

As he had done several times before, Nathaniel got up before dawn one morning and went fishing. It gave him opportunity to sort out his emotions about Snow Deer and the decision that was still to be made by the Council. Although he had little reason to anticipate the events of the morning that lay ahead, they would be embedded in his mind forever and would be the pivotal factor behind the Council's acceptance of his petition.

It was dark when he left his lodge. As he passed through the village, the dogs that he had befriended by throwing scraps of food to them, either ignored him completely or got up and greeted him and then returned to the fire before their lodges. They had come to know the smell of the white man and were not nervous as he made his way through the village. That is, all of them except Bear Claw's dog.

As he passed by the lodge of his friend, the dog jumped up as Nathaniel approached and wagged his tail and then dutifully followed Nathaniel. It was fishing time, and the half-breed wolf-dog knew that Nathaniel would share his catch with him. They entered the path leading from the village and continued toward the river, carefree and happy until they heard the owl screech. Instantly, Nathaniel stopped and the dog froze beside his leg, alert and hair bristling.

He reached down and spoke softly to the animal. "You heard it too? We must go quietly." Moving forward they heard another call, and almost to himself Nathaniel said, "There is something out there for sure and I don't think it is an owl." Hearing the man's voice, the dog stopped again.

Nathaniel listened for another call, trying to pinpoint the sound. The owl hooted again, and this time got an answering cry. Then he knew! There were Indians in the woods and at this black hour they had to be looking for a fight. Perhaps it was a Creek raiding party, or some other band of marauding invaders, but he was sure they represented a threat to the sleeping village. He guessed they were waiting for daybreak and had sent out an advance party to survey the layout of the area.

In any case, he had to act fast. There was no time to return and awaken the tribe. If he started shooting, that might alert them and give time to get in position for the battle. He started moving quietly, hoping to surprise the Indians as they got closer to the village. The dog bounded ahead, the scent of the enemy warrior on the trail.

He was in luck! Almost immediately he spotted the Indian. He was standing with his back to Nathaniel, concentrating on something ahead of him as the dog leaped. The dog surprised Nathaniel as much as it shocked the Indian, and before the raider had a chance to move, ninety pounds of canine fury hurtled through the air and knocked him down and tore at his throat. The Creek died quickly, thrashing on the ground as the dog stood before him watching the lifeblood drain away.

There was another one not too far away. Nathaniel glimpsed him in the dim light as he waited for some one or some signal. Nathaniel patted the dog, reassuring the animal that he had done well, and he looked up, his eyes shining in the starlight, as if to acknowledge that he and Nathaniel had become a killer team. Nathaniel motioned for the dog to stay, and was rewarded when it dropped beside him. As Nathaniel moved ahead, however, the dog slunk along behind him, and when they had gotten within range for Nathaniel to throw his knife, the Indian heard and turned and looked in his direction, just as the knife found its mark. The Creek screamed once and fell, but the Indian was in his death throes, and the dog stood over him until the body stopped convulsing.

The final scream alerted the third raider, who out of fear for his life raced away. Nathaniel could hear him thrashing through the forest, and he lifted his rifle and fired once in the direction of the fleeing

Indian. It also alerted the war party that there would be no surprise attack on the Cherokees this morning. Retrieving his knife, Nathaniel quickly removed the Indian's scalp and then retraced his steps to where the first one lay. He repeated the procedure and tied both to his belt.

The sky had become lighter and he could clearly see the signs of the war party. Then he heard the sounds of two or three Cherokees coming along the path leading to the river. He called out as they approached. He told them quickly of the raiders in the woods ahead, and they fanned out and started running after the Creeks. Suddenly he felt tired. He sat and leaned against a tree, waiting for the second group of warriors to appear. They were not long in coming.

"Na-tan, where are they? Who were they?"

"You surprised them, huh?"

"How many were there?"

The questions came fast. Nathaniel repeated the story. Red Arrow, who was leading the warriors, was eager to go after the Creeks. "We will track them down, Na-tan. Wait for us here!"

"Let them go, Red Arrow," Nathaniel suggested. "They are already across the river, and the scouts are after them. They will not be coming back soon."

The other men straggled back. The first one looked at the scalps dangling from Nathaniel's waist. "You killed two more, Na-tan!" he exclaimed.

Red Arrow shook his head and added, "Soon all the Creeks will be after your scalp. That makes five of the devils since you came here."

Nathaniel interrupted. "One belongs to the dog; he did the killing. As for the dead Creeks, you know I love them little, so no great loss." He grinned, "Besides, they ruined my morning of fishing."

The Indians laughed, and one bright lad pointed to the dripping scalps and said, "Use those for bait, Na-tan, you should catch many fish."

"I think I'll wait for another day. I don't like Creeks for breakfast."

The small group of warriors headed for the village. The men were excited and one was sent ahead to inform the village of what had happened. Nathaniel was tired, but proud that he had foiled an attack. They stopped when they reached the Chief's lodge.

Chief Oconostata raised his hand and grinned as he looked directly at Nathaniel. "Na-tan, we heard that your fishing was interrupted this morning." Then glancing at the scalps, ". . . and that you caught some Creeks instead."

"Yes," he replied, "but give Bear Claw's dog credit for one of them."

The Chief continued to beam, but growing serious he said, "The tribe thanks you for warning us. If the Creeks had come, we would have been ready."

"I figured you would hear the shot, but I was trying to hit the last one I saw," he said.

"How many did you see, Na-tan?" the Chief asked.

"Just three, but more were out there. How many? I do not know."

"It is good you left the village early—to fish, but since you have nothing to show for the morning, come sit by my fire and I will share my pot. You must be hungry now."

"I am hungry, and I will gladly sit with you," Nathaniel said.

Snow Deer, who had been standing beside her father during the exchange, smiled at Nathaniel. "Na-tan, I am proud of you for doing this for my people." She dropped her eyes, adding, "And for me."

Her father waited for Snow Deer to finish. Stepping closer, he placed his hand on Nathaniel's shoulder. "I too am proud of what you did, Na-tan. You are a brave Cherokee warrior."


The Chief called the Council together the next morning. Nathaniel had been told late in the day that he must come before Council to explain why he wanted to stay with the tribe. Bear Claw also told him that he and the Chief and Red Arrow would speak for him and ask the tribe to accept him as a member of the Cherokee Nation.

All night long Nathaniel tried to put his thoughts together. He had known since he came to the camp with Snow Deer that he had found his place in life. He did not want to leave. He was sure that the maid had much to do with his decision, but it was much more than the girl. As he lay in his lodge, his mind turned to England and what he had left behind. He wondered what changes had occurred there, what had happened to his family and Jenny. Since leaving he had received no messages, nor had he tried to communicate with them. Was this really what he wanted, or was it some kind of inner escape? No, he finally decided, his family and friends were all a thing of the past. He could never go back. What use would there be in that? And for what? He decided that the bonds had severed at the moment of sailing, torn irrevocably by his departure.

Now he was here, lying in a lodge within a Cherokee village. His thoughts swirled around him as he tried to put together what he would say on the morrow. And finally he knew. First he would remind the Council that he had lived in the white settlements, and that he had seen the "blanket Indians," as they were known, trying to retain their way of life, but with little success. Their failure to live in the way they wanted was the catalyst that made him reject his own race and head west. Then he would tell them that he came to the village of his own volition, that he had learned what their freedom meant, and he could no longer return to the white man's way. He would remind them that he had not been captured in battle, and therefore, should be permitted to stay as one of them. Finally, he would say that he had gained that right and had proven to be worthy of their trust. With this last reflection on the matter, he turned over and slept.

He was standing before the Council, confident that he could speak clearly of his desire to stay. As he looked around the room, he could not discern from the stoic countenances on the Indians what would happen.

The Chief had the first word. "I have called the Council to hear Na-tan's words. He has told us he wants to stay here. We have never looked upon the white man and his ways as something we wanted to be like. Now this man comes to us and asks us to take him in. I myself have thought much about this man before us.

"He was not captured by us. He carried my daughter from the Creek war party. He has been a warrior among us, and he has killed our enemies. He gave the village warning before the morning sun rose. I think he is a good man. Now, let others speak for or against him."

Bear Claw stood. "Many suns ago, after we first saw this man in Council, I sat with him by the river. We said many things to each other that day. He told me that he wanted to stay with us, and when I asked him why he said that his heart told him he could find peace in his heart. I do not know how much peace he has found, for he has killed five of our enemies. How many of us have killed as many? I liked him that first day, and he has become my friend. I think he is a good man too. Perhaps, the Great Spirit has brought him to us for some reason. We must decide now whether he stays with us or must go."

Bear Claw had barely spoken the last words when the shaman jumped to his feet and shouted, "I say he should go. The Long Hairs have brought nothing but trouble to our tribe. He is one of them. Do not say the Great Spirit brought him. That is wrong!" he snarled. "Perhaps the Dark Spirit who lives under the ground brought him! I believe he was sent by the Long Hairs, and will stay only until he learns our secrets. Then he will scatter like the wind and bring much misery upon us." Then he conjured up all the anger and hate he could muster and pointedly screamed at Nathaniel, "Again, I say he should go."

Now the Indians commenced shouting. Many leaped to their feet, trying to drown out the shaman. They heard the bitterness in his voice and could not understand why he appeared to hate Nathaniel. One cried, "Sit down, Old Man, you have had your say." Another shouted, "How many Creeks have you killed?" The shaman muttered something more and then scurried off to the side of the house.

Red Arrow stood to speak. "I have seen and heard what this man has done since coming to our village. He has learned many of our ways If he wanted to tell our secrets to the whites, he would have gone many suns ago." Red Arrow continued. "He has been a brave warrior, and there will be other battles to fight. I do not like the whites. The Long Hairs, as the shaman says, may come against us again, and if that day comes I would rather have this man beside me than fighting me. I want him to stay, both as friend and warrior."

When Red Arrow sat down, there were a few other who wanted to speak. Each one praised Nathaniel for his exploits of the previous month and offered their support. When they finished the Chief motioned for Nathaniel to speak. Only the shaman raised an objection to this, but was quickly shouted down.

The Council grew quiet as Nathaniel rose to his feet. He thanked the men who had spoken on his behalf. Then turning to the shaman he said, "Much of what you say about the whites is true. I do not know if the Great Spirit brought me to help you, but He led me to this village. That is enough for me. I may not have your trust, Black Crow, but we are the same in that respect. You do not have mine. Yet, I believe we can live together as friends, rather than as cautious enemies. That is your choice, if the Council allows me to stay here."

Returning his eyes to the Chief, he continued. "What words can I speak now that I have not said before? Many know my thoughts. Last night, I had many things on my heart to say, but they have been spoken here today. If the Council decides that I should go, I will leave you, today. Now I would like to go to my lodge so that others may speak freely."

After he left, the vote was taken. It was unanimous that he should be allowed to stay, provided that he undergo the tribal rites. Even then, since he had proven himself thrice-over in his time with them, they agreed to make an exception in his case.


Now that he was an accepted member of the tribe, Nathaniel found it quite simple to speak Cherokee. The transition from Iroquoian to Cherokee was rather painless. Their culture had a profound effect on him. As he came to understand the customs and traditions, and even the nuances of body language and signs, he realized how little he had learned about them before his arrival. He was so comfortable with them that he was rarely surprised at anything they did or said to him. When they tried to shock him by some outlandish action or scheme, he generally could see through their purpose quite easily.

They loved to play games on him, or tease him, trying to get some outcry or reaction from him. They would wear masks and want him to guess their identity, or set simple traps for him, both in camp and on the trail. They would try to catch him off guard and use some stunt to fool him. They seemed never to tire of the games.

One day he went hunting with two young men of the clan. An Indian he recognized as Two Arrows and another brave came upon him as he practiced with his bow. Two Arrows was already a warrior Sub-chief, the younger brother of Red Arrow. He had counted coup, and was being groomed to lead in battle. Tall and well-built, he wore two feathers, a certain sign of warrior status. He was one of the guards who had taken him to the first Council meeting. The second man was shorter by a head and possessed a slight limp, but when he came up to Nathaniel he grinned and raised his arm in salute. Nathaniel liked him immediately. Both Indians carried their bows carelessly. They decide to have some fun with him.

"Hai, Na-tan," Two Arrows cried, "Are you ready to use your bow?"

"Yes, why not?"

"We are going hunting. Come along and see how well you can shoot."

Nathaniel, caught up in the jesting, replied, "I have heard it told around the village that your name has meaning. What does it mean, Two Arrows?"

Before he could answer, the other brave said, "Hai, he needs two arrows to hit anything, Na-tan."

Two Arrows thrust out his hand and sent the brave sprawling. "Oh, is that so?" he exclaimed. Then he reached down and scuffed the man on the ground.

"Perhaps, I will need only one arrow to fetch a deer!" Nathaniel said.

Two Arrows, not yet ready to concede the point to the white man, replied, "We will see about that. Are you sure you want to come with us?" Then he turned up the path leading away from the camp.

When they had gotten deep into the woods, they stopped near a fallen tree. "Stay here, Na-tan. We will go up the trail and chase a nice fat deer to you. If you are as good with the bow as you think, it will be an easy shot."

"Why don't you wait, Two Arrows? Then you can use both arrows for the kill," Nathaniel teased.

"No, it is for me to decide. You wait," he ordered.

Nathaniel thought it to be a wise maneuver. The Indians slipped off into the forest while Nathaniel waited for some sight or sound of the approaching animal. Mid-afternoon came, and the day was growing shorter. The first hour passed, and then another. At last he realized they had no intention of chasing anything toward him. They were toying with him again, wanting to prove that he wasn't much of a hunter.

Nathaniel found their innocence and child-like actions refreshing, and he chuckled to himself when he guessed what they intended.

With that realization came discovery, and Nathaniel decided two could play at the game. He studied the woods around him, suspecting that they had circled him and had gone to ground to see what he would do. He watched for some movement, although he knew they had infinite patience and would try to remain hidden and quiet for hours if need be.

His plan started to take shape. He first removed his shirt. Quietly, he set himself the task of weaving several grass ropes. He moved around gathering the long stems, making sure they could see him, and then sat braiding the grass together. He pretended he was bored and needed something to do, but all the while he scanned the forest. He knew the watching eyes would soon get curious and one of them would move. He saw the first one, a quick glimpse of something white, and he knew that he had been right.

When he finished the work he pulled the shirt over his head again. He tied all the ropes around his waist, exaggerating each movement, except for a longer one that he tied to a low branch. Scanning the ground, he scuffled around the small clearing looking for his next piece of the puzzle. Then he saw the second hunter! Luck was with Nathaniel and he found what he needed: the skeleton of an old deer. Picking up the dried head, he brushed off the leaves and returned to the branch where he tied the rope to the skull beneath the tree and started it swinging to and fro. This would certainly draw their attention!

So far, so good! The tree, when it fell, had not crashed to the ground. It was held at an angle, supported by other trees around it. This gave Nathaniel the cover he now needed to play out the game. Moving behind the trunk he stripped off his shirt and quickly filled it with grass and leaves from the covered ground. He then propped the stuffed shirt above the fallen tree so that it could be seen by the hidden hunters.

The sun was falling and Nathaniel knew that he had to move fast. It would soon be dark. Sliding to the ground he started making a long circle to get behind the first Indian he had spotted. He crept forward slowly and quietly, and when he was within a few feet of the unsuspecting man, dived on his friend and clamped a hand over his mouth. With a swift motion, he gagged and tied the ropes around the hunter. Nathaniel was much larger and stronger than the Indian and quickly had him trussed and tied to a tree.

Now for the second! Remaining on the ground he slithered toward the other man. It was not as easy. Every few minutes Nathaniel would stop and listen, and try to orient his position to the fallen tree. He knew generally where he would find the Indian, but it was slow going. Again his sense of direction was right. His victim had chosen to relieve himself seconds before Nathaniel attacked, and could do little as the apparition flew through the air and landed on his back. Quickly, as he had done with the first one, Nathaniel had the second hunter bound to a tree. There was no need to gag him.

Leaving the Indians he returned to the fallen tree and laughed and shouted and made all kinds of threats and taunts to the trussed hunters. He told them he was leaving them for the night, that they would become prey for the wild animals that roamed the woods, and that he would tell the clan they had been killed while hunting. He teased them unmercifully and they could only lie on the ground and listen to this wild, screaming man who had bested them.

"Hai, my friends, how do you like the game?"

"Come on, Na-tan, cut us loose and we'll finish the hunt," the ungagged Indian yelled.

"Why should I let you go, so that you can trick me again?" Nathaniel asked. "No, I think I'll leave you for the night. I'll tell the clan you were killed. You know, that's not a bad idea," he smiled to himself.

Through the gag the first Indian moaned loudly. Nathaniel shouted, "Maybe I'll tell the tribe where I left you, and they can come fetch you. On the other hand, I could tell them that you got lost. Yes, I think I will do that."

"Na-tan, you can't leave us here," one pleaded.

"Hai, how do you like being my prisoners? Think about it after I'm gone."

They were silent then, not knowing what this crazy white man had planned for them. They had underestimated him and now the table was turned. He had convinced them he was leaving them for the night. They struggled to free themselves, but the ropes held them where they lay and their movements were futile.

"Have a good sleep, my friends. Tell you what! If no one comes for you tonight, I'll come back in the morning."

He left them then and quietly headed downhill toward the creek where he waited for the deer to come in the gathering dusk. When a large buck appeared, Nathaniel was able to kill and gut it quickly before returning to tell his two friends. When he finally cut them loose and removed the gag, they pretended to be mad at him, but as they descended the hill together to fetch the deer, they laughed at the joke Nathaniel had pulled on them.

He had won them over and it would be a story to tell many times in the long nights ahead. In the village he gave them credit for the kill. After all, if they had not played a game on him, he could not have gotten the deer; and when he divided the meat he gave them the choicest parts to show them that he bore them no enmity.

## 8

# SHAMAN AND THE GREAT SPIRIT

The absolute belief of one Great Spirit as the authority of their lives impressed Nathaniel. Still he found it difficult to reconcile some of their actions, especially the cruel and vicious ones, with their profound respect for this Supreme Being to whom they paid homage in everything they did. Nathaniel paid careful attention to them, trying to understand to what depth they revered or knew their god. He suspected they had rather vague conceptions of two divinities, one good and the other evil. He sensed that all worshipped the good one, quietly for the most part, while the tribal medicine man or the conjurer attended to the evil influences which fell upon the tribe.

The shaman, a priest or medicine man or woman, was accepted as an important member of the village. According to legend, they possessed extraordinary powers based on the belief that good and evil influences attended the tribe, and the shaman had the ability to communicate and influence these spirits for the good of the individual or tribe. In Nathaniel's judgement, the shaman encouraged and reinforced this belief because of his or her power of perception, physical presence, and the ability to create illusionary situations of mystical proportion. He found this man to be totally unscrupulous. In his opinion, the village shaman was little more than a poor magician, who carried his sleight-of-hand bag of tricks around for all to see.

This simple fact was to become one of the most serious matters Nathaniel would face after he joined the tribe. For whatever reason, the shamans were respected and had become an integral part of the society. This caused Nathaniel no end of problems, for while he recognized the shaman's knowledge and use of medicinal herbs and plants for healing, and even the medical procedures the shaman used, he could not condone the medicine man's rituals that came close to witchcraft.

All medicine men and women possessed uncanny psychic powers over their patients, as well as keen knowledge of anatomy, but the application of remedies for some disorders was highly questionable. They used any number of blood-letting techniques because they believed, and had the patients believing, that evil spirits were held in the body, and by cutting veins or scarring the forehead, they could then suck the blood along with the evil spirit from the body.

Cherokees believed that animals were the cause of disease, but that plants provided the cure. Thus, the shaman used various plants to heal the body. Many indeed did have medicinal value, and these were used frequently to relieve fevers, to stimulate healing, to cause vomiting, and to alleviate headaches. The shamans knew how to apply unguents, relieve constipation, and treat other maladies. If they had stopped there, Nathaniel could have tolerated them, but he vigorously opposed their strange gestures and incantations, their imperious attitudes, and their pretensions of knowledge well beyond the average Indian.

The exhortations and contortions and rites of exorcism, which he had seen the shaman inflicting on other members of the clan since his arrival, had convinced Nathaniel that the medicine man was more a practitioner of witchcraft than a healer of medicine. In fact, White Horse had told him that the power of the shamans had been seriously eroded after they had failed to cope with several earlier smallpox epidemics that had wiped out large numbers of the tribe. He was more than ever persuaded of the medicine man's deception and dishonesty, and vowed that somehow he would reduce or eliminate the shaman's influence in tribal affairs. He did not stop and consider what he would do, but he was determined to try, nevertheless.

In fairness to the shaman, however, he had seen what happened when whites came to live with other tribes. White man's customs were different, and he feared for changes in his own culture and what it meant for the integrity of the Cherokee Nation. The shaman suspected that Nathaniel's interest in remaining in the village was Snow Deer. He saw the seeds of friendship beginning to flower into more—a love relationship between Snow Deer and the white trapper.

After the Council had accepted Nathaniel's plea, during which the shaman was the only man to object and was voted down, the medicine man realized he had lost some influence in the tribe. He was also acutely aware of Nathaniel's popularity. While he was still respected by most of the villagers who were accustomed to his ways, he sensed that he was not the central performer he once had been.

Nathaniel learned that the Great Spirit was the creator of the universe. He provided them the sun and the moon, he was the giver of light and life and fire, all that was necessary to living. This cycle of life never varied, for He gave them game and all plants and every provision the tribe needed. Every season—the New-born-Leaf, Sun-high-in-the-Sky, Fall-of- the-Leaf, and Cold-in-the-Ground—was a time to honor the Great Spirit.

Nathaniel found the child-like acceptance of this Supreme Being in everything they attempted to do, for they recognized that as He gave, so could He also take away. They had no images or idols that he had observed; they believed the Great Spirit sat above the clouds, but could easily walk upon the earth.

One day Nathaniel sat with Snow Deer's brother, Nanatola. He needed to know more about the religion and what it truly meant to each of them. While he had watched the religious festival, and knew that a certain season was set apart for it, there were many questions gone unanswered.

"Across the Great Sea, where I once had my home, we too knew a Great Spirit," Nathaniel said. "What do you call God, or this Spirit of yours?"

Nanatola's features softened, and he replied, "He Who Sitteth Above, 'Hianequo', is our Great Spirit. From Him comes everything: the lights in the sky, the sun and moon, the wind and the rain, and the great fire and the snow."

"But how do you explain Him? You cry out to the Spirit during your solemn festival—so how do you know He exists?"

Nanatola made a deliberate gesture toward the sky and spoke softly, "Na-tan, we know the Great Spirit is everywhere, He governs everything; He watches each one of us. If we hunt well, provide for our family, make war on our enemies, are honest and brave, then we will go and meet the Great Spirit in the sky."

"And what of those in the tribe who do not do these things?"

"Then, if they have not listened to Him, they will have to shift for themselves and will never meet the Great Spirit. They will find few animals for food and clothing, and little fresh water to drink, and will wander aimlessly and never know peace."

"So you believe there is a heaven and a hell!"

"Na-tan, we know nothing of this word you speak. We know that when we die, our spirit goes the way of the sun, to the west, and there our friends and family will meet us and we will be happy together."

Nathaniel needed to know more. He said, "But Snow Deer told me her soul would wander aimlessly if I had killed her, and yet she knows the Great Spirit."

"That is certain! If we die and no one cares for us, if no one pays tribute to us, then our spirit cannot enter into the hunting grounds."

"In the Council House, on each of the posts, there are carved faces. What do they mean to the tribe?"

Nanatola hesitated before he answered Nathaniel. "Na-tan, you think they are idols to us. They are not! The Great Spirit has not need of such things. Those faces you speak of are dedicated to our people who have gone before us, those who have hunted well or fought well in battle."

Nathaniel did not say anything. For long moments he tried to comprehend what Nanatola had told him. Finally, he arose from his seat quietly and said, "I am happy that you spoke of these things. I count you as a brother, and my brother has enlightened me again."

"Listen Na-tan, when the sun is high and the wind is whispering, when the moon is bright and the corn is green, when the solemn festival is next come, see well with your eyes and hear well with your ears, and then, you will know our Great Spirit too."

* * *

The medicine man was involved in every facet of village life, and the shaman called upon, or made entreaties to, the Great Spirit whenever tribal activities demanded his services. Every impending raid, hunt, festival, marriage, illness, birth, death, or game was occasion for the shaman to participate and attempt to divine the will of Hianequo. The priest was the intermediary to the Great Spirit, or at least the people thought so. His attendance at, and involvement in these events was accepted as a pre-ordained requirement. This included the game of stickball.

The most favorite and competitive game, and one which gave the players a chance to expend excess energy, was stickball. The Cherokees called the games 'the little brother of war', for it was a rough and tough game that frequently caused serious injury to the players. They played regularly against teams from other villages, and frequently took on teams fielded by neighboring tribes, especially when they were not engaged in fighting war with these enemies. Nathaniel watched the games with a great deal of interest.

One day late in the summer, after a game had been played, he approached one of the players coming off the field. "You played a good game, Grey Fox. I was watching and I would like to try it sometime."

The Indian, pleased with the compliment, lowered his head and said, "I think you would be good at it, Na-tan, but you need a ballstick."

"So, that is no problem. I will ask Bear Claw for his."

Grey Fox shot a glance at him. "No, you cannot play until you make your own. That is the rule. Then you must follow the ritual of cleansing and training. Perhaps, before the snow flies, you can be ready."

This was required for all players. The training lasted for nearly a month, during which time he was forbidden to eat certain foods, touch a woman or infant, or undertake any other activity that might divert his attention from the required regimen.

The first thing he had to do was to make the stick. He sought out Bear Claw. "Uncle, the 'little brother of war' the men play interests me. Would you help me make a ballstick? I don't know how to get started."

"I will help, Na-tan, but only that. You must make it yourself. It is important to gain experience and only by creating the ballstick will you know its strength and the way it handles."

They walked to the woods together. Bear Claw helped him select the wood and agreed to guide him through the construction steps, but refused to make the stick for him. The first one they found was about two feet in length, at the end of which was a slight fork. They they returned to the clearing. Nathaniel waited while Bear Claw went to his lodge and returned with the material to complete the task.

"Now I think we have everything we need, Na-tan. Come, let us sit in the shade." He selected a place where the sun came through an opening and formed a bright beam. "Let's work here. You will be able to see better."

He handed the leather strips to Nathaniel and said, "First, you must weave the webbing for a pocket . . . like this." Bear Claw's hands quickly wove the leather together. "Pretend you are making a basket, but make it a bit larger. It has to look like your man-sack."

He laughed as Nathaniel clumsily attempted to weave the thongs together. He was making a small pouch. "Is that the size of yours? Hai, you have to fashion a pocket to catch and hold the ball when it is thrown by the other player, or to receive it from your own man. Think of it as an extension of your arm. It provides leverage to the thrower as the ball leaves the pocket."

"Uncle, will the training be as bad as this?" he asked as he worked on the pouch.

"It is worse, Na-tan. You know that you may not touch a woman; it will weaken your spirit. But if your man-sack is no larger than the ball-stick pocket, you have no worry," he giggled. "Now, attach the webbing to the stick. Here, I will show you."

As he listened to Bear Claw giving him step-by-step directions, Nathaniel finally got the stick together into a reasonable-looking replica of others he had seen. He leaned back and looked up from his labor. "Now that I have made this, Bear Claw, do you think it will play?"

"It is a good ballstick, Na-tan. You have done fine work."

"I hope so. I'm not sure I want to try the game now."

Bear Claw looked hard at him, surprised at Nathaniel's outburst. "The training will be good for you. It makes a man's head think clear. It is also a hard game, and if you do not want to play, the men will believe that you are not too strong," he replied.

"Look, Bear Claw, the men know what I can do."

"Na-tan, whether you play the game or not is for you to decide. But do you ask me to help you make a ballstick so that you can hang it in your lodge, or walk through the village with it tied to your belt, or carry it when you go fishing? I think not!"

Nathaniel thought for a moment at what his friend had said. "As usual you are right again, Uncle. If I am to play well so that you will place bets on me, then I must learn the game, huh?"

He jumped up from the ground and swung the ballstick back and forth, and over his head, imagining how he would slash and throw the ball. "Like this, Uncle? Do I have a strong arm, Uncle?" he cried.

"You will do well, Na-tan. Now let us find a good teacher who can show you how to do better. I want to bet only on a sure thing!"

While men and women played stickball, it was considered to be a male-dominant game because of the injuries suffered during the competition. Frequently, players sustained severe bruises and broken bones. Nathaniel also discovered that the Indians loved to wager on the outcome of the games, whether they were held within the tribe or with other village teams. They were born gamblers! Frequently they offered everything they possessed as stakes in the games, including jewelry, personal items they had made, even some of their household goods.

Nathaniel's first invitation to play came after his training was completed. Bear Claw had found the right teacher for him, and Nathaniel followed his instructions to the letter. He practiced diligently for long periods, and whenever he could find another brave to hurl the ball toward him, Nathaniel continued the practice sessions. He studied every move his opponents used, and quickly learned their strengths and weaknesses, and he pushed himself hard in order to get ready for the game.

Snow Deer, who had come to love this white man, was very supportive and said little as he focused attention on the training and not on her. She thought, soon, when he has played his game, I will have him to myself.

Another game soon was scheduled and Nathaniel was asked to play for the village team. It was his first time and he got caught up in the excitement immediately. His testing was to commence! The opponents from another Cherokee village arrived yelping and shouting, accompanied by many of their supporters. Their shaman came too; he would chant prayers and assist in the pre-game activities and urge his players to win the game. All of the visitors gathered to watch them play.

Nathaniel's team was assembled and led by the shaman to the Long Man, the river near the village. He cut each player's flesh to bleed the demons and evil spirits from the men. Then, taking the root of a tree or bush, he blessed them and intoned a special prayer until each player had reached a high spiritual level. Certainly this would provide him with the necessary skills and mental outlook to excel at the game. Nathaniel thought it all quite humorous, but he followed along with the instructions of the shaman. After all, his shaman was servicing the team for battle, and he did not wish to appear to be different.

Returning to the village, the shaman accompanied the team onto the playing field. The shouting and screaming noise of the opposing teams climbed to a loud crescendo. Nathaniel was caught up again in the festivities and enjoyed the camaraderie of his teammates as they slapped each other and danced around the field and got ready to play. An elder of the village pitched the ball into the thick of the players. It was the signal to start!

The players scrambled, and the duel between the teams was underway. The players raced from one goal to the other—running, slashing, catching and throwing. Chiefs and sub-chiefs served as referees, and followed the ball as it flew between the opposing teams. The ballsticks clattered, stick upon stick, sticks upon bodies, a never-ending duel of tempers and physical beatings.

Nathaniel was knocked down and a pack of Indians smothered him. Then he struggled from under the pile and was back on his feet, attempting to find the goal of his opponents. He threw hard and long, his ballstick performing as Bear Claw had designed it, and he laughed and pushed and played the game for all it was worth. the game continued, hour after hour, neither team allowing goals to be made easily. As the afternoon wore on, the players could barely generate energy to move the ball or to score the runs, and the game ended, the opponent vanquished into the dust of the playing field.

The shamans, who had removed themselves from the playing field when the game commenced, now performed a final ceremony and chanted to the Great Spirit, asking that the victors would be protected from the wrath of the losers, and that the team having lost would not be hungry for revenge. Then the fires were lighted and the tribe gathered for feasting and dancing.

The players recalled the things they had done, or others had done, and who had made outstanding plays or had scored goals, and who had not. Nathaniel found this time to be very important, for it gave them a chance to celebrate victory together and to build solidarity within the tribe.

# 9

# GAME OF WAR

Shortly after arriving in America he had heard the story of the tribes of the Iroquois who had opted for peace among themselves. It was said the Indians had formed a confederation, one which brought together many of the eastern tribes, and one that could bring considerable trouble to the colonists. After years of war and many battles, the confederation of the Six Nations was created. It was no legend.

The confederacy comprised the great eastern tribes: Mohawk, Cayugas, Oneidas, Senecas, Onondagas and the Tuscaroras. Then the People of the Longhouses, the Ho-de-no-sau-nee, met in the Great Council and pondered the decisions necessary for resolving tribal issues. The time of the Great Peace descended upon the Iroquois and all was well.

The fraternal tribes now could no longer wage war and were forbidden to war with non-members. If an injustice was perpetrated by an outsider the Great Council would sit, the issue debated, and the decision made. No longer could a member take it upon himself to exact revenge on an enemy. Prior to the union being formed, it was expected that any member could mete out personal justice whenever wronged. The act of maintaining balance in all things was a primary focus of the tribe. When a member was killed his family would kill in return. But that had ended. Now the Council would meet and decide what action would be taken by the offended party. The member was obligated to heed the wisdom of the elders. There was no appeal.

It was not the same for the Cherokees. Having inherited their fighting skills from the Iroquois, they enjoyed the excitement and thrill of battle and refused to consider giving it up. Peace escaped them, but they wanted it no other way! They warred with many tribes: Shawnees, Creeks, Choctaws, Chickasaws, and Catawbas. The Cherokees considered fighting to be the chief happiness of a man, and the ceremony of preparation of war was elaborately undertaken to assuage the spirits who would guide the war party on its path. War was a beloved occupation, and the Cherokees were less than fulfilled when they could not engage in the fight.

Nathaniel found there were three major passions of the Indians: they waged war, hunted, and played games, not necessarily in that order. Each of them provided the participants a chance to exhibit strength, tenacity, and in some cases, intelligence in the particular pursuit.

As for the game of war, the Cherokees waged it to avenge the death of one of their tribe. In their long history they had been attacked many times by other tribes, and when one of their numbers died they believed that only if they retaliated in kind could they maintain harmony and peace within the tribe. The Council passed judgement on the incident, and then called for clan members of the relative who had been killed to carry out the act of retribution and avenge the wrong committed. When several of the clan were killed, the war to be fought required an equal number of the enemy to be destroyed. There was no other way if harmony was to continue.

Preparation for war called for the chiefs—the War Chief and other men who had distinguished themselves with valor, fighting skills, and success in battle—to meet in Council and debate the issue that had precipitated the action. When the announcement of the meeting was made, the chiefs and braves gathered in the Council House. War bonnets and lesser designations of rank were worn. The headdress consisted of multiple rows of feathers, tied together into a strip of netting made of woven bark. These adorned the mantle, and ornate lappets fell on the shoulders of the chiefs. Single or double feathers were allotted and worn by the braves to signify their position in the tribe. They had likely been won for bravery or skill in battle.

The men who wanted to participate in the battle came together. Male members of the clan had the right to attend, but could not speak unless the warrior had struck a living, armed opponent in battle. He likewise could not take a bride until he had proven himself in this way. The action was intended to show valor in fighting and maturity for the marriage couch. All young males in the tribe wished for the chance to go into battle for the first time.

Any brave had the option of deciding whether he would go on a raid, with the possible exception of one who had lost a clan member earlier. These braves had an obligation to seek revenge and generally went on the raid. If one of the party had a dream or a vision that something might happen, however, he was free to speak of the dream in Council. Every Indian respected the man for the telling. The dream might portend a bad omen and could mean failure in battle. Many would try to interpret the dream, or what the vision meant, and the discussion could continue for hours.

Nathaniel found the Cherokees to be very superstitious. The shaman, or medicine man, would be asked for his interpretation of the signs, for the Council never made the decision to attack an enemy without the shaman's counsel and agreement. The Indians placed great faith in the words and incantations spoken by the shamans. They were thought to have great wisdom and be able to communicate with the invisible spirits, and to foresee the battle before it began. All of the Council members carefully considered their views.

When everyone in the Council had been heard, the War Chief, along with subordinate leaders of war parties, would make the decision on what would be done. Now it was time for the planning of war. The number in the war party would be decided, and when and how the attack would be initiated. There was much drinking of 'asi', the black drink, as the warriors cleansed themselves, and much shouting and pushing as they rehearsed what they would do in battle. The rituals might last for several days; and when the men were spiritually pure and mentally prepared for the war, they left the Council House.

"Hai! My tomahawk is thirsty—it wants to drink the blood of my enemy. It will be filled soon."

"The Creeks will fight like old women!"

"We will count 'coup' tomorrow, and they will not know what struck them."

"We will avenge the death of our brothers. Many of the enemy will die. There will be much wailing when they die. This we believe."

"We will surprise our enemies. The Great Spirit will not protect them from our attack."

"Perhaps there will be prisoners to trade or to tie to the slave posts. Hai, that will be a good game to play tomorrow."

"May the Great Spirit give us courage to fight our enemies!"

When the meeting adjourned the men returned to their lodges to prepare for the fight. War paint was applied: eyes ringed in black and red circles; bodies striped in white and black and red designs; arms tattooed with more splashes. There was no set pattern; only the imagination of the warriors who created face and body designs to scare an enemy and to avoid recognition by the enemy. The braves' hair was plaited and greased and sometimes shaved, leaving only a topknot, to make them appear more fierce. Weapons were inspected and tested, knives and hatchets sharpened, charms to ward off injury or death retrieved, and the warriors were ready to do battle.

After the preparations for the raid, Nathaniel was surprised by the departure the men made as they left the camp. The raiders yelped and howled, but Nathaniel didn't know whether it was for show or whether to reinforce the braves' courage. He too had painted and prepared for the expedition, said goodbye to Snow Deer, and fallen into file as they departed the village. His adrenalin was flowing; it was his first raid. He had killed before but only in response to a threatening act. This was different. He was part of a raiding party going on the attack. He wondered how he would perform in battle.

Nathaniel had heard the tales around the campfires, stories of the battles fought and won, but rarely lost. He knew the tribe loved a good fight and would attack the enemy fiercely, offering no quarter and expecting none in return. He suspected that he would be the focus of the raid, not only from members of the tribe who would be watching to see how he performed, but also from the Creeks if they discovered his true identity. He thrust the thoughts from his mind and decided he would do the best he could, whatever lay ahead.

He carried his rifle, and strapped to his belt was the long knife and a hatchet. He hoped he would not have to use either one of them. The other warriors carried bows and arrows, a club or tomahawk, and a spear. Some of the Indians had guns, but had chosen the bows for their silence. Red Arrow led the way. When they were about a mile from the village, he directed the raiding party to deploy to ambush positions. He dispatched the warriors quietly, directing them on either side of a ravine through which a trail ran into the village. Silence was the pass-word, and stealth and deception the game being played.

Taking Nathaniel aside, he told him to take his place on the side closest to the village but to wait until the Creeks passed him before shooting. The war party, now completely camouflaged, blended into the brush lining the ravine. It was still dark, but first light was only a few minutes away when all were settled. They waited.

The village started to awaken. Soon Nathaniel smelled the food being cooked, and he felt hungry. He popped a few grains of parched corn in his mouth and chewed quietly while he waited. The sun was rising fast when the head warrior passed the signal that the Creek hunt-ing band was coming. Now was the time for action.

It was a sudden, fierce attack, the arrows quickly finding their tar-gets. Nathaniel fired too, and the first Indian dropped. Then the sec-ond victim fell, and at that moment an Indian was upon him with hatchet raised to crush his head. Nathaniel twisted and fired and the hunter's head split apart as he fell forward. The battle was joined, but the Creeks were finished before they had a chance to react. Several turned and started running back toward the village and Nathaniel fired again, and another dropped to the ground. Suddenly, the battle was over.

Nathaniel felt weary but elated. He knew that he had killed four Creeks, and it was time to scalp the dead. His mind and stomach rebelled at the thought, but he knew he must do it. He started on the Indian who had attacked him, and moved down the slope to where the others lay. While he was taking the hair he heard the screams in the camp where the raiders had gone. The screams mingled with a fearful succession of yelps and howls as the Cherokees indiscriminately slaughtered the Creeks. Then the smell of smoke engulfed him, and he knew the lodges were burning.

Shortly after, he spotted his tribesmen coming up the ravine with their prisoners, a ragged column of a half-dozen blacks who had been held by the Creeks. He felt pity for them and their fate that lay ahead.

The raid was a decisive victory. The warrior chief led the party home, bringing the captives who were tied together. The warriors laughed and shouted. None had been killed today. Red Arrow, walking beside Nathaniel, was excited about the fight and the way it had gone.

He congratulated Nathaniel. Nathaniel accepted the praise, but his heart was not in it. He wasn't sure if he wanted to go on another raid. He was sick of the massacre, and while he understood the reason for going, the killings bothered him.

"Na-tan, it was a good fight. You did well," the head warrior shouted.

"My thanks, Red Arrow. I think our braves surprised the Creeks."

"It is true, my friend, but none have as many scalps as you!"

"Red Arrow, you had a good plan. A battle is won because of the plan. No one deserves more credit than you."

The Indian looked at Nathaniel. "Na-tan, it takes more than a plan; it takes courage to fight as you did today. I watched you. You did not want to take the hair. It was different for you, but you took them anyway. Snow Deer will be proud of you; as I am proud."

"Right now, I am more tired than proud. I will find peace at my fire."

"You are right, Na-tan. Fighting makes us all old and weary, but we did well today. I am glad you came with us."

"My thanks to you, Red Arrow. I am happy that you allowed me to come."

It had been a successful raid, and Nathaniel was pleased the war party was returning without any dead or wounded. He knew from the stories told that while the Indians tried to remove their dead after a battle, they usually were too far from home to carry the bodies with them. When this happened the war party would take the dead from the battle site and then cover the bodies with stones. They could not allow the spirits to carry the warrior away, nor for that matter, the wild animals that roamed the land. Whenever possible, they treated the bodies with great respect.

Weeks or months later, whenever they had the opportunity, the Indians returned to the cairn of stones and retrieved the bones and carried them to the village. There they would be put to rest in the tribal burial grounds as clan and family members gathered and chanted the funeral song. They would be accompanied by the shaman, who would chant and hiss and make all kinds of entreaties to the Great Spirit in order that the warrior would find a suitable path to the stars.

The tribe believed it was important to honor the dead in this way, for then the warrior would not wander in the spirit world. Nathaniel also learned of the Indian's belief that the bones of their ancestors revealed the story of their history, and thus, the very existence of the tribe. The remains were sacred and must never be desecrated, and the bones in the burial tomb were venerated beyond any personal possession. The tomb was to become the single, most important honor that all Indians hoped to receive when they died. Nathaniel wondered how he would count in their scheme of things.

At least for this time Nathaniel thought as he trudged home, there won't be any bones for the burial grounds, nor the wailing of widows or mothers. All were coming back alive. It was a good feeling, for the fires would burn high and long tonight and a great feast and dancing would be celebrated for the success of the raiding party.

The captives were turned over to the Chief who would decide their fates. Some might be sold into slavery. Another might be given to a widow as a personal slave. Others might be held as ransom and traded at a future date for a clan member held prisoner by another tribe. A final solution for a captive was death! Nathaniel was happy that none of the prisoners would die. Because the raiding party had suffered no deaths or wounds, the Chief decided to be merciful once again.

Several weeks after the raid, the tribe decided to fulfill its second passion, the Great Hunt! It took place late in the season of Fall-of-the-Leaf, usually before the snow fell. By then, the vegetation and the acorns and roots had fed the deer well, and they were heavy with fat.

The overriding preoccupation of the Indians, and the basis for much of their activity for finding food, was the hunt. They spent hours fashioning the hunting implements needed for the kill. The tribe or clan was normally split into several hunting bands, and each had its own leaders and structure. Hunting was considered man's work, and from boyhood the Indian male was taught and trained how to use the hunting weapons, and how to pursue the animals and make the kill. It was a highly-skilled activity. The hunter had to understand nature intimately, and the Indians used sight and sound, smell, knowledge of the terrain, animal behavior, and weather as their allies in the hunt. The hunter learned to decoy birds and animals, imitating the cries of the young animals and mating calls to coax the game to come within killing range.

The hunt was not confined to daylight hours only. There were animals and fowl to be taken at night. Hunters carried torches and used sticks to club unsuspecting sleeping birds. Beavers and raccoons and porcupines were much sought after, and were hunted after dark also. Deer tracking and killing was a well-honed art. Deer herds, which once had been plentiful and scattered throughout the land, now were less abundant and required more skill by the hunters to kill what was needed for the winter months ahead. Frequently the Indians laid an ambush on deer trails, in thick cover or in gullies, and waited for the deer to move past their hiding places. After the kill the hunter would speak to the slain animal, and tell it that he needed meat, and to forgive him. It was a ritual to purge the Indian's soul and maintain balance in the land. But more importantly, the Indians believed that the deer's spirit would bring crippling rheumatism if they failed to ask forgiveness for the death.

While the Indians did not like inclement weather, they used it to their advantage and set traps and ambushes for animals, with great success. In his high, hunting moccasins or on snowshoes, the hunter was able to stalk the elusive game even when it snowed.

The winter was a particularly good time to hunt bears. The Indian never underestimated the bear, an animal that possessed great courage, strength and defiance. If the hunter spotted the ice formed by the bear's breath as it lay sleeping in its winter den, he could kill it easily.

The hunter might then pay special homage to the brute or offer prayers to the giant animal. Some called the bear grandfather or grandmother in reverence to its strength and beauty. The bear meat was sweet and the yellow fat could be melted for cooking. It was great occasion for the tribe when the meat was shared.

The days were drawing short. There was a chill in the air that meant winter was fast approaching. The women of the village had started preparations weeks before when the days were longer and warmer. As the corn ripened the ears were braided together and hung up to dry. The beans were scattered in flat baskets or on a hide and placed in the sun. The yellow squash and pumpkins were sliced and dried on racks over the fire. All the berries had been gathered—choke berries, june berries, which tasted like apples and were preferred as an addition to the dried meat in pemmican, and blueberries—and were stored in baskets for use during the winter.

Grapes and wild sunflower seeds had been collected and placed in the sun to dry, and then stuffed into rawhide bags to hang from the lodgepoles. The hollyberries had been gathered, ready to make 'asi', the black drink, that was used by the warriors as an emetic to cleanse the body of evil spirits before going to war. The women of the village were busy from dawn to dusk, preserving and saving, and the fires burned throughout the day as the food was prepared and dried for the cold months ahead.

This hunt, the last of the year, would provide the meat and skins needed for the coming winter. The men were excited about the hunt, and preparations were carried out almost as if they were going off to war. On some hunts, women of the village accompanied the hunters, but none would participate this time. Dogs went along behind the main party to assist in hauling the meat home.

The chase went exceedingly well. Nearly every hunter had made his kill, and there was tremendous exhilaration as they dragged the deer to a central place and commenced the job of gutting the animals. Then the dogs were brought up and hitched to the travois, used to transport the meat to the camp. A runner was sent ahead to alert the villagers of the huge kill. Cooking fires were heaped high, for tonight there would be much feasting and dancing for all to share. When the weary hunters returned, the villagers gathered around to wait for their share of the bounty. The leader and sub-leaders now began skinning the animals and distributing the meat.

It was an exciting time for the tribe gathered there. Even the leader was happy. "Hai, this was a good hunt; we have much meat and everyone will share tonight."

"The women will have much work to do," another promised. "But it is good to have meat for the months ahead."

A sub-chief announced. "No one will go hungry tonight!"

The women stood, waiting for each share to be given, and they were laughing and giggling as the men cut the animals and made hugh stacks of meat. One grinned, "We will have no rest tonight. The men are hungry for more than roasts!"

Another replied, "Tomorrow will be time enough to preserve the meat. Now is the time to eat and dance and whatever will follow."

"It is good to have the men home," one ventured hopefully.

"It is too long to wait until the feast is over. I will have a warrior before we eat," a young, pretty woman declared.

"You know nothing," an older woman scoffed. "You do not have a man. Who would want you, anyway?" she added.

"It will be easy to find one tonight," the maiden answered. "Wait and see for yourself!"

The division of the hunt was serious business. It was based on the traditions of the tribe, on family custom, and on gratitude for the meat being provided. The person or persons who had killed the game had first choice, and others who had participated in the hunt were then awarded their portions. Certain parts of the animal went to the shamans for their religious rituals. Depending upon the animal killed, they might receive the hooves or tails, the ears or eyes. There was never a dispute about the portion or the amount of meat given; the boiling pots accepted whatever was offered. Everyone was happy with whatever he got.

Late corn was picked and roasted on the coals, large chunks of flesh were placed on green poles and suspended over the fires, and hearty stews of wild potatoes, squash and corn simmered in the pots. There was bread, made from ground corn or acorn meal, wrapped in green husks and baked in the ashes. A pudding of dried beans and cornmeal was set on the fire. Finally, chunks of dripping honeycombs and wild berries were brought to the feast to honor the hunters who brought much meat to the villagers. Then tribute was paid to the Great Spirit in the sky, and every member of the tribe ate his fill until late in the evening.

The following day, fires were kindled early. The hunters, and the women they hunted or chased after the night before, were exhausted, but there was much meat to be preserved from the kill. The women and children set up drying racks over the fires and sliced the meat into strips several inches wide and laid them above the coals. Drying racks were set up in the sun as well. There was abundant meat, and it made for much work. The sun and fire converted the raw meat into 'jerky', a blackened and leathery meat that was stored for long periods. If it was needed for a hunting or war party, the jerky was pounded into a softened mass, and mixed with fat or marrow and dried berries to make pemmican. Stored in a rawhide bag, it was carried on a belt to provide nourishment on the trail.

The men sat in groups throughout the village, recounting the hunt in infinite detail while the women looked after the meat. After the wearying hunt and feasting of the night before, they gathered in camp to rest and talk. The Indians loved to explain in detail what they had seen and done, and those who had not been on the hunt enjoyed vicariously the action that had taken place.

"So how many animals did we kill, Bear Claw?" one of the men shouted.

"Ask the leader of the hunt. It is not my place to know."

Red Arrow heard the question. "We brought home forty-two; that's a lot of meat for winter."

"Hai, we got some big ones," another said.

"How many did Two Arrows kill, Na-tan?" Bear Claw asked. He was trying to goad the Indian into talking.

"Who knows?" Nathaniel answered. "But he came home with no arrows. He needs plenty to shoot well."

Two Arrows accepted the jesting. "True, my friend, but I got two of them. Mine were clean shots. I did not have to chase them all over the land—like others I know."

"You were lucky! We saw you waiting by the trail, and the deer walked right up to you. How could you not kill them when you could almost touch them?"

Two Arrows wanted to draw the attention away from himself. "Did you see Red Fox? He shot at the small deer. But it was a rabbit!" Then he laughed, "He thought the big ears were small antlers." He chuckled again. "It was a big rabbit, though."

The men burst out laughing. "Where is that boy," one of them asked. "Making rabbit stew? I'm getting hungry thinking about it."

There seemed to be no end to the tales. When one hunter told his version, another would interject his own. There was much good-natured bantering, and the stories grew in size and exaggeration with each telling. Occasionally, one of the men would get some food, or leave the discussion and go to his lodge, or simply ask his woman to bring him water or his pipe. The men believed they had done their work, and did not intend to do anything more.

The skins were saved too. After stripping the hides the skins were scraped to remove residual flesh before tanning. They were first soaked in water and the hair removed and then placed in containers holding a mixture of deer brains and water. After becoming saturated with the mess and thoroughly soaked, they were removed and slowly dried, all the while being worked with the hands. When the skins were soft and pliable; they could be easily sewn. Many of the older squaws worked at this task. Bark was also used for tanning. Some skins were bleached white and made into clothing to be worn on special occasions. Others were cured with the fur intact. These would be made into a cloak to be thrown over the shoulders when it was cold or raining.

The women made the clothing and footwear for the family. Winter leggings and high-top moccasins that laced to the knees were prepared for the men. In warm weather, both men and women wore a short skirt, although when it was unseasonably hot, the men wore only a breech-cloth. Waistbags, to carry provisions for the hunt and for fighting, were cut from the hides and sewn together. Nothing was wasted from the animal. The bones and antlers were made into ornaments and tools, the sinew was used for sewing and other uses, and the hooves of the deer provided glue for baskets, bags, and other items that were needed. The women went about their work, happy to have so much meat and many skins to prepare for the cold season that was quickly arriving.

# *10*

# *MARRIAGE VOWS*

As the raiding party returned, Nathaniel spent much of the time on the trail thinking about Snow Deer, trying to sort out his affection for her and her feelings for him. He had finally come to accept the fact that he was in love with her. He had known it for some time but had not yet told Snow Deer, nor had she responded to him openly.

He would tell her tonight! He became excited at the thought and tried to rehearse the words, and wondered what her reaction would be. He rationalized his love for her. It was time for him to take a wife; it was certainly time for her to have a husband; to start a family. As he thought about it, he realized that he wanted her more than he would admit.

She was an enigma to him in some ways. There were two sides to her. There was the woman part of her – someone whose keen mind knew without question what she wanted from life, a mature woman whose expectations allowed little room for change if that change made difficulties for her otherwise well-adjusted role. Then there was the child in her – an innocence and wonder that allowed her to seek out the fun of life, and which gave her a special grace and sweetness and yes, vulnerability that only the young possessed.

This was the part of her that Nathaniel liked best, for he found in her the ingenuous child who pushed away complications and pretenses and problems and accepted life in total harmony, unused and unspoiled in any way.

He reconciled himself to the absolute truth that she had become an intricate part of his life. He realized how much he missed her and longed for her—her presence and her touch. He wanted to be with her, to watch every movement she made, to listen to her voice that was so lovely that he heard its tone rather than her words. Whatever she did, however she moved, was so beautiful that it was sheer pleasure to watch her. Nathaniel felt shy and sometimes clumsy around her, unsure of himself, yet completely sure of his love. But he kept those feelings to himself until he returned to the village.

The tribe welcomed the raiders as heroes. As soon as Nathaniel saw Snow Deer, he went to talk to her. The Indians pressed in on them, and he was alone with her for only a few minutes. There was much yelling and laughing and celebrating over the return of the warriors. Then he was rushed off to rest and bathe for the evening's festivities.

When the fires burned high, a feast was laid and the dancing began. Nathaniel stayed beside Snow Deer, fascinated by her beauty and jealous of the attention the young braves of the village paid to her. Finally, as the fires burned low, he led her away and told her of the raid and that he had missed her, and how much he loved her. She listened to him and told him she had worried about him and was happy to see him back, but beyond this she was not able to say how she felt. She asked him to be patient with her. Then the Chief called out to her, and she left him sitting there, alone and lonely.

His thoughts turned to the women in the village. Those who were unmarried were sexually active and frequently made it clear to Nathaniel that they were ready to be taken if he so desired. He had, however, practiced abstinence from the beginning, as he came to realize that he was falling in love with Snow Deer. There was none other in whom he was interested.

He had been with the tribe long enough to know how marriages worked. If a brave took a fancy to a maiden he would make some overture to her by bringing her a gift. If she liked it, she would give something in return. Frequently, she would leave something she had cooked outside her lodge. If the man tasted it, the marriage was agreed upon. That was the sign of willingness on her part. The clan to which the man belonged would construct a lodge for them and they would move in together. If the couple shared connubial bliss and still liked each other, a ceremony of marriage would take place. If, however, either decided they had enough of the relationship, at the next Green Corn Ceremony the man would move out and the woman retained possession of the lodge.

As thoughts of Snow Deer and his feelings for her tumbled around in his mind, Nathaniel knew that as a white man he could not follow these customs exactly and would have to approach the marriage proposal differently. He was aware of the implications of mixed marriages, but he had seen a number of these unions in the frontier settlements. He was sure that living together was workable. He had to talk to Bear Claw. Perhaps his friend would know what he should do. Nathaniel frequently sought him out, asking for guidance in some matter or another, and he would be able to shed some light on Nathaniel's next step.

Bear Claw was indebted to Nathaniel, but more than that he liked him because he had brought Snow Deer home and had not asked for anything in return. He loved Snow Deer as much as he could have loved a daughter, and he devoted much of his time to the girl. After his young wife died in childbirth, he had never taken another wife. Since that time of deep sorrow, Bear Claw considered his sister's children to be equally his, but Snow Deer was his favorite and he indulged her without restraint.

Now he had a big problem! Nathaniel thought that Snow Deer was willing to accept him, but he did not know what he was supposed to do to seal the union. He needed Bear Claw to give him some advice. One afternoon he found the old man in his lodge.

"Dear Uncle," Nathaniel said, "I need your counsel. Tell me what I should do about this that is happening to me."

"So Na-tan, what is happening to you?"

"I love Snow Deer and I want to marry her," he blurted out. "I want it to be done under the tribal laws, and I am at a loss to know what is required of me."

"Na-tan, I have known for some time of your interest in Snow Deer. An old man's eyes can see how you are when you are together.

She has talked to me about you. She believes in her heart that she loves you, but I could not tell you this before."

Surprised by his friend's reply, Nathaniel asked, "Then why did she not speak to me about it?"

"You should know that is not our way, Na-tan."

"Tell me, what is your way, that I might do what is expected of me, Bear Claw."

"There are some problems, Na-tan. You may not speak to her directly. If you were Cherokee, you would ask your mother's sister to talk to Snow Deer's mother's sister. She, in turn, would talk to Snow Deer's mother and the rest of the clan. I am her uncle, and because you are my friend, I will talk to my sister for you."

"You say there are problems. What else must I do?"

"Na-tan, it is not a question of what you can do. And I am not sure how to settle it myself, but it is a problem," Bear Claw sighed.

"So? Tell me."

"The shaman."

"The shaman! What does he have to do with this?" Nathaniel exclaimed.

"He must be a part of the ceremony. Have you not seen him before at the weddings? And he does not like you much!"

"As I do not like him."

"Everyone knows that too. He did not want you to become a member of the tribe. He voted against you, remember? He will oppose the marriage, and I believe he will tell that to the Chief. He will speak against you and try to turn the Chief's thoughts away from you."

"Why can't we be married without him?"

"That is not our way, Na-tan. Snow Deer would not agree to a marriage without him."

"What should I do, Uncle?"

"I think you owe something to the shaman. Kill a deer! Take him the best part. Let him believe there is kindness in your heart. Sometimes it is better to overcome your pride before your pride overcomes you! Think about it Na-tan."

"Thank you, Bear Claw, for helping me."

"Since you have come to me, I will speak for you. You must have some gift to offer, something you value much. You will take this to her lodge as a sign of your love. Snow Deer will not look at you. My sister will tell the clan that Snow Deer is willing to marry you. This is the way of our marriage, Na-tan."

"When can I do this, Bear Claw?"

"Wait until after the Festival of the Green Corn, Na-tan. Then if you have decided what to give her, I will tell Chief Oconostata of your intentions. His consent is not needed, but since he likes you, I think he should know. Then you will marry my niece."

Nathaniel had not long to wait for the corn to ripen. Planting and cultivation of corn was a regular and necessary activity. Maize was the staff of life and brought happiness to the Indians. Without it they would have suffered badly. They spent a lot of effort clearing land and getting it ready for the spring planting. Near the village was the common cornfield. The soil belonged to all and each family was expected to participate in the digging and sowing, the hoeing and harvesting. No one but the Chief was exempt. The men broke and raked the soil and the women followed with their digging sticks and planted the seeds of sustenance. Whatever was raised—corn and beans and pumpkins and squash—was for the benefit of the community.

The Festival of Green Corn, or Busk, was held after the first mid-summer harvest. It was a time for jubilation and for honoring the Great Spirit for bringing bounty to the tribe. It was an occasion for dancing and feasting and wild singing far into the night. The Indians considered this to be a sign of future prosperity and what the land would yield throughout the new year. It was held in the season of Sun-high- in-the-Sky.

The annual event was a time of renewal. Each lodge was thoroughly cleaned, broken implements discarded, hearth fires extinguished, and food that had been stored, destroyed. The cleansing signified the time when feuds and disagreements among the villagers were ended and placed aside, except for the crime of murder. That action alone was not exorcised; it was too serious to be forgiveable.

The feast centered around the new, ripe corn that had just been harvested, but other foods were prepared to give substance to the meal. The fresh, young corn, thrown into the hot coals and eaten hot or dipped into melted bear's fat, was so tempting that huge quantities were consumed before the Indians had their fill.

The festival, held in the open on the village square, provided a special opportunity for dancing and singing, and the music featured was both harmonic and discordant. The Indians could produce that which was sweet and low, or raucous and loud, depending on the dance that was to be performed. Nathaniel could never get over the sounds that erupted during the festival. Some drummer would start the dancing by pounding or beating the drums incessantly, while others would blow on a reed instrument or shake gourd rattles.

Then the dancers would spin and jerk uncontrollably around the fire, howling and screaming as if on the warpath or the hunt. At other times they might be replaced by dancers accompanied by rattles and smaller drums, who shuffled slowly and sedately around in a circle. Often there were two concentric circles, with maidens and braves moving in opposite directions, each ring of dancers having its own signs which they made to the other as they passed by.

Aside from the festival, dancing was a nightly affair and anyone in the village who had energy or inclination could gather and dance until the fires burned low. There were special dances held: dances in the spring when the seeds were planted; in the fall when the fruits of their labor were harvested; and those in commemoration of battles fought, or of successful hunts. There were hideous and frightful dances, held for captives who had been sentenced to die, and solemn, slowly-executed dances to honor the Great Spirit, or to elicit his intervention in the affairs of the tribe. Dancing was a form of catharsis for the players, and provided a sense of community that otherwise they would not have experienced.

The forthcoming wedding of Snow Deer and Nathaniel was scheduled to be held within a few weeks. As the Chief's daughter, the ceremony promised feasting and dancing on a scale rarely experienced, and nearly everyone in the village was excited, especially, the women.

All wanted to be involved. Snow Deer's mother and other family members took great delight in parceling out the fashioning of the wedding dress, the ornaments for the lodge and the various foods that would be prepared. The Council House had to be decorated, and there was a multitude of details to arrange.

Nathaniel and Snow Deer had little time to be alone. This was frustrating to both, but whenever they had the chance, they would slip away from the village together. Snow Deer attempted to explain how the ceremony would evolve, but when Nathaniel tried to relate what she told him to the traditional ceremonies in England and the colonies, he was at a total loss. Finally she suggested that he talk to Bear Claw; perhaps a man's viewpoint would be easier for him to understand.

A great feast had been prepared to honor the bride and groom. The occasion was a perfect opportunity to eat and dance. Nathaniel expected the festivities to go on for a long time, but little did he know they would continue for hours on end. Bear Claw, who had described the wedding activities to Nathaniel, had withheld this crucial fact until it was too late! In fact, Bear Claw did not consider it important enough!

His plan was to pick up Nathaniel and escort him to the Council House. He went to Nathaniel's lodge to fetch him.

"Are you ready, Na-tan?"

"Yes, Uncle, is it time?"

"Snow Deer is waiting and it would be good if you went now," he suggested. "Try and remember our customs. Do you remember what you are to say and do?" Bear Claw quickly sketched in the details.

"I understand, Uncle, but thank you for telling me again. After the wedding, you must come to our lodge."

Bear Claw looked at Nathaniel and smiled, "Na-tan, I don't think you want me to visit on your wedding night, do you? I'll come later. You cannot get rid of me so easily."

Some of his nervousness disappeared as Nathaniel and Bear Claw walked to the Council House. They laughed and talked, completely at ease with one another. Bear Claw chided Nathaniel about Snow Deer and wondered aloud why Nathaniel hadn't just left her in the river.

Then he suggested that now Nathaniel would learn a lot about wildcats, and he could become a great warrior after his training by Snow Deer.

Bear Claw stopped before they arrived at the Council House. "Do not be afraid, Na-tan," Bear Claw laughed. "After you are married you have only to wait until the next Green Corn Ceremony."

"And what does that mean, Uncle?"

"You know that Busk is a time of cleansing. If you and Snow Deer can't get along together, you have only to wait until next year! Your marriage can be ended then."

"Bear Claw, you need a cleansing! I love the girl, and your foolish words mean nothing." He pushed the older man forward. "Come on, Uncle, take me to my wedding."

His heart leaped when they entered the Council House and he looked across the space and saw Snow Deer. She smiled at him, and he knew for certain that she was the single most important person in his life. He could scarcely refrain from going to her immediately.

The pre-nuptial ceremony commenced. As was the custom, the bride and groom were separated, each seated on opposite sides of the room. They were to remain there until the feast began. When the signal was given that the food was ready, the shaman opened the festivities with a long prayer, beseeching the Great Spirit to come into their midst and to look favorably on Snow Deer and Nathaniel. Chief Oconostata spoke at length about the bride and groom, reminding the audience of Nathaniel's many brave deeds and how great a warrior his daughter was marrying. As soon as he sat down, Bear Claw presented Nathaniel to the gathering and wished long life to the couple.

Now was the moment for Snow Deer to be presented. The Chief and Nanatola escorted her across the room. As she approached him, Nathaniel arose and took her hand and led her to the seat beside him. Bear Claw stepped back, but not before Snow Deer breaking all traditions, leaned over and kissed her uncle on the cheek. She moved closer to Nathaniel and squeezed his hand, happy to be so close to him.

The feasting started; everyone was hungry. Snow Deer fed bits of food to Nathaniel to demonstrate her commitment to him, and he reciprocated by offering morsels of the same food to her. Then, the dancing began. The shaman dedicated a dance to the Great Spirit to bless the marriage with happiness and fertility. He danced and chanted and implored until at least he dropped to his knees and his incantations stopped.

The drums commenced; a slow, soft beat that promised something more. The village maidens came to the center of the house and danced for Nathaniel and Snow Deer. The drums kept up a steady beat as the girls, in perfect step and movement, chanted a song of fertility and love. They were lovely, and Nathaniel felt his juices racing as he watched the sensuous dance. He squeezed Snow Deer's small hands in his mighty ones, and looked at her with great yearning and love.

It was time for the bride and groom to come forward. They danced together, telling a story as old as mankind—that of a warrior taking a woman, fresh and beautiful, as his wife. The open space soon filled with braves, then family and clan, until many were dancing to the beat of the drums and flutes.

Finally, late into the night, the dance ended and Snow Deer, escorted by her family, left the Council House and was taken to a small lodge where she remained alone. In the morning her mother came to the lodge with new clothes and helped her bathe and dress for the wedding and took her to meet Nathaniel.

He arrived early with Bear Claw and was seated when Snow Deer entered. She was absolutely stunning as she came to him, dressed in bleached white deer skins, decorated with colored beads and silver. Her hair gleamed and Nathaniel thought she was the most beautiful woman he had ever seen or known. She was radiant as she reached Nathaniel and took her seat beside him.

Again, the shaman started the ceremony with dancing and incantations, but this time when he finished, he handed Snow Deer a thin slice of meat. She quickly seared it in the fire and gave it to Nathaniel. He cut it into two pieces and offered half to her. Then Snow Deer and Nathaniel tied the blankets they had brought with them, signifying they were of one bed. They were now married. Accompanied by the hum of laughter and murmuring from the assembled guests, Na-tan picked up Snow Deer, kissed her soundly and carried her to his lodge. They were not to be seen until late the following day.

## *11*

# *P*EACEFUL *P*RELUDE

The first year of marriage was a special time for Nathaniel. His love for Snow Deer grew daily. He could sit and watch her for hours as she assumed the responsibility of running the household, and he never tired of talking to her and listening to her voice. He was hopelessly, unequivocably, in love with this Indian maiden who responded in kind.

On a raw, rainy day, with a hint of winter in the air, Nathaniel awoke to find Snow Deer gone. It was a rare occasion when he over-slept, and when he reached for her the skins were empty. "Oh well," he thought, "she has gotten up early to build the cooking fire."

He lay still, not wanting to leave the warm shelter and go outside. He stayed there, relaxing in the knowledge that he and Snow Deer were experiencing something that had eluded him for many years; that was the love and intimacy of a perfect union.

How right it had been for him to pursue and marry the girl! She had brought to him a totally satisfying meaning to his existence, and they were so hopelessly in love that he wondered why it had taken him so long to discover this one whom he had chosen to marry. For three months now he had been consumed by her. He liked her too. He liked her as a person, and what she had become to him. What wonderful gifts she had! Nathaniel pushed the hides away and got up from the couch and went outside to find her.

When he saw her, Snow Deer was retching beside the lodge, obviously sick to her stomach. He went to her and put his arm around her waist as if to tell her that he shared her misery. His first thought was that she had eaten something which had made her sick. Then she straightened her body as the convulsions stopped.

"What is it, Snow Deer?" he asked. "Do you feel better now?"

The spasms had ended for the moment. "I think so, but my stomach is not so good."

"Wait, I'll get some sassafras and make you some tea. Come sit here," he suggested. He led her to a fur rug that lay before the door of the lodge.

She took his hand. "Na-tan, it is the morning sickness. I have had it for some time, but it will soon be over."

Ignorant in the ways of women he looked at her sharply and said, "I do not know what you mean. Do all women have this sickness?"

Snow Deer smiled at him. "Only those that will have a baby," she said quietly.

As her words got through to him, he jumped up and stood looking down at her. His mind raced. She was beautiful . . . her face soft and lovely. Her expression was one of amusement. "What are you telling me, Snow Deer? Are we having a baby?" he shouted.

She laughed then as she saw the look on his face. "Not yet, my love," she said, "but before too many moons you will have a son or daughter." She deliberately teased him, ". . . or perhaps both!"

"Why did you not tell me before?" he asked.

"I thought you would know soon enough, and I did not want to bother you. We will have a baby and you will be the father."

He reached down and picked her up and held her close to him. "You are my dearest wife and I love you very much. I am happy for us. Oh, what shall we name him?"

"Don't be silly Na-tan. We will have plenty of time for that. I am not going to have the child tomorrow! And it may be a little girl. Now run along, and get me the tea you promised. After all, I am the one who is sick!"

During the next six months Nathaniel found it increasingly difficult to leave Snow Deer when he was invited to hunt or to participate on a raid. He was excited about every facet of her pregnancy and the growing child in her body. He offered excuses whenever some activity was suggested, and if she could not attend an event he stayed at the lodge.

Unlike the other married men of the village he talked about the forthcoming birth as though it had never happened before. While the other males remained stoic and quiet about their wives, Nathaniel shared every move the baby made, or any reaction of Snow Deer with any and all who would sit and listen.

He showered her with love and attention. As the birth approached, Nathaniel and Snow Deer talked endlessly about the baby and how it would affect their lives. He went on quick day trips and snared a rabbit, or dug certain root vegetables for her to eat, and even prepared food for her and the 'boy' that he knew was coming. He talked to the midwives who would attend Snow Deer, wanting to know every procedure relevant to the birth, but he refused to talk to the shaman. As far as he was concerned, the midwives could take care of the matter, and he distrusted the medicine man to the point of loathing.

The shaman, however, would not accept not being involved in the delivery of the child. His reputation was at stake, and he was certain now that Nathaniel did not like him. He also knew the tribal customs demanded that Snow Deer would choose him to be present. The midwives could not be persuaded to assist at the birth without the shaman. Nathaniel tried another approach.

He talked to Snow Deer about his concerns, and attempted to gain her support to exclude the medicine man, but her cultural habits would not allow it. He was disappointed in not getting his way in the matter.

One morning, after a sleepless night of twisting and turning and dreaming of the impending birth, he shook Snow Deer awake. "Wake up, Snow Deer, I want to talk about our son."

"Na-tan, it is still early. Let me sleep a bit longer. Can it not wait for the morning?"

"It is about Black Crow," he said urgently. "I have bad feelings about him. He does not like me and I think he is still angry that you married a Long Hair."

She sat up then. "You are being foolish, Na-tan. The shaman must be there when the child is born. That is our custom. I cannot have the baby alone, and you . . . you will be . . . you are not able to help me," she added hesitantly.

"How about the women?" he asked. "Why can't they deliver the boy?" he argued.

She pleaded with him. "You must try to understand. The shaman must be there to breathe life into the baby and to protect it from evil spirits. That is our way," she reiterated.

He listened, but he knew the shaman could do nothing of the sort. "It is hard for me to hear what you are telling me, but I promise you I will be standing by watching for any tricks Black Crow might try. I do not trust the man. I think he tries to take advantage of the clan at every turn."

"I know what you want to believe, my love, but you must let me do what is right for us. Now come here and hold me, Na-tan. I am as much afraid as you are." Then he acquiesced to her plea, and lay beside her and cradled her in his arms.

The birth of the baby went well. When her labor began early one morning, Nathaniel called for the two midwives who arrived with the shaman. With Nathaniel's help they carried Snow Deer from the lodge and laid her on some skins arranged as a bed. The medicine man commenced his chanting back and forth and around the women, but Nathaniel thought that he was more subdued than before. The midwives proceeded with their preparations.

Suddenly, in the midst of his incantations, the shaman stopped and announced that the Great Spirit was happy and the baby would come soon. The women, one of whom sat at her feet smoking, told Snow Deer to push hard, harder still, and the baby started to emerge. Then the first midwife wiped the baby's face with her hand, and grasping it by the feet, turned the child and spanked it lightly. The baby cried aloud. Then the second midwife tied string in two places between the mother and the baby, and cut the cord. She handed the child to Snow Deer. As Nathaniel kneeled on the ground beside her, she cradled the boy and placed him at her breast. Their son was born on a beautiful morning, in the season of Sun-high-in-the-Sky, 1782.

At the moment of the baby's birth, a small, young eagle swooped low over the lodge, and regaining its strength, landed on a convenient branch. There it sat, looking down on the scene, announcing the birth of the boy.

Snow Deer looked up as the bird gained its perch. "Look Na-tan," she urged excitedly, "it is an eagle the Great Spirit sent as our son was born."

"Yes, it is a pretty one, but not very sure of its wings, I'm afraid," he replied.

"But don't you see what it means?" she continued. "The eagle is the greatest of all birds. It has intelligence and fleetness of wings, and is a great hunter! It is what we will name our son. He will be known as 'Little Eagle'."

Nathaniel readily agreed for he was so thrilled that a son had been born that he would have assented to any name. "That is a good name for the boy. I am proud to have my son called Little Eagle. But more than that, my love, I am proud that you are his mother, and I love you for giving me a son."

And so it was that Little Eagle joined the Deer Clan, and became a member of the Cherokee Nation. The boy spent much time in his early days being transported on his mother's back, or on the childboard hung on a branch of a tree or lodge pole where, when his eyes focused, he could observe the activities about him. By the end of the second month, he could recognize or distinguish the voices of Nathaniel and Snow Deer, and when they talked to him he smiled and sometimes giggled at them.

Both parents delighted in their new-found joy, and spent hours just looking at or talking to their son. He quickly became the focus of their lives, and his parents carried, bathed, fed, and entertained the boy. It was a rare moment when one of them was not hovering over him. By the seventh month he was crawling throughout the lodge and on the ground, and they spent much of their time preventing the child from eating bugs or sticks or assorted stones that lay around. In his tenth month, Little Eagle stood and walked on shaky legs for the first time.

Nathaniel was pleased that this milestone had been reached, but Oconostata was excited beyond belief. "The boy will become a great scout or tracker one day, and a great chief of the tribe," he declared to Snow Deer. Then he proceeded to start teaching him how to be one.

Oconostata took an interest in his grandchild early, and spent many hours holding him or playing with him. As soon as he could walk on his wobbley legs, the Chief held his hand and escorted him out of the lodge and through the village, proudly showing off his first grandchild. It was a dear sight, the old man and the boy, walking together, but it quickly passed.

The Chief was ill. Many suns he lay in his lodge, dreaming of bygone days when he led the nation in war and peace. In his youth, he had fought the whites aggressively, but in his prime he had become the consummate leader, negotiating treaties that he passionately believed would benefit the tribe. Now he reclined on his bench outside the lodge, fading in and out of his reverie, as members of his tribe came to humor and to honor the Great Chief.

He was dying, that much he knew. Somehow, he gathered his strength and made one last effort in 1782. He again met with the whites and negotiated and signed the Treaty of Chote. And then he was finished. In the season of Fall-of-the-Leaf, 1782, he called the Council together for the last time. Nanatola, supporting his ailing father, helped the Great Chief to his bench where the old man slumped.

His clothes fit him no longer. They hung from his body like those on a scarecrow. His long grey hair fell freely on his shoulders, exaggerating the dark skin of his face, now terribly wrinkled and brown. His black eyes were deep in their sockets, round orbs that peered out from his sunken face to look upon the gathering. Yet, as he straightened his body upward, there was an aura of power as he started to speak.

"My Brothers, I come before you for the last time. We have had good hunting and fishing together. Many snows we have been together, many that have run red with the blood of our enemies—and our own. But the Ani'-yun'wiya stand here today—brave and strong—as the whites come around us, forcing us from our lands. My eyes no longer want to see what lays before us and my ears no longer want to hear the cries of our people. Before I go to the hunting grounds in the setting sun, I make known my thoughts to you.

"I would wish my son, the Tarripine, whom some know as Nanatola, to take my place as chief. He has sat with me in Council and when we have met with the Long Hairs. I want my new son, Na-tan, to be a warrior chief. He has fought well for us; and he will stand with us against the whites. Together, they will represent peace and justice for the Ani'-yun'wiya. I ask that you grant me these wishes. Then I will go peacefully to the Great Spirit."

When the old chief finished speaking, the Council members remained silent. What he had just asked of them was strange, The Cherokees normally selected the Chief on the basis of his leadership abilities and persuasive skills, and although they respected both Nanatola and Nathaniel and had little disagreement with the request, it had come as a surprise. They would have to think about it.

In the season of the New-born-Leaf, 1783, Oconostata died. In the old tradition, Snow Deer and her mother washed and anointed the old chief and placed him in a sitting position facing west, resting on furs in front of the lodge. Beside him, they placed his rifle and bow and his quiver of fine arrows, and other implements of war and peace he had collected over the years. They would go with him to his tomb.

Nathaniel, who had come to love and respect the old warrior, even from that first meeting when he stood before the Chief and and pleaded his case to remain in the village, mourned the old man deeply. Snow Deer, after many attempts to assuage his grief, left him alone as he went off into the forest to suffer the loss and the loneliness that the old man's death had brought.

In the end, Nanatola became the Peace Chief, but it was not until years later that Nathaniel was made War Chief and waged a final battle to bring peace to the village.


A traditional custom of the Cherokees was for the mother's brother to play a paternal role in helping to rear a son. "Uncles" were considered to have a special relationship to a child, and willingly accepted the responsibility. Nathaniel, however, had such love for his son that he could not forfeit the right completely. He deferred to Nanatola and Bear Claw, the boy's great uncle, but the culture of the white man was too deeply imbedded to allow them to take over the job.

Except for schooling. In the Cherokee culture the child was taught at home, and everything he needed to learn to equip him for life in the tribe—hunting, fighting and playing—was introduced to the child at an early age.

The boy was no exception. Almost as soon as he could walk and understand simple instructions, Nathaniel and Little Eagle's uncles commenced the training. His first bow was a simple piece of wood that the boy found and brought to his father, asking if Nathaniel could add a string and make it into a bow. From that day on, Little Eagle pretended to shoot anything that moved within the village.

By his third birthday, Little Eagle was fast becoming acculturated in the ways of his people. He was a precocious child, and Nathaniel started to instruct him in the tribal customs early. And so it was, when Little Eagle was about four, that Nathaniel took him into the woods close to the village. There he spent hours and days with the boy, teaching him the skills necessary to his survival. He taught him patience, and how to remain still and wait for the animals that lived there. Nathaniel showed him how to slip quietly through the forest, conceal himself in the trees and bushes, recognize a sign of an enemy, and how to hunt and fish and track an animal.

A few months later Nathaniel took Little Eagle to search for proper wood to make a bow and some arrows. They found a slender sapling and fashioned it as he had watched Bear Claw make his own bow a few years before. As the shape emerged, Little Eagle danced around his father urging him on. When it was finished, Nathaniel showed the boy how to hold it and told him to keep his left arm straight as an arrow, and to pull the string repeatedly. Only then, he told the lad, could he strengthen his shooting arm.

The boy practiced incessantly, using heavy, short arrows with thick blunt heads that Nathaniel made. He learned how to snap the bowstring, compensate for a strong wind, and look for unobstructed targets. He went into the woods near the village every day to try his luck with the bow. Little Eagle's arm grew stronger. One day, when Nathaniel had seen the boy hold the string to his nose waiting to shoot, he took him on his first hunt.

It was late afternoon when they came to a clearing and sat down to wait. As they sat quietly, several animals stirred in the heat of the day. Squirrels played in the shade of the trees, daring Little Eagle to try his arrows. Nathaniel cautioned him to wait. Suddenly a rabbit came into range, and he motioned the boy to shoot. Little Eagle drew back the string and let it go. As the bowstring snapped the rabbit jumped, squealed once and dropped, and the boy ran to it and held it up for his father to see. It was a proud moment for Nathaniel, and an even greater one for the boy.

The first time Little Eagle saw a fawn with its mother, he was so excited that he could scarcely wait to get home and tell his mother.

"Hai, Mother, guess what we saw today in the forest?"

"You saw a squirrel or a bird, huh?" his mother asked.

"No, we saw a baby deer and his mother. They were so pretty, and if I had a big bow I could have shot them. Father said we didn't need the meat. Anyway, I'm glad we saw them."

Snow Deer was proud that her son realized the beauty of the animals and the need to kill only for meat, and she said, "You are right, Little Eagle, and I am pleased you would not kill a deer so young." His happiness was so real that she wanted to encourage him.

"I think it is time for your father to make another bow for you," she suggested. "Would you like that?"

Nathaniel, standing outside the lodge was listening to the exchange. "You don't have to give the boy any ideas . . . he's got plenty of his own. For now, I want him to learn to use the blowgun. Come on, Little Eagle, let's finish it first so that you can practice."

They collected the gun and the materials needed for the darts, and then found a large tree to give them some shade. Nathaniel had taken a hollow cane from the river's edge a few days before and pushed out the pulp inside so it could dry. Now he fashioned the darts. Taking a small, straight stick he cut it into pieces about a foot long and then attached feathers tightly around the shaft. On the opposite end he sharpened a point. Now it was ready for testing.

Placing the dart in the tube, he took a deep breath, placed the cane in his mouth and blew hard. The dart fell to the ground a few feet in front of the man and boy.

"What happened, Father?" the boy asked.

"The dart needs to be thicker here," Nathaniel pointed. He tied some feathers and trimmed them into a tight wad encircling the shaft.

"Now, let's try it again."

This time the dart was propelled into a tree about twenty feet away. Little Eagle, who had been watching Nathaniel, was anxious for his turn. "May I try it, Father?" he ventured.

"Of course. Now, hold it between your hands and take a deep breath; then put your mouth . . . here, you have to load the dart carefully at this end . . . and then get ready to blow. There, you've got it. Go ahead!"

Little Eagle took a breath as he had watched Nathaniel do, and then expelled it into the mouth of the tube. Nothing happened. "Take a deep breath and hold it," his father cautioned, "and then blow through the tube."

He blew as instructed and this time the dart left the tube and fell on the ground about six feet from the end.

"That's good!", he encouraged the boy. "But you have to practice a lot . . . especially when you take a breath before blowing. Also, you have to learn to aim the tube; otherwise, you won't hit anything."

Gathering up their things the two of them returned to the lodge, where Nathaniel told Snow Deer that now Little Eagle had a blowgun and would soon be hunting animals for the pot. He was proud of their son and wanted her to share in the learning he had just undertaken. She reached for Little Eagle and tousled his hair and he beamed up at both of them, secure in the knowledge that they loved him very much.

Another weapon of the tribe was the lance. Since Nathaniel had never learned how to use it, either for hunting or fighting, he asked Nantatola if he could help Little Eagle make a lance. Nantatola agreed and took it on as his project. Early one morning, after the morning meal was over, Nathaniel took Little Eagle to Nantatola's lodge and left him for the day.

He challenged Nantatola. "Here is the boy. He needs to watch you work and learn how to use it. Teach him well, I'd like to see him take you on one day! Besides, I have never learned how to make one."

"He'll be fine." Turning to Little Eagle, he said, "Come on, Nephew, let's go find ourselves the right wood and then we'll get on it."

"Bring him home when you're finished, will you?" Nathaniel asked.

"Sure, Na-tan, as long as you invite me to share your supper. Tell Snow Deer I'll be there early!"

When the uncle and nephew returned to the lodge later in the day, both were happy and excited. The boy carried a small lance and a ball made of a skin stuffed with hair. The ball was pierced a number of times, and the lance had seen some rough use.

"So the great hunter has returned," Nathaniel exclaimed, "and with an old ball and worn lance? How many beasts did you kill today, Little Eagle?"

The boy beamed. He was covered with sweat and dirt. "Uncle and I made the lance and the ball, and we have been practicing all afternoon. He sure is good."

Nantatola placed his hand on the boy's shoulder and smiled down at him. "You should be proud of him, Na-tan. After we made the lance, I had him try it out. He's a natural thrower. He could not throw it to the top of the pole, but his accuracy was good. Even the warriors watching him try for the first time were impressed. He'll have me beaten fast."

"How about the ball? Did he try that too?"

"Most of the holes are his. I showed him how to throw ahead of the ball as it rolled down the slope, but I only threw the lance a couple of times. I swear it; he is good! Very good!"

Nathaniel looked at his son. "I am proud of you, Little Eagle, very proud. You have the best teacher in the tribe. No one is as good with the lance as your uncle. If he says you are able to throw it well, then I know it is true. I hope you have thanked him for his help. Now get down to the creek and wash up for supper. Your uncle is hungry and I bet you are too."


This was a peaceful time for the tribe. Only a few raiding parties were assembled and dispatched against other tribes, and it remained relatively quiet. Occasionally, Nathaniel would accompany a patrol as the Cherokees made rounds of their lands, or to participate in a skirmish when an intruding tribe or war party was detected. Most of the tribal activity centered on getting animal hides to exchange for goods with white traders who continued to travel into Cherokee territory.

But for the most part it was quiet and all was well. As Nathaniel and Snow Deer and Little Eagle watched the seasons come and go, supremely happy with the bounty the Great Spirit had provided them, they could hardly guess or imagine how soon the tranquility of the land would be shattered, or how the distant drums of war would affect their lives and fortune.

# *12*

# *T*HE *B*ROTHERS

After a peace treaty was signed in 1785 between the Cherokee Nation and the government, trading posts were established to assist in commercial activity between the Indians and whites. Fair prices were established for the goods traded, and for the most part the Indians were treated decently.

In 1786, a small outpost village was designated as a trading town for the exchange of goods. Two brothers, Ben and Amos Awkerman, were rough and nasty frontiersmen who had seen the treaty as a way to cheat and corrupt the Indians, and seized the opportunity to establish the village as their own personal fiefdom. They made it clear that their primary aim was to force the Indians off the tribal land.

Both men were large, unkempt, and boastful, and they decided that rule by fear was the only way to survive and make a living. The townspeople, those unfortunate settlers who had arrived in the village looking for a better life, were confronted by the brothers who announced in no uncertain terms that they could stay only if they remained subservient to the Awkermans. Whatever the villagers did or said or believed was known to the brothers, and no one was willing to run up against the infamous duo.

The Indians who traded at the post were treated miserably, and the brothers cheated them by assessing exorbitant levies for skins, crafts and other items the brothers wanted in exchange for inferior goods. Frequently, after consuming large quantities of liquor, the men would go through the village threatening the townspeople for some

infraction of the conditions imposed on them, exacting tribute—money, liquor, or food—before departing the premises.

The men of the village, many of whom owed the Awkermans for
purchases of supplies, could not bring themselves to act collectively
against them. The brothers, knowing the fear of the townspeople, grew
more mean-spirited and proceeded to institute a tax on each member
of the town. Still, the villagers failed to confront the brothers and
demand their rights, knowing that if they did the brothers would exact
a penalty. So they were prisoners within the town, unable to get on with
their lives, becoming increasingly indebted to the brother wardens,
until that fateful day in the season of Sun-high-in-the-Sky.

The morning started innocently enough. Two young Indian girls
had been sent to the outpost village carrying packs of baskets to trade
at the post. They were happy to be making the trip. It was exciting to
have the day away from the village and the endless chores that occupied the women from morning to night. The Cherokees were expert
basket makers. The girls had collected the reeds used in the weaving
and had created several they would trade that day. They ventured out
with joy in their steps, never realizing how the day would end or the
bitter experience that would soon alter their lives.

As they left the camp, they passed Nathaniel's lodge carrying their
loads. He knew the girls' families were not overly concerned about the
day trip, but he cautioned the girls anyway.

He called out to them. "So you are going to the village?"

"Yes, we have baskets to trade," one of the girls answered.

"You are leaving very early. Why don't you wait and go in with the
others?"

"If we go now," the girl countered, "we will have more time to
choose what we want in trade."

"And more time to get in trouble, I fear," Nathaniel said. Be careful. Those men in the village are always waiting for pretty girls to come
along."

They laughed at him when he told them to be careful. After all
they were sixteen, of marriage age, and perhaps they would meet an
eligible brave during the trip. Nathaniel did not think it a good idea for
the girls to visit the outpost village—he had heard stories of the place

and the two brothers who controlled the people and everything that went on there.

It was late afternoon when the young male Indian struggled into camp, whipped horribly about his face, and tried to blurt out a story about the two girls at the trading post. As one of the women administered to his wounds, he described the horror of the day and what had happened to the girls.

"The traders have them!" he cried. "No one wanted to help me. Everyone is afraid of the brothers."

Nathaniel and several villagers gathered around the youth. His worst fears were confirmed. The brothers had taken the girls hostage, and he knew someone had to go into the village and find them. Stepping forward, he demanded, "Tell us what happened." Then to one of the squaws, he said, "Give him something to drink . . . can't you see he is thirsty?"

"I don't know everything that happened. I saw them come into the trading post with their baskets. I spoke to them, but the older brother told me to shut up. Then he called to his brother who was in the back, and he came out. They started to talk with the girls. The younger one said that since they had many baskets, and were so young and pretty, he thought he and his brother could make some good trades. I tried to talk to the girls in our tongue, but the men caught on right away and said something to each other which I did not understand."

"What were you saying to the girls," Nathaniel inquired.

"I told them not to trust the traders. I think the girls were getting frightened, but the men tried to be friendly then. They told the girls to look around the trading post and choose anything they wanted, and they would look after the baskets in the back. Then one of them motioned to me to follow them. He said that I could explain how the baskets were made, and then maybe they could pay more."

"Did you agree to do that for them?" another brave asked.

"Yes, because I wanted the girls to have a chance to leave . . . I motioned them to go, but they stayed. Ow! Be careful." He admonished the woman putting ointment on his bruises.

"And then what happened?"

"When we got back to the storeroom, the first one grabbed me and started to hit me. He was big and strong, and I tried to get away, and then the second one beat me and pushed me to the floor. I tried to scream to alert the girls, but they knocked me unconscious and threw me in the corner. I think they thought they had killed me because they did not bind me."

"How did you get away?" Nathaniel asked.

"When I finally came to my senses, I hurt all over. The girls had been brought to the storeroom and the men had undressed them and beaten them, and were drinking from a jug. Then they started to touch the girls all over. The girls were crying and begging the brothers not to hurt them, but the men just laughed and laughed and paid no attention to their cries. I pretended to be unconscious, but I could see what was happening."

Nathaniel was trying to make sense out of the boy's story, and he knew that the tribe had to get a plan together quickly if they wanted to rescue the girls. "Try and be clear now. When you got out of there, what did you do?"

"I did not have very long to wait. One of the brothers stopped drinking and came over and kicked me. He told the other that when it got dark they could get rid of my body. They thought I was dead. Then they took the girls and left the storeroom. I could not hear them, so I crawled to the door and got out. I saw some men of the village and told them what had happened, but they said they could not help me. When I pleaded with them for the girls, they walked away. They were frightened too. Those brothers are beasts, and should be killed like any other wild animal!"

There was no time to assemble a raiding party. Nathaniel had already mentally sketched a plan of action, but he felt that it was necessary to explain it to the few villagers assembled around the man-boy. Perhaps the lad had not gone through the formal initiation rites, but he had suffered from the men and Nathaniel wanted to give him a chance to avenge the happening.

"I would like to go to the village tonight and get the girls. If we wait until we meet in Council or arrange a raiding party, I fear it will be too late. Hear me! I want to form a small party— three men—and this lad if he is well enough to go. He knows the layout of the trading post, and can help us. Choose among yourselves! I want to leave within the hour. That should get us to the post when the moon is high. Get your weapons . . . I will tell you my plan as we move to the village."

Nathaniel's plan was simple. The party would slip into the village, enter the trading post and bind and gag the brothers. Then after collecting the girls, they would leave quietly. The men would be brought back, sentenced to death, and simply disappear forever. Nathaniel doubted if the villagers would know or care what had happened to them, and whether they did or not was of little concern to him at that moment. If during the raid an alarm was raised, the brothers would be summarily executed, and the raiding party would carry the girls from the outpost.

As the party moved toward the outpost village, Nathaniel went over the plan very carefully with each man. The lad wanted nothing more than to face the men again at the post. Nathaniel had decided that a swift entry into the trading post was necessary. He called for each man in turn to walk beside him as he laid out the details for the action. When one had been briefed, another came up to take his place. About a quarter mile from the village Nathaniel stopped, and in the moonlight brought the warriors together and reviewed the plan and the role that would be played by each. Then they started on again.

It was not difficult to gain entry to the outpost. If there were guards, they had fallen asleep at their posts and the gate was unlocked. Nathaniel was concerned about the dogs that might be lying about. They would likely start barking and alert the villagers. The lad said that he had not seen any near the trading post, but that was a chance they had to take. Nathaniel hoped they would not have to kill any.

As quickly as they had gotten inside the village proper, they moved to the trading post. A dim light from a candle or lantern issued from a window. Nathaniel sent the young boy to see what was happening inside. He returned to Nathaniel quietly and told him that both men were seated at a table drinking from a jug. The girls were nowhere in sight. Looking through the window the boy had checked the door, and there was no bar across the planks. It was just a matter of entering and catching the men before they had a chance to react.  Which is precisely what they did!

Nathaniel kicked open the door and entered, and the young boy followed and slammed the door shut.  In two strides, Nathaniel was across the room facing the brothers.  The look of surprise changed to recognition as two pairs of eyes saw the boy, and then returned to the taller Indian.

The first one to react pushed his chair back and started to stand when Nathaniel slammed him hard against the table and said quietly in English, "Sit down!  I did not give you leave to stand."

"What the hell are you doing?" the second brother yelled.  "You got no right bustin' in here like you own the place."

"Yeah, this is a trading post. and we're closed for the night."

"What the hell d'ya heathens want?  Get outta here."

"We're going nowhere," Nathaniel said.  "Now shut up!  You're open for us!  We want the girls."

The man looked up at Nathaniel, trying to see him in the dim light.  "What are you, Injun or white man?" he asked.

"It makes no difference.  We want the girls!  Where are they?"

To reinforce the question, Nathaniel had removed his long knife and extended it toward the man.  "You have not long to speak the truth or you're dead?  I ask you again, where are they?"

The first brother who had not moved from his chair said, "We can make a deal.  We'll give you the girls, and you leave us alone."

Nathaniel motioned to the lad who had been standing near the door.  "Bar the door, Son, and bring the rope."

To the men he shrugged.  "It is not important that you tell me where the girls are.  We will find them.  And you, my friends, have had your fun for today, but tomorrow you will face something far more exquisite.  Then I am sure that your memory of this night will return!  Now get on the floor!  Face down."

The brothers were slow to act, and Nathaniel slammed the butt end of the knife against the man's chest.  He doubled over and tried to catch his breath, and Nathaniel pushed him onto the floor where the boy tied his hands together.

"Did you not understand, my friend?" He looked at the other one, who quickly slid to the floor.

Again the lad deftly tied his hands behind him. "Go find them, Son. They have to be here someplace." Looking down at the brothers he said, "They had better be here, or you will never see another sun!"

The older brother heard the threat in Nathaniel's voice. "I told you we could cut a deal. Don't you want it?"

"It is too late, my friend. You had your chance. Now it doesn't matter what you offer."

He picked up the lantern from the table and moved over to the window. The he waved it back and forth once. A muffled knock sounded at the door. Nathaniel opened it and two other members of the raiding party slipped in. "Look for bullets and powder and knives," he ordered. "That's all we want. The rest will be left for the townspeople."

One of the brothers on the floor started to object. "You cain't do this to us. We got rights too."

"Yeah, that's right, Injun. You be sorry tomorra' if you don't let us go . . . you got no right to tie us up," the second chimed in.

To one of the Indians, Nathaniel said, "Bring me a piece of cloth, Brother. I'm tired of hearing them."

Then he bent down and stuffed gags in their mouths. The boy came into the room. "I found them, Na-tan, but I think you should come see for yourself. It is not a pretty sight."

"Are they alive?"

"Barely so. I don't know how we can get them out of here."

Nathaniel handed the boy his long knife. "Stay here. If they so much as move an inch, use it. Kill them!"

He almost retched when he saw the girls. They were stripped and tied to the center post of the storeroom, back-to-back. They were unconscious, heads hanging on chests, their long hair falling over their breasts. Streaks of blood covered their bodies. Of all the killings and fighting he had seen, nothing was the equal to this maddening scene before him. Their bodies had been violated, but worse they had been desecrated almost beyond belief, tortured and hurt until overwhelmed by pain they had lost consciousness. He shook his head, trying to regain his senses that for a moment had rebelled at the sight of the young women, and then he stooped, withdrew the small knife from his ankle sheath and slashed the ropes that held them to the post.

Tenderly, he laid them on the floor and removed the rags stuffed in their mouths and wrapped them in blankets. Then he went to the door. "Son, see what medicine and bandages are here. Don't worry about those two. I look for the chance to kill them myself. Bring some water. We must move quickly and leave this hell on earth!"

Nathaniel turned to the other Indians. "Hurry! Get the packs together. We will have to carry the girls, so keep them as light as possible. I will try and get them ready to leave. Keep an eye on these animals. They will never forget this day, that is for certain!"

The water refreshed the women and the ointment soothed their tortured flesh. Nathaniel helped them stand and exchanged the blankets for some muslin sheets he found on the shelves. They whimpered as he covered them again with new blankets, but he told them it was cold and they would need the body heat and they accepted whatever he said. He and the boy helped them into the main part of the trading post, but when they saw the brothers lying on the floor the girls cringed and cried out.

The physical condition of the women caused Nathaniel a change of plans however. They would have to be carried, one by each of the older Indians. The boy would carry the packs of ammunition and powder, and Nathaniel would escort the brothers. He quickly got the two men on their feet and tied together at the waist. They tried to get his attention by posturing and rolling their eyes, but Nathaniel said nothing to them except they were his prisoners and were being taken to the tribe. He saw real fear in their eyes now, but after the scene in the storeroom he had no pity for them.

He hoped they would try to escape on the way to village; shooting them would be more humane than what they would experience at the hands of the tribe. He shuddered as he thought of what lay ahead, and for a moment he was tempted to tell the brothers but decided against it. His mind flashed back to the horrible vision he had dreamed when he first came to the tribe, and he knew that these men would soon know pain many times over what they had inflicted on the girls.

The raiders exited the trading post and the village without incident. The brothers meekly followed Nathaniel's instruction and moved at the same pace as the Indians. Every hour the party stopped and rested, for carrying the women was not an easy task. The girls moaned softly and sometimes cried out when the carriers slipped, but for most of the journey accepted their deliverance without making a sound. Nathaniel wondered if any of the braves could endure a similar ordeal and be as strong as these two women. He was proud of them and he promised himself that he would tell the tribe how brave they had been. Perhaps it would help reduce the pain of their suffering and shame.

About a mile from the village they were met by another party which had started out to find them. Dawn was just breaking. Nathaniel told them quietly what had happened and turned over the prisoners. Two members of the new party shouldered the girls and Nathaniel's group followed along behind. When they arrived at the camp, he thanked those who had gone with him and told them to get some rest. Then he went to his own lodge and sat with Snow Deer for some time, telling her of the raid and the girls. He was utterly exhausted but happy that he had accomplished the mission. Soon after his recital to Snow Deer, he was fast asleep.

The Council was called the following afternoon. During the early morning hours the story about the successful raid, the brutality inflicted on the girls, and the prisoners who were now in custody, had reached nearly everyone in the village. The villagers were seething with anger and loathing for the white men who had committed the atrocities, and were ready to kill them without having a Council meeting. The Chief suspected what the outcome would be, but the decision to be reached had to be unanimous. The meeting allowed everyone to have his say in the matter.

The two sullen, badly frightened traders were led into the Council House. Their hands had been tied in front and attached to a leather belt around their wrists. Their feet were hobbled with a short length of rawhide which allowed them to shuffle forward when they were called. Another strap had been placed around their necks and drawn snug, and it was attached to a leather rope which was used to control their movement. The gags had been removed. As they dropped to their knees in front of the Chief they were no longer the powerful and arrogant traders of the outpost village, but weak and subdued prisoners before the high court of their chosen enemies.

Nathaniel was called to speak first. The Chief asked him to tell the story again, although all of the members of the Council had heard the tale. The tension in the Council House was high. While few had seen the victims, their condition had been described by those who had, and the fate of the prisoners had already been decided. Nathaniel told how the village outpost had been approached and how they entered the trading post and taken the men. Then, reliving the sight that met his eyes when he found the girls tied to the post, he heaped scorn upon the white men at his feet and grew angrier still.

"Listen, my Brothers, for what I want to say is not easily spoken. I am ashamed of what they have done. They represent everything that is wrong in the white man's world. They are despised by the other Long Hairs in the village, and I doubt if they will be missed. But they are like us! Some are bad and some are not. These two are the worst! Not all whites are like them. I have no pity for them. They are animals, and should be slaughtered like any other animal.

"If there is a bad wolf that comes into our land and carries off a baby, do we not go after it . . . to kill it? If a snake with rattles strikes at one of us, do we not cut off its head? I would not wish these men to be treated the way they used our women, but their dying should be long so that perhaps they will understand what is right and what is wrong."

Now the oldest brother screamed. "You cain't do this to us! We are your friends. We got to drinking and din't know what we were doin'. Look, we trade with you. We're good people. You cain't kill us. Let us go, please! We'll turn over the trading post to you. You can have anything you want there. Free. No trades. Just take whatever you want. But let us go. We'll leave the village." He started to cry and thrash around.

"As I said before, it is too late. You have not even said that you were wrong for what you did to the girls."

"But we are sorry. Look, you're one of us. Please tell the Chief here to let us go. We'll do anything you ask. Just free us."

Nathaniel turned away from them and spoke quietly to the Council. "The Great Spirit of the white man has said, "an eye for an eye", and I believe they should die, willingly or not, but die nevertheless!"

The brothers died, unlike how they had lived, begging for mercy and forgiveness for every sin they had practiced against the Indians. Their pleas went unheard. They died as few wish to die, living in a conscious state of pain that had no end. It took them two days before their spirits left them, but the Indians would not let them rest. They mutilated the bodies and hung the heads on posts in the clearing for all to see, before tossing the broken bodies to the dogs and wild animals to devour.

# *13*

# DRUMS OF WAR

The tribe remained much to themselves in their isolated village, and seldom had contact with other tribes beyond their boundaries. They were content on their land, and did not seek out others unless they had to for some specific purpose.

It was the season of the New-born-Leaf, 1788. All was well, and the tribe was happy and enjoying the new year.

On rare occasions, a clan member from another village would find his way to the camp, and become the single, most important event of that moment. Early one morning the camp was awakened by the dogs. The barking was sustained, and everyone was immediately alert to the intrusion. Dogs frequently set up an alarm when some stray animal trespassed during the dark, but the villagers knew that something was very wrong. Dawn was attack time, and all were aware of it.

Throwing his cloak around his shoulders, Nathaniel reached for his rifle and powder horn and shouted to Snow Deer, "Hurry, something is happening!"

"What is it, Na-tan?"

"Get Little Eagle! Run for the river!"

She reached for the boy. "Are they dog soldiers, Na-tan?"

"I don't know, but run. Quickly now." He lifted the flap and disappeared into the clearing.

He quickly caught sight of a group of men converging on some creature, who was surrounded by the pack of snarling dogs. They had corralled the hapless figure in their midst, and were staying out of the reach of his stick. As Nathaniel approached the scene, he looked down on the ragged intruder. He was a pathetic animal. His clothes were filthy and rags barely covered his body. Nathaniel had seen destitute Indians in the colonies, but none had looked worse. The man showed little fear as he stood there, encircled by the men and dogs. There was something proud, almost regal, in his bearing despite his rags, that gave pause to the men before him. As Nathaniel pushed his way forward, he sensed something familiar about the man, and he thought perhaps they had met before. And then came recognition; he knew for certain that it was White Horse, a Cherokee he had not seen for many years.

At that moment White Horse looked up, his eyes meeting Nathaniel's, and as he opened his mouth and said, "Na-tan," his eyes closed and he slumped to the ground. The Indians, who had gathered around the old man, drew back as Nathaniel pushed forward and picked up his friend, surprised at how frail and thin he had become, and carried him through the crowd to his lodge.

Now the tribal members dispersed. The men slipped away to meet in the Council House, and the women and children, relieved that no attack had been made, returned to their fires and commenced preparing the morning meal.

The camp was soon alive with noise and people bustling about. Everyone was excited about the man who knew Na-tan. From where had he come? What news did he have about the outside world? Why did he cry out to Na-tan? Was this a good omen, or did his arrival portend some great evil that would sweep through the village? The visitor had quickly become the subject of their questions and the focus of their thoughts.

Nathaniel, carried White Horse to his fire, and was soon fussing over him like one of the squaws. He stripped him of his rags and washed him. This was woman's work, but Nathaniel needed to do it. It was small payment for the friendship extended by the old man years before. He found clean skins and wrapped White Horse in them and sat quietly and waited for the man to open his eyes. Snow Deer had quickly put water on to boil, into which she threw the neckbones of a deer that Nathaniel had brought home the night before, adding wild onions and wild potatoes to the broth. When it was ready, he carried a bowl to White Horse, and watched as the famished old warrior devoured the food.

Nathaniel knew that when the tribe met in Council and he told them of this man, all would want to honor White Horse with gifts of food and clothing. But that would have to wait, for White Horse needed to rest and gain nourishment after his long journey. Until then, Nathaniel would not allow other members of the tribe to get close to his fire. Except for the Chief! He could not be denied the pleasure he found as he looked upon his uncle whom he believed was dead. With tears in his eyes he embraced White Horse, and then told him there would be time for talk later.

Nathaniel and White Horse had eaten and talked late into the night the previous day, and White Horse was still exhausted from his travels. It was good to have his old friend back again, but Nathaniel sensed White Horse's soul was deeply troubled. Sometimes, in the middle of a conversation, he would stop and look away, as if in the telling of the story, there were bad things that could not be said.

"You are not well, my friend. The fire has gone from you. and you look weary. You have come a long way. It is good to see you again and to have you by my fire. Stay with us, Uncle, as long as you choose." He waited for the old man to speak, and when he did not answer, Nathaniel continued. "Now my mind tells me this: you have experienced some bad times and much troubles you. You must tell these things at Council."

Now White Horse spoke. "Yes, Na-tan, I think it would be good to speak before the Council."

"Good. I will ask Nanatola to call the meeting. But you did not travel here with good news. Am I right?" Nathaniel asked quietly.

"I believe what my eyes have seen in the settlements. Old they may be, but they see clearly on a cloudy day, and what they tell me hangs heavy around my neck. It is not good, Na-tan, and . . ." White Horse closed his eyes as if by the act he could forget his fear and the words he was about to speak, "and I am afraid that soon, in ten seasons or twenty, the Cherokees will be gone from these lands, washed away forever."

He stopped and looked at Nathaniel, studying his face, and then he started again. "Na-tan, you are right, my heart is heavy. It seems to be crushed by a giant oak. The winds followed me as I have looked to the west, and I am afraid for the Cherokees."

"Tell me, White Horse, but only as your heart opens to me. I make no demands on you."

"I know, Na-tan, and I thank you for understanding. You have brought strength to these weary bones and happiness to my soul. There is much to tell, but for now, Na-tan, let me tell you that the Great Spirit is crying for our tribe. The white man is making many changes and the Indian is being crushed, and there is little we can do."

A deep fear washed over Nathaniel as he listened to White Horse speak. The seriousness of what he said caused a great chill to envelop him. He wondered what White Horse had seen or heard to cause him such anguish and pain. Nathaniel wanted to ask his old friend but he sat quietly, engulfed by the prophecy, afraid that some unfathomable power would destroy the peace he had found with the Cherokees. He was not able to shut out the dreadful feelings that overcame him.

At last he said, "Dear friend, you have come to the right place, and here you shall stay. I am afraid for you, afraid that what you know has brought disease to your heart. I fear for the words that you speak, but I will wait until the Council sits together, that we might find strength in our numbers."

Standing then, Nathaniel reached for White Horse. "Come, my friend, it is late now, and we must rest for the morning."

The Council met the next day after the morning fires had been put to rest. There was great expectation as the elders of the village gathered in the Council House. They knew that something was important and many were agitated as they waited. White Horse had remained with Nathaniel since his arrival, and the tribal members were impatient for the meeting to start. The Council House was packed, and many of the villagers waited outside to catch what was being said inside. The murmuring voices subsided as Nathaniel and White Horse entered.

Nanatola raised his hand for silence. He told the Council members that White Horse was a clan member, and that he had lived with the whites a long time.

"My uncle, White Horse, has returned to us. We believed for many seasons that the Great Spirit had taken him to the hunting grounds. When Na-tan came to us, he told me that my uncle was still alive.

"Now he is here and he makes my heart happy. It is a good thing that he came. He has words for us, and the Council must listen to what he says. They are words he does not want to speak, for they hang heavy on his heart. We must hear them and decide what must be done. Now he will tell us his story."

White Horse stood before them and started to speak. "My Brothers, my heart is heavy and my spirit is weak. I have traveled for nearly a moon to come to you. The land to which I return gives me great joy and I thank you for taking me in. But my heart is not happy. My blood brother, Na-tan, I have known for many seasons. He gives me strength now. We have smoked the pipe together. You do not know me, but it is right to tell you of my fears, that you might know what we are to do.

"We are the Ani'-yun'wiya, and this land is given to us to use by the Great Spirit. He blesses us with fertile lands and much meat, he brings the sun and the rain to keep us happy. We live on this land now by his providence, but it may not be our land much longer.

"I have come a long way to tell you this. The white man wants the land, and makes settlements on it, and gives us nothing. The treaties mean nothing. They say forget treaties. Our once proud spirit is broken by the white man's guns. We no longer want to fight. Our bows hang quietly in the lodges. The tribe has lost its will to stand.

"Try to think as they think. Many of our brothers have seen enough war. They want to be like white men. They wish for harmony in their lodges and are willing to give up land rather than fight. Skins and furs are not so plentiful now. They no longer cover our people. Our braves have become farmers. They keep cattle and horses and grow the corn now. They ride in wagons. The women live inside the lodges and go to trading houses when they want goods.

"I do not judge them. They believe if they take the white man's ways, the white man will think better of them. Some do not know what is best for the Cherokee in the long run.   ·

"But I say now that seeds of desolation and great calamity have been sown and are growing fast in this land. The white man spreads the wrong spirit. My heart is sad. Our ways are going fast, my Brothers. Soon, we will lose more land and lose more spirit. I tell you this. We must stand together and decide what to do. If not, our young people and their children will lose the spirit, and we will be gone from this land. I do not want to fight the white man, but the Council must decide what to do. We cannot give our land without battle, but if we fight again, we will lose. That is all I want to say."

When White Horse had finished speaking, no one said anything. In Council, when a man had spoken, the members waited for a few minutes in case he wanted to add something more. It also gave them the chance to think about what had been said. His words carried a sense of doom; they had not known what was happening in the east. As his words began to sink in, many of the tribe started to speak at once. The Chief called for silence, saying he would speak, and then each would have his turn.

"My Brothers, I speak from my heart. I thank White Horse for the words he has spoken. Three snows past, the Ani'-yun'wiya met with the white men and agreed to a new treaty. They said our boundaries would be held sacred, and that we could govern ourselves as a nation. The new whites are no longer under a King Red Coat. A great White Father now governs the country. Perhaps, we must give the new White Council a chance to honor the treaty. They want to live in peace as we do; they do not want war. We must be clear about what we do. Now, we will listen to our men speak. That is what I want to say."

The Council debated the issue before it. Many words were spoken; many ideas offered. The sense of foreboding experienced by Nathaniel, when White Horse and he had talked, could not be shaken. He listened to the men, but could get no clear sense of how the story had affected the members. Some of the braves were ready for war. Others wanted to wait to see if the treaty conditions would be honored. The words of White Horse had cast a shadow over the meeting, and the arguments for and against the issue before them were intense and emotional. Nathaniel, who now had the same right to speak, listened carefully to the discussion until it was time for him to say what was in his heart. He chose his words carefully and his voice was strong.

"My Brothers, the words of White Horse lay on my ears. I share your fears as I share your life. When I came to your village, it was because I saw what was happening in the east. Everything White Horse has told you, I have seen myself. It is true what he says. I am white of skin, but I am Cherokee of heart, and I believe what you believe. I have lived with you by choice, and I want no other life. Your fire is my fire; your hunting grounds, my hunting grounds; your wars, my wars!" Nathaniel added emphasis with his gestures.

"I covet the peace that we have, and I do not want to war against the whites. But if the Council says that we should, then I am ready to fight with you." Nathaniel paused to let his words hold their attention.

"We have a treaty. It states that the boundaries are not to be violated and that we are an independent nation. Therefore, we should remind the great White Father of this and tell him that if the terms are not kept, the Ani-'yun'wiya will fight, and there will be no peace in our lands. We should be strong in saying this. Let us send a delegation to tell him. When they return, they will tell us what the whites are saying."

When Nathaniel finished speaking, others followed. Finally, after hearing all who wanted to speak, the chief asked for a vote. The debate was finished, and the Council voted to follow the course set out by Nathaniel. The Council adjourned.


The decision reached by the Council was to be postponed indefinitely. Cherokee raiding parties were already being put together, and strategies of war formed. Farther to the west, local chiefs had initiated plans that would result in a number of raids against white settlements. Time was fast running out for the tribe. The settlers had pushed westward, bypassing tribal lands, always wanting more land. White Horse had described what was to happen; he did not know how prophetic his words were or what the results would be.

Thus, he was as surprised as Nathaniel and the rest of the Council members when they received the word that raiding parties were already attacking white villages along the French Broad and Holston Rivers, and even the settlement of Knoxville. The treaty of peace that had been signed was quite specific. White settlers were ordered off Cherokee lands, but their farms were thriving and few left. The Cherokees, realizing that any new treaty would precipitate the forfeiture of more land, believed simply that they could no longer wait for the government to forcibly remove the foreign tenants.

It was not only the colonies that were putting pressure on the tribe. The English had been beaten in the east, but even after Cornwallis' surrender at Yorktown they continued to have a strong presence in the lower Mississippi valley. Along with the French and the Spanish, they staked out claims for tribal lands and ignored the young American government and the Treaty of 1785. Perhaps the English had decided to become assimilated into the new democracy. Whatever their destiny, the Indians sensed that whites would continue to establish new settlements, and nothing short of war would stop the encroachment. They were right.

The Cherokees had established a government represented by a central council. It was made up of independent chiefs who met annually, debated critical issues that affected the tribe, and attempted to reach consensus. It was hardly an acceptable or workable political forum to represent the many villages, or to resolve the issue of white tenancy on their lands. The upper and lower villages of the Nation were in disagreement.

Now in these changing times, separate village councils, especially those in close contact with the white intruders, met and decided on war. They believed, rightly or wrongly, that there was no other option. Use force of arms; negotiate from strength: That was the way to reinforce tribal possession of these lands. Let the whites know that the Indians would fight!

The war drums began rumbling in 1788. More than two hundred warriors gathered to form a raiding party. Not all were in favor of attacking the white settlements; The old men knew of battles that had been fought before and the disgrace of failing to win when they went against the whites. The older hands cautioned patience, but it was in short supply at the moment. The young warriors could not be dissuaded; they were ready for war, and the objections and arguments offered by the elders fell on deaf ears. At times, raiding parties were assembled without authority of the chiefs, and went off to search for whites wherever they could be found.

Then Dragging Canoe, Chief of the Chicamauga faction of the Cherokees, who had refused to cede any more land, gathered a great army of hundreds of Cherokees and Creeks. The slaughter continued. For months the attacks and counterattacks continued. The whites fielded an army, and the Indians not to be outsmarted, forced it to divide its strength and went after the two parts.

The Indians attacked Gillespie's Station. Using arrows, guns, and lances they moved on, killing and slashing their way against the settlers. They struck pack trains carrying goods to the settlements and killed whites without remorse. The skirmishes continued for months as the Cherokee raiders raged along the Holston.

Blood fever ran high in many of the warriors, and blood begat more raids. Whites were mutilated and tortured and scalped; severed heads and other indignities were heaped upon the victims. The forts or stations that had been built to protect the white settlers were under attack; prisoners were taken for ransom; and the peace that had endured for just a few short years was broken. It seemed like a repeat of the 1760s, when raids launched by the white army destroyed at least fifty Cherokee towns.

In the late 1780s, Colonel John Sevier, a skilled Indian fighter, joined the battle against the Cherokees. The whites retaliated in kind, and hit and devastated many tribal villages, including the central village of Chote. The soldiers burned and ravaged the villages, torturing and mutilating the Indians. If anything, their brutality upon the "heathens" was worse. The frenzy continued; the blood ran deep. When would it all end, for whites and reds alike?

Then in the season of Cold-in-the Ground, 1789, the tide of battle turned. The winter encampment of the Cherokees was attacked and overrun by Sevier, and the Indians suffered a devastating defeat. Many warriors died; women and children were taken prisoner. The months of war was a loss not only of life, but signaled the beginning of the end of the Cherokee Nation.

The Indian raids had been hit-and-run affairs aimed simply at creating fear and havoc on the white settlers, and they had been successful in doing just that. But the whites were indiscriminate in their attacks on the Cherokees, striking peaceful villages and even killing peaceful chiefs under deceitful flags of truce. The army that was brought against the Indians caused immense suffering.

The tribe understood the game of war and accepted the losses stoicly. Dragging Canoe was not to be stopped totally. He and his band continued to fight Sevier until 1794, ranging along the Tennessee-Alabama border, striking and withdrawing, hitting again and again.

But what they could not understand, however, was the natural disaster that would visit them shortly. The calamity would come suddenly, without warning, and create in the Ani'-yun'wiya as much anguish and pain than any raid ever undertaken.

# 14

# $E$ARTHQUAKE AND $F$LAME

In the season of the New-born-Leaf, the first tremors raced through the area. Few of the Indians noticed the slight movement of the ground. Once before, while living in the settlement, something similar had happened. When he inquired about it Nathanial was told that the earth was just shifting and there was nothing to worry about. Along the shelf jutting into the Great Water, the giant land plates had moved, but as no damage had occurred there was little concern over the trembling earth.

Nathanial expected the shaman to make some comment about the event, but for the first time since he joined the tribe the medicine man said nothing. Regardless of whatever happened in the land, the shaman explained that the spirit world had caused the disruption. Whether it was a wind storm, a rain storm, a drought, a long winter, or whatever, the shaman attempted to reinforce his position in the tribe by conveying the idea that he was able to commune with the spirits. Perhaps there had never been a tremor before, and the high priest was not able to comprehend the significance.

Nathaniel went to see Bear Claw. He had read something about earthquakes and remembered that frequently earth tremors would be felt before the main event. This might be a precursor of something worse, but he wasn't sure how to tell the tribe without sounding foolish.

He spoke quietly to his uncle. "Hai, my friend, have you felt the earth grumbling today?"

"Yes, but it is nothing."

"I'm not so sure, Bear Claw. The shaking earth could be followed by something much greater."

"What do you mean, Na-tan?" the old man asked.

Nathaniel wasn't sure how he could explain it simply to his friend, but he had some premonition that he could not ignore, however false it might be.

"Bear Claw, I have a bad feeling about this. I do not want to frighten our people and yet I feel the need to tell them. So what should I do?"

Bear Claw thought for a moment and said, "Na-tan, the Great Spirit has not brought suffering to our people because the earth moves."

"You are probably right, but what if something happens? How would the tribe react?"

"They will be afraid, but what can we do, Na-tan? We can't move to another place. If the earth moves beneath us, then, it is the will of the Great Spirit."

"That is true, Bear Claw, but I think the people should meet and be told. There will be less fear and surprise if it does occur."

Two days later, in early afternoon, Nathaniel left the village to look for swarming bees which could lead him to a honey deposit. He hoped that Bear Claw's dog would tag along, but when he went to the lodge the dog did not greet him as before. The animal's behavior bothered him. The dog was nervous about something and whined when Nathaniel approached, but it could not be coaxed away from the lodge. Always before the animal was ready to go into the woods with him, but now he slunk back. He seemed to be frightened of Nathaniel and kept his distance. Oh well, Nathaniel shrugged, he is just not interested, and so he turned and walked away from the village.

He had only gotten a short distance into the trees when suddenly he was aware of a roaring sound breaking the stillness around him. Then the earth beneath his feet moved sideways, and he heard a loud noise like distant thunder echoing in the wind. He knew the earth's crust had shifted and would never be the same again. The wind increased in intensity, trees bent under the force in the ground, and in those first few awful moments the smell of raw earth and vegetation encompassed him.

Although he had never experienced such a phenomenon before, Nathaniel feared what was happening, and he stood rooted in place anxiously watching the grinding of the world around him. The first shock lasted only a few seconds, but in that time he sensed, rather than saw, trees toppling and crashing to the ground, uprooted by some gigantic force. The earth undulated before him. He was stunned by the upheaval and the ferocity of the shifting earth. He was thoroughly disoriented by the earthquake.

Finally as the earth settled, he came to his senses and heard the screaming around him, coming from some great distance. He moved toward the village, but had not gotten far through the tangled underbrush when he saw a large jagged slice in the ground where the earth had split apart. Small fissures emanated from it. He was reminded of a story told when he was a young boy, of a giant so immense that he could lift the world causing it to crack. As he stood staring at the slash in the earth, it looked like the giant had raised his back and stretched, and a wild smell unlike anything he had ever known leaked from the crevice.

With a gnawing fear he approached the fissure cautiously, uncertain of what he would find, and dropped to his hands and knees to crawl closer. When he got to the edge and looked into the bottomless pit, he felt uneasy and started to move away. The first aftershock hit, and far beneath him the bowels of the earth shifted again, and Nathaniel started to crab backwards as fast as he could go. Then the earthen walls of the split came together and settled into place. The waking giant had rolled over and was asleep again. Certain now that the worst of the earthquake had passed, Nathaniel ran for the village.

He was wrong! Two minutes later, another powerful aftershock rumbled underfoot, and he was thrown off his feet and smashed to the ground headfirst. He shook his head to clear it. As the wave moved past, Nathaniel stood up and dusted himself off, astonished that the blow had been so strong. The ground continued to undulate; he was reminded of his voyage aboardship, and how the waves had swept them along in a storm. At least he was on dry land, he thought, however bad it would get.

As he reeled drunkenly forward, sure that somehow the village offered more protection, another mighty shock struck the ground and uprooted several large trees directly ahead of him. Then he saw a large herd of deer stampeding across a clearing in the woods ahead. Incredulously, two deer raced by on his left close enough to touch, running wildly with several great wolves to escape the terrifying earthquake.

He stopped and stood transfixed as the subterranean thunder increased. The wind rose in intensity, blowing leaves and dirt against him. Another fissure lay ahead, but as he looked at it trying to figure how to get across, it slammed together with such force that the ground under his feet shook violently. When he looked again, a shallow mound of dirt outlined the intensity of the closing. He was frightened now, not for himself but for the people in the village, and he swore softly, convinced that the quake had destroyed his world.

Then for the first time he was aware of the unworldly stench rising from the ground. Penetrating his nostrils and his throat, the sulphurous fumes made him think that the Gates of Hell had opened wide for where else could such a smell originate.

Arriving in the village from the west, he saw a scene that conjured up the worst of hell. For there on the side of the clearing, near one of the lodges, a great fire was roaring into the still air. Reaching higher than the Council House was a pillar of flame that dwarfed any fire he had ever seen, sucking up the air around it, fed by escaping gas from the ground. It was so monstrous that the few Indians who had not escaped into the woods were huddled far from the spewing inferno, crying to the Great Spirit to save them from a fiery death.

Surveying the scene quickly, he saw that the earthquake had done little damage. Because of the way the lodges were built, the upheaval of the ground smashed or splintered some of the posts supporting the roofs, but remarkably only a few of the lodges had been shattered. He guessed they could be repaired quite easily. While the destruction to the buildings had been light, the shock and fear of the moving earth had devastated the tribe. They appeared to be in a daze, not comprehending that the village had been spared and they were crying and howling to the shaman to do something for them. A small boy ran by, alternately crying and laughing, and he was reminded of Little Eagle, and his heart sank.

He ran to his lodge, fully expecting to find Snow Deer and Little Eagle, but they were gone. His fear grew. Where were they now? Had they run into the forest, trying to escape the churning earth? He screamed their names but there was no reply. He looked around the lodge, trying to see if they had taken anything with them. It was a shambles. Food pouches and hunting weapons were torn from the lodge poles and strewn on the ground. Utensils and pots were piled together in a cluttered mess. He could see nothing that might have been taken by Snow Deer when they departed. Then he left the lodge, screaming their names, and they were coming down the path toward the lodge. He ran to them and scooped them into his arms, and hugged and kissed them and held them to him, relieved they were safe and with him.

Nathaniel felt that somehow he had to get the villagers functioning again. He had heard the legends of earth rumblings and flaming spires of death caused by the Great Spirit when he was upset by the evil spirits of the Underworld. Indian mythology told many stories of major geologic events.

The Indian tribes believed this was all part of the Great Spirit's plan, that rocks and rivers and lakes were all living beings, and that they possessed immense powers. They said that the Great Spirit used these objects to maintain harmony in their land, that the heavens and earth were bound together with the Principal People, and that only when these were in harmony was the Great Spirit fulfilled.

Nathaniel knew how the tribe would feel about the earthquake that had just struck them. They would believe that something was out of balance, or otherwise they would not have been visited by such a force. Since the Great Spirit controlled the physical world, He could cause the earth to move whenever they displeased Him. He would have to explain this happening very carefully since he had been the one to raise the concern before the earthquake hit.

Taking Snow Deer and Little Eagle with him, he went directly to the clearing. The fire was still roaring out of control, but the villagers were returning and coming out of their shocked look. The shaman huddled alone, still far from the blaze, muttering incantations to himself. Nathaniel walked toward the group and raised his hand to get their attention.

"Do not be frightened," he counseled. "The worst is over as you can see, and the village has been hurt little. The fire will soon burn out!"

"How do you know that, Na-tan?" someone shouted.

The shaman had appeared in the crowd. "You do not know. The Great Spirit has brought this upon us because your white men have taken our land. We will suffer because of them."

Nathaniel looked directly at the medicine man and spoke forcefully. "It is true. I was born a white man, but I am Cherokee now, perhaps as much as you. You know that! Do not bother me with your foolishness. Go back to your silly world."

The assembled Indians were startled by Nathaniel's words. It was the rare Indian who questioned anything the shaman said or what he interpreted. Now they were seeing undisguised loathing coming from Nathaniel. While they respected him greatly, his comments bothered them. For his part, Nathaniel wanted to show the people that the shaman had no more insight or control over the Great Spirit than he had. He was fed up with this man who took advantage of the tribe, pretending things that were not so.

Regaining control, he said in a quiet voice to the shaman, "Tell us why the fire rages. Do you have the power to put it out?"

The priest could not be denied his chance to recoup his position. "It burns because the Great Spirit wishes it to burn. He is unhappy with the tribe. The people must regain harmony with the land and all things in it. Then the Great Spirit will quench the fire."

"And what must the people do to stop it," Nathaniel asked.

The shaman smiled smugly, "They must make sacrifice. Perhaps we could kill you. That would appease the Great Spirit!"

At this statement the people gasped aloud. Snow Deer, who was holding Nathaniel's hand, squeezed it hard and cried, "No! Perhaps, it is you who should die. I too am sick of your ways. You cause the people much hurt, all in the name of your stupid practices. Put out the fire, if you know so much!"

Nathaniel realized the shaman had to prove his point and he wanted to terminate the matter. Nathaniel had noticed the flames diminishing, and he guessed that soon the eruption would end. He spoke again to the crowd, "The fire is burning from something under us. I do not know what, but it is deep in the ground and the earth's movement has opened a hole for it to escape."

The shaman failed to grasp what Nathaniel was saying and could not let go. "I will ask the Great Spirit to put out the fire."

He moved toward the flames and began dancing in a circle around the blaze, exhorting the spirits to stop the scorching discharge. He danced closer and closer, unmindful of the heat generated by the flames. Then suddenly the wind shifted, and he was engulfed in the spewing gas. He screamed once, a heart-stopping cry of terror and death, and then vanished as the powerful winds sucked him into the base of the funeral pyre. The smell of burning flesh overspread the tribe, and they were stunned and cried at the roaring flames and knew fear again.

The shaman had disappeared into the flames, and the legends would tell of the medicine man and how he had provoked the Great Spirit. He had died in the holocaust that consumed his body before the fire burned out. Minutes later, the flames tapered off, and then stopped completely. The ground around it was scorched bare and there was no sign of the missing shaman. He had simply been incinerated.

Calamity and death were no strangers to the Cherokee Nation. Wars between various enemy villages or tribes, famines, disease, and pestilence had given the Indians a recognition of their mortality, and the hand of death was never unexpected. So it was with the earthquake, an event that struck an indelible fear in their bones, and then was gone before they could fully comprehend what had happened.

The fire had extinguished itself, but not before the enormous power of the wind that fed the flames had lifted the ashes into the sky above and scattered them over the village and the surrounding forests. The scarred ground was all that remained, a circular patch burned into the earth. The shaman had vanished, along with some of the prejudices and superstitions he had brought to the tribe. The people clustered around the still-smoldering earth and fell on their knees and offered supplication to the Great Spirit who had granted them life. There was little need for the medicine man now.

Many of the villagers, humbled by the death and disappearance of the shaman, were shocked by the force of the earthquake and the pillar of fire. They had been frightened badly and did not know what was to come next. For that matter, Nathaniel didn't know either!

As Nathaniel and Snow Deer and Little Eagle stood on the fringe of the massed villagers, her brother approached them and said, "Na-tan, now that the worst is over, I think you should talk to the people about the shaman's death."

"Why? What can I say that they do not already know?"

"They know you were not friends and that you did not approve of him, and that is the reason. Our people heard you trading words, and you should explain to them why he died."

"He died because he was arrogant and wanted to prove that he had the power to put out the flames. He wanted to prove that only he could speak with the Great Spirit."

"The people believed him, and still do. Since he has disappeared they will believe that Hianequo, the Great Spirit, has taken him."

Nathaniel thought about what Nanatola said. He was aware that superstitions played a major role in the lives of these simple folk. The earthquake and flames were imbedded on their minds, and whatever he said would be important. Otherwise, a legend would be born, and the shaman would be made into an heroic figure. He did not want the people to think ill of the shaman; on the other hand, he would not encourage the belief that the man possessed extraordinary powers.

The Chief called for the villagers to gather around him. He did not know what Nathaniel would say, but when he looked at him, he knew Nathaniel could be trusted to say what was in his heart. He raised his hand for silence. "I have asked Na-tan to speak now. The earth below us has stopped moving and the flames are gone. The fire took one of our people."

"Do our eyes see everything they should see? I do not know. Let us listen to what Na-tan has to say."

Nathaniel knew that he could not mislead the people. He had to explain what he believed had happened. The spoken truth was always best.

"My friends, the earth is still. When the fire burned high, I told you that it would soon burn out. Some of you believed what I said; the shaman did not! There are some of you who think I did not like the shaman. That is not true. I did not respect him. Hear what I say! The man had great power in the tribe, but I do not think he used it wisely. If he had been wise, he would not have gone to the fire to be caught up in it. The flames burned high and took him prisoner, and he is gone. Now we must get back to our lodges and live again. We must select a new medicine man or woman, one who will have our respect, not one who would gain power and use it against us! It is time to do this. That is all I want to say."

When he finished speaking, Nathaniel turned and leading Snow Deer and Little Eagle, started for his lodge. The tribe must get back to living, and he knew the people would think about what he said. He could set an example by going to his lodge and putting things back together again. Before the day ended, nearly all the lodges had been cleaned and repaired. The cooking fires were lit. A sense of gratitude and peace replaced the gloom and fear that had weighed upon the villagers. The people were now strangely quiet, awed by the terrible nightmare they had experienced. When the sun fell, they settled by their fires, content to be with family again. Night quickly enveloped the village, and the fires burned low. Like the others, Nathaniel and Snow Deer sat late into the night, quietly re-living the day's happenings.

The day following the earthquake a few tremors shook the village, but the people seemed unconcerned and went about their daily work and play. Hunters took to the forest, looking for animals for the cooking pots, and returned with tales of great destruction and death, along with several deer. The women and children worked the fields, gathered wood for the fires, and collected food for the evening meal. A few remaining lodges were repaired and the Council House inspected for damage. Not one person shirked the work assigned. It was as if in the tragedy of the moment the villagers regained a sense of a cameraderie and an understanding of each other's needs that temporarily had been lost. That evening a communal feast was planned, and the people came together to thank the Great Spirit for giving them life.

# *15*

# *TREATIES OF DISSENSION*

The earthquake had a debilitating effect on the tribe. While it had not caused any appreciable damage or loss of life, except for the shaman, the people considered it an omen of great proportion.

There was open discussion about why it had occurred. Many believed that the Great Spirit was displeased about the white intrusions and had brought it upon them as the shaman had predicted. Some Cherokees believed that the Great Spirit was warning them with the earthquake that they were becoming "too white," and that they should return to th old ways. In the Cherokee villages all across the land, the Councils met to deliberate what was happening around them. The net result was that several raiding parties were formed to attack white settlements.

The great White Father and his government far to the north had found the Indians to be implacable. The Indians had simply decided that war was preferable to giving up land that the Long Hairs wanted. The Creeks were also on the warpath and had united in principle, if not design, with the Cherokees against the white intruders. They had little time for the Cherokees, and had never accepted the Cherokee boundaries between the two nations, but they found in their northern neighbors, perhaps for the first time, a commonality of purpose. It was to fight the whites! They too were tired of losing their lands.

At the same time, a spirit of disunity and fear swept throughout the tribe, especially between the upper and lower villages. It may have surfaced because of the truce that had been reached between the whites and the Cherokees. However it occurred, it too was to have an effect upon the Nation.

In 1791, the Treaty of Holston was signed. This treaty promised perpetual peace to the tribe, and stated quite simply that the government wanted the Cherokees to pursue a new lifestyle and become sheep and cattle herders and take up farming. In this way, the treaty promised, the Nation would attain a higher level of civilization. Of course, the government people pledged that much assistance would be provided in these matters, but certain concessions must be made. Some Cherokees believed that by adopting the terms of the treaty, they would gain more respect from the whites and save their remaining land. But after more land was sold, dissension among the villages threatened to break into open dispute.

As word of the treaty and its implications reached the village, Nathaniel called on Nanatola. He was concerned there was more to this move on the part of the government than appeared on the surface.

The two men sat before the Chief's lodge. "I came to you," Nathaniel said, "because of the treaty we have signed. I have not read the words of the white government, but I fear they may mean something more than my brothers will accept."

"But the Ani-'yun'wiya have agreed to the treaty. We believe that the Long Hairs will honor what the words speak. Besides, we cannot do otherwise."

"It is true that we believe what the words speak, but is it true that we understand what the words mean?"

"Na-tan, I hear concern in what you say, but we must accept what the White Father tells us. The whites have accepted a truce. We are tired of fighting them. They are strong warriors and they are asking us to be at peace with them."

"Brother," Nathaniel said, "I am not ready to be a farmer or a sheep herder as they ask. If we agree to this, then we have lost our pride. Why can we not live the way we have always lived? Why must we change?"

Nanatola sat quietly for a few moments and looked away. Nathaniel had the sense that he was reliving memories of the past. He could not intrude on the man's thoughts. He waited.

Finally the Chief came out of his reverie and said. "We cannot . . . and must not forget the past, Na-tan, but we must also live in the present. Perhaps the Great Spirit wants to give us a new life . . . one that is better than the old." When he had finished saying this, he seemed to slump where he sat and again retreated into his memories.

Nathaniel believed, and the future was to affirm it, that the whites were using this promise as a ploy to gain even more land from the Cherokees. "You may be right, but I think we should bring this before the Council. Will you call us together so that others may speak of this treaty?"

"That I will do," the Chief replied. "I will ask my brothers to meet when the next sun sets. I would ask that you be the one to speak."

When the Council convened, Nathaniel addressed the assembly. The mood of the people was somber. They had come to respect this white man who stood in their midst. Perhaps he could interpret what these latter events would mean for the tribe.

"Everyone knows that when we last met in Council, White Horse told us what was happening in the east. His words were those of a prophet. We did not send a delegation to the great White Father. And now, here in our land, raiding parties have fought the white soldiers and as White Horse told us, we have lost. The white man's army and their guns and cannons are too strong for us to go against with our few guns, arrows, and lances. We cannot stop them!"

White Horse stood and motioned that he wanted to speak, and Nathaniel deferred to his old friend. "I would ask to continue, but first White Horse will say what is in his heart."

"I understand the treaty. The words do not say that if we stop hunting and take up the ways of the white men in the settlements the Nation would require less land, and what we did not use or need the whites could take. But that is what they mean! Do not be mistaken and believe otherwise. The whites think they are better than us. They have a powerful God, and they read his words in a book. They believe their God will give them what they need. I do not know if their God tells them to take from the Nation, but as I spoke before, the whites will take our lands. Listen! Our days are numbered! And we may not have too long to live."

"White Horse speaks well," Nathaniel continued, "but we must give the treaty a chance to work. I believe as he does that more land will go. But let us be patient and wait for the great White Father to give what has been promised. Other villages may not listen. We have peace now. We can continue our ways for the present and enjoy the land of our people for yet another sun.

"Yesterday, when I asked the Chief to call the Council, he said to me, 'We must not forget the past, but must live in the present.' Today is the present, and today other chiefs are talking about what the treaty means. It is true the drums of war are speaking. We may honor the treaty, but there are others who will not!"

He stopped speaking for a few minutes, but no one said anything. Then he continued. "My brothers, whatever happens we must think of the future. What will become of the Ani'-yun'wiya when all our lands are gone?"


By 1792, the acculturation of the Cherokee Nation was in full stride. But the ink was barely dry on the treaty before both white and Indian raiding parties went on the roll. Along the Watauga River the settlers had built many stockade forts or stations close to its junction with the Holston. They had not stopped there. Along the Holston and the Tennessee rivers, other stations were added. As the whites moved into what they called 'the new West', bypassing much of the Cherokee lands, claims and counter-claims precipitated more battles for possession.

In the season of Cold-in-the-Ground, 1792, another Cherokee village was destroyed. The president of the new American nation and his secretary of state signed a proclamation denouncing the attack and offered reward money if the perpetrators of the destruction were found. The killings did not stop and no one claimed the bounty. A militia company, ignoring the tentative truce, hit Coyatee and killed both whites and Indians in the settlement before departing. It was too much for the Cherokees.

In 1793, Warrior Chiefs Benge, Watts, Vann, and Benge's uncle, Chief Doublehead, a brutal chief of one of the lower towns, assembled a large war party comprised of Cherokees and Creeks. The latter, having set aside their enmity toward the Cherokees, attacked Sevier's and Cavett's Stations, ranging up and down the river striking frontier posts in a frenzy.

Then Watts moved across the Clinch River and on to Etowah where he entrenched his warriors and waited for battle. He had not long to wait. Sevier again set a trap for the war party, and a final humiliating defeat was administered. Not willing to accept the defeat for the Nation, Benge went off with his own war party and launched raids against settlements to the north in Virginia, killing whites and taking slaves, until finally his luck ran out and he was killed in the action.

The Treaty of Tellico Blockhouse was signed in 1794. The federal government, frustrated in its attempts at reconciliation, met with the tribal leaders and settled on an agreement that led to a factory system for the Indians. It was supposed to establish fair prices for Indian goods—pottery, baskets, cloth, and other trading commodities. The assimilation of the tribe and the adoption of the white culture had begun. What had happened to this proud race, beholden to no man, that it should be reduced to commerce of this nature!

The Council met again at the request of Nathaniel. The Chief opened the meeting. "As you know, our Brother Arcowee met with the whites at Tellico. They have decided to help us trade with them. Trading posts will accept what we have to offer. Our people have begun to act more white than Indian, and keep cattle and sheep and horses. They have farms now and can make these things for trade.

"Some of us do not agree with their ways, but the old ways are disappearing, and we must decide what is to be done. The issue before us is whether we trade now and have some peace, or whether we will continue a running battle that goes nowhere and has no end. Now I will listen to what your hearts speak."

"I am tired of fighting," an old warrior said. "War is for the young for they have the eyes of an eagle and the strength of the bear, and they can run like the deer. But my old bones are weak and my eyes cannot see as before."

A younger brave stood, "I am for fighting. We continue to give up our lands and the Long Hairs want more. What do we have to trade?

Why are we forced to sell to the factors? I do not believe the treaty is good for us."

Another man spoke. "Where is our pride? We have fought well and have lost a battle. But there will be other battles to stop the Long Hairs. If we take up the white's ways, we will soon have lodges where we must go to learn new things and to pray to the white God. I too say we should fight!"

Nathaniel rose to his feet. He had fought this battle in his mind many times. He knew the tribe was losing its self-respect as well as commitment to its culture. He hurt inside as he saw what was happening. He sensed what was to come. Some village chiefs could be bribed by the white land companies, and as they gained in power and influence would sell more land and adapt to the white culture completely. The inexorable wave of settlers had commenced, and there was little the tribe could do about it.

"Listen to the words spoken by our Chief. He speaks the truth. For many seasons now we have traded with the whites, as have your fathers before you and their fathers. They have given us guns and hatchets and knives, and even cloth for our wives to use. Pots made of iron for cooking they have given us. And many things that we did not have before.

"But they have also brought famine on our people and death from the white man's diseases. They have destroyed our towns and cause us much sorrow. They have brought our brothers strong drink, and then talked them into giving up land for little in return."

There was murmuring now in the Council. Nathaniel knew that his litany of transgressions by the whites had struck some chords of discontent. He raised his hand, and the Council quieted.

"Hear me, Brothers, for I want to say more. And what did we give them in exchange? We gave them hides from deer and bear and beaver. We exchanged many things for the goods that we wanted, and we offered them much more—our hand of friendship and trust. They turned against us. Yes, we could continue trading with them, but that is not enough. They want more land . . . and they will take it from us whether we want to give it or not.

"I am sad for the Nation, for I think we have lost our sense of purpose. Now the towns fight with each other. And so we split apart as the white man drives an arrow between us, and we break from our ways. The Great Council meets, but the village councils can no longer agree on anything together. That is not good.

"There was once a sense of honor when we fought our enemies. I think there is little honor left. I am tired, but I am more sad because we seem to have lost our way. How have we come to this? What can we do now?"

As he spoke to the Council, Nathaniel's mind was already forming the words that might offer a partial solution. He chose his words carefully.

One night, weeks before, Snow Deer had planted the seed of the idea and now, coaxed along by the treaty of the trading posts, it was starting to bud. They had lain awake on the sleeping bench, holding each other close.

"Morning comes soon."

"Yes."

"What do you think we should do, Snow Deer?"

"You are sad tonight, Na-tan. What causes it?"

"The Chief has said the old ways are disappearing. And he is right. I do not want to trade our ways for that of the white man. There must be something that we can do."

Snow Deer was quiet for a moment. As she lay in his arms, he could hear her breathing and felt an almost imperceptible movement of her body against his. Finally she spoke. "There is something, Na-tan, but I am not sure that I should say it."

"What?"

"We could go deeper into the mountains, and start a new life there. Where no one could find us."

"What about the tribe? Are you talking about us or the village?"

"I think others in the village will want to go."

"And give up the good living for something strange and terrifying and new?"

"Perhaps. We have had a good life here—summers of love and laughter and good food."

"Is it easy to forget the rest, Snow Deer? How about our friends? Are we to leave them behind?"

"Ah yes, but we will have them with us. At least, some of them will go."

"I'm not so sure, my love."

"I think you are making yourself sad. Go to sleep. We will talk more in the morning."

Nathaniel had gotten very little sleep that night. The ideas whirled around in his mind, one never stopping until another surfaced. They piled up on top of each other as he discarded and saved, altered and chose, until nearly dawn. Maybe Snow Deer was right! From that moment on, he readily accepted that the idea had possibilities, and it was something that he had to do.


"Listen, Brothers, there are some here who want to fight and others who wish to trade. As for me, I think there is another way. I do not want to fight the whites just now. As I said, we must give the treaty a chance to prove itself. But I do not want to trade with them. I do not want my woman to make baskets and pottery and weave blankets for the white man. I am not yet ready to become a man who lives so.

"I am afraid that disagreement among the villages will grow over the treaty, and I think there will be chiefs of the Cherokees who will trade land for money or strong drink. The new great White Father and his chiefs have promised us many things in their treaties, but all know what has happened in the past. Our lands grow smaller. The deer and the bear are not so plentiful now, and we fight among ourselves.

"Hear what I have to say! I have spoken to no one about this except to Snow Deer. For many suns she and I have talked together. We believe we can keep our ways if we go deep into the big mountains. Some of you may want to go too. In two suns I am leaving the village to travel into the mountains. Perhaps I can find a place that welcomes us. I do not know. I ask you to wait until I return. A man has to do what his heart tells him to do, and this is what I must do."

A hush had descended upon the Council as Nathaniel spoke. But when he announced that he was going west, the voices erupted. The Chief tried to calm the gathering and when he finally succeeded, he rose from his place to speak.

"Na-tan, has spoken wisely again. His words come as a burst of heavy rain to me. I did not know what was in his heart, but I know he speaks well. Whether he will find such a place in the mountains for us to go depends upon the Great Spirit. He does what he has to do. I will pray to the Great Spirit to guide him well. That is all I can say."

White Horse spoke. "Na-tan speaks for me and many of us. My friend wears the white skin, and since he came to us he has taught us much about the white man. His eyes are open and he sees what is happening around us and to the tribe. I think that maybe we are too close to understand as clearly as he seems to understand. I too wait for his safe return. If he finds a new land where the waters run deep and the wind blows free, there I will go with him."

There was more discussion in the Council. Many questioned Nathaniel about where he was going, and it was late when the Chief signaled a stop. The Indians went out into the night and returned to their lodges, and many were filled with both anxiety and a sense of anticipation of what Nathaniel said he was going to do.

Nathaniel's preparations for the journey required little work. He decided to carry his rifle and not the bow, a small blowgun and darts, his hatchet and both knives—the long knife that he could wield with great accuracy, and the short knife that he strapped to his calf. It was only after his acceptance into the tribe that he had removed it from his body. Now he thought it might be an ally on the trail. He took it from the peg in the lodge and spent nearly an hour sharpening the blade and oiling the hard leather. If he needed it quickly, he wanted it handy and ready for use. Although he did not know at the time, it was to save his life on the expedition.

Snow Deer fussed over him interminably during the day. He sensed in her some anxiety about the impending journey, and he spent a good deal of time trying to allay her fears. She went about the lodge packing pemmican and parched corn in separate bags for him, and added some jerky. She brought the provisions outside the lodge and laid them on a hide for his inspection. He first assembled his weapons, food, an extra pair of moccasins, and a lightweight, oiled deerskin that could serve as both a poncho and a ground sheet. The skin was rolled tightly into a small bundle. Nathaniel looked over the items.

"Where is the flint and steel? And the small water bag? I will need both," he said.

"How long will you be gone, Na-tan?" she asked quietly.

"I think for several weeks, at least."

"I will miss you much. The days will be long."

"And I will wish sometimes for you, Snow Deer, but it is better that I go alone."

She accepted his comment stoically. "Yes, it is better that way. Little Eagle and I will wait. There is much to keep us busy. It will be good if you find a place for us."

"Ah, my Little One, I will find it—that I promise."

"Na-tan, be careful. Do not take any chances."

"Come here! The only chance I want to take is for you to love me before I go."

"I think that is a good choice."

Later in the day they were visited by Nanatola, Bear Claw, and White Horse. All of them wanted this white man, who had married into the tribe, to have good fortune on his journey. The three men sat with Nathaniel before the lodge.

"This is a good thing you do for the tribe, Na-tan," the Chief said. "We want you to find a new land where we can go."

"I did not think the village would move. That is not the reason for making a search. I was speaking only for myself and Snow Deer."

Bear Claw interrupted. "When you spoke at Council, you said what many of us wanted to hear, and you were brave in speaking so. We too, do not want to live this way. When we give up our manhood, then we become nothing. I would rather fight and die than do this."

Nanatola continued. "I do not think that I should remain your chief." As Nathaniel started to speak, the Chief raised his hand. "No! No, hear me. If you find a place that some of us can go and live, Na-tan, then we will leave here together. Another can be made chief."

"You cannot do this, Brother! The people need you to lead them," White Horse exclaimed.

"I think not, Uncle. There are many who will be happy to see me go."

White Horse continued. "Na-tan, the last time you left me, many seasons went by before I saw you again. I hope it will not be that long this time."

"No, my dear friend, I expect to be gone a few suns. I think I will know the place when I find it."

Bear Claw spoke again. "Na-tan, what can we do for you while you are gone? What can we give you for the journey?"

"All of you can look after Snow Deer and Little Eagle for me, and ask the Great Spirit to guide me on the trail. That is what I want you to do and nothing more."

"Go then, my Brother," Nanatola declared, "and know our prayers are with you. Come back safely . . . the tribe needs you and your wisdom now more than before."

The men got to their feet almost at the same moment, and took Nathaniel's hand and grunted their goodbyes. They felt good about this man, and they were confident he would find a new land for them. Each man had decided to go when the time came, and they were already anticipating his return with good news. As they turned to leave Nathaniel felt great love for these dear friends, and he offered up a silent prayer that he would be able to fulfill their dreams during the journey.

# 16

# THE MORAVIANS

Daybreak. Nathaniel strapped on his belt laden with weapons and food, said a sad goodbye to Snow Deer, and left the village before sunup. Bear Claw stood in front of his lodge and watched the man as he passed by his lodge. Under his breath he called upon the Great Spirit to care for his friend, and spoke aloud, "Go with the Great One, Na-tan; this may be the only way out of this madness." And then Nathaniel was gone.

To reach the mountains Nathaniel started east along the river. He had no set goal to reach that day. His intent was to make a long, wide circle generally northeast into the hills, and then head south for twenty or thirty miles before returning to the village. He was not concerned about losing his way, simply because he would make his own trail as he proceeded. He knew settlers had moved into the area, but he planned to avoid them as much as possible. His major concern, and one which had caused Snow Deer the most apprehension, were the raiding parties. They too were moving throughout the region, and he did not want to get involved with them, whether Cherokee or Creek.

The going was relatively easy the first day. That was good. He needed to get the kinks out of his legs, and it allowed him time to think about the tribe and what was happening to it. As he moved along, his thoughts turned to the reason behind his adventure.

Changes were occurring at an alarming speed. The assimilation of the tribe had intensified. The latest treaty proved that. Although the land belonged to the Nation, members of the tribe had taken up farming and staked out claims for their piece of land. They were becoming too much like the whites, he thought. The word had been passed to the village: the separate village chiefs were leading by example and persuasion, and for the most part, ignoring the instructions of the Great Council.

He believed that dissolution of the tribe would happen because of the inability or disinterest of the local chiefs to adhere to guidance passed down from the Great Council. There was much disharmony. Where was it all to end? There was a breakdown in authority, and that final thought lent a sense of urgency to his journey and affirmed for him that what he was attempting to do was right.

Nathaniel moved along at a rapid pace. He felt good. He was in Cherokee country and felt reasonably safe, but at the same time he kept a low profile as he walked along the river. The going was easy. A few times he had to detour away from the water's edge to get around a massive thicket blocking his path or a creek that intersected his travel, but the delays were slight and bothered him not at all. By noon he figured he would head north for a bit and leave the river. There was too much opportunity to come upon whites who might have settlements near the water.

He made the decision at the right moment. He had gotten less than a quarter of a mile from the river and into the undergrowth of the forest when he heard men yelling to his left. He knew they were whites, but could not discern what direction they were moving or whether they had stopped. He stood quietly under the branches of a great balsam tree, and waited. The voices died, and then several shots sounded and the yelling commenced again. A few minutes later several deer flashed by him running scared, and he decided a hunting party had spooked the animals. While he stood there waiting, he ate some parched corn. There was no real hurry, and it was pleasant under the tree.

There were no signs of pursuit, and he guessed the men had gone back toward the river. He could move on. As he went farther into the woods, it got darker. The canopy of hugh virgin trees extended as far as the eye could see, and the sunlight diffused below onto the thick-carpeted ground. Occasionally, where a tree had fallen, the bright light came pouring through the opening above like a gigantic reflected lamp.

What a magnificent place, he decided, untouched by the woodsman's axe or any other tool the whites used. He was immersed in the grandeur of the forest primeval, wanting to possess the stand of trees, but then he realized he had gotten caught up in this thing of beauty and started walking on beneath the covering.

He crossed several small streams, and each time he came to water he drank deeply and filled his water bag. Gradually the stand of giant trees started to thin out, and Nathaniel's senses heightened. He had not felt threatened for there was peace in the dark, great woods, but the openness of the forest now caused him to move more cautiously, alert to every smell, every noise, every sight around him.

It was getting late in the day, the sun beginning to drop behind the tall mountains in the far distance. It was time to stop. He had traveled since early morning and he could feel the fatigue washing over him. "I am feeling tired," he reminded himself, "and I had better get settled before dark. Besides, I'm not as young as I once was!" He was also hungry.

Caution and experience led him to decide against making a fire. He found a large fir tree and crawled upon the thick pile of needles that had fallen to its base. Taking off his belt, he slung it over the lowest branch, and then leaned back against the trunk to rest. It felt good to sit. He took from the bag of pemmican a portion for his supper. He chewed slowly, feeling the strength returning to his body, and washed the mixture down with water. Then placing his rifle on the ground beside him, he raked the dry needles around and on top of his body and fell asleep.

Nathaniel slept well and when he awoke he went to the stream and washed before he ate. He considered having some parched corn for breakfast, but he didn't find that very exciting. First he rearranged his belongings for he needed to make them easier to carry on the trail. He reasoned that if he packed everything in the skin except for his rifle, he could then sling it over his shoulder. That would free his hands and make travel easier. He would keep the knife and hatchet on his belt.

When he unrolled the skin to make the pack, he was pleased to find several baked corn cakes. Snow Deer had placed them there to surprise him. He was! He sat and ate two of the cakes and thought of her and Little Eagle, and started to miss them terribly. "Better get on the move," he thought, "then, I can get back to them."

He continued his trek in an easterly direction. Maintaining his alertness, he did not run into either whites or Indians during the day. The areas he moved through were not heavily wooded, and he was able to make good progress. By late afternoon he began looking for a place to stop for the night, when suddenly he came upon a rushing stream that tumbled over a small waterfall. Close by was a stand of small pine trees. It was a lovely sylvan setting, and he decided to stay and go no farther.

Shedding his pack and belt under a tree, he drank the fresh, cold water and refilled his water bag. He saw some berry bushes near the water's edge and plucked some to eat. Then he realized how hungry he had gotten, and he decided he wanted something more than a cold corn cake or jerky. Meat! That is what would give him strength. Maybe a fish. With that thought he unrolled the skin and found some twisted deer gut and one of the two hooks that Snow Deer had packed.

Using parched corn for bait, he quickly caught the first fish. He wasn't sure it would be enough to satisfy his hunger so he cast again and was rewarded with the second one. He slit them open and washed them in the running water before wrapping them in green grass. He placed them aside. Taking his rifle and blowgun, he set off upstream hoping to find something more. He was in luck! Near the bank of the stream a small water hole had formed, its waters placid and deep. He hid himself and waited quietly where he could observe the animals as they came for water. Several deer came close, but he would not use the rifle and they were too large to kill with the blowgun. His mouth watered, thinking of the venison that was his for the taking.

He waited patiently, and finally a rabbit came into range. The blowgun was already to his mouth loaded with a dart, and as the rabbit stopped to nibble, Nathaniel aimed and the dart found its mark. Retrieving the animal, he quickly dressed and washed it in the cool water. Then he headed downstream to his camp and the fish that awaited him.

From a dead tree he gathered some dry bark, and from his waist-pouch he extracted flint and steel. Deftly he struck a spark into the shredded wood, and the pile commenced smoldering and the tinder burst into a small flame. He added some dry grass and leaves, and the fire grew. Then he took his knife and cut some green branches to cook his supper. He was careful to keep the fire burning clean. He did not want smoke to give away his campsite. When the fire had burned down, he placed the rabbit on a spit low to the bed of coals until he had seared the meat to hold the juices. Then raising it, he rolled the stick between his hands as he roasted the meat slowly.

His saliva flowed as he conjured up the taste of the meat, and he kept swallowing as he waited for it to cook. He took the fish and laid them on the outer edge of the fire. They needed less cooking and would serve him well as a first course for his banquet. Almost before they were finished, he grabbed them and wolfed them down. Then the meat was roasted and he leaned back and ate his fill. He saved one small piece and wrapped it in leaves. That would be a good beginning for his breakfast in the morning, along with the corn cakes, he reminded himself.

When he finished eating, he gathered pine branches for his bed. Before he fell asleep, he listened to the night sounds—the cicadas and frogs croaking their mating calls—and once he thought he saw an owl sitting above him quietly, waiting for its prey to move beneath the branch where it sat. It was peaceful there, and before he knew it he was fast asleep under the tree.

The next day he reached a deep gap slashed into the earth. On both sides, steep hills tapered into the valley, and he guessed that he was getting close to the mountains. The going was a bit more difficult. Looking around, trying to get his bearings, he decided he would stay where he was until morning. Then he could move through the gap that appeared to lead into the mountains. He hoped it opened wide on the other side, but he had no way of knowing what he would find there. He reckoned he had traveled nearly fifty miles since leaving the village, but there were many more ahead of him before he could return home.

There was a single narrow path leading through the gap. It was well-worn, an indication that it provided easy passage through the mountains. He considered leaving the path and striking out parallel to it, but discarded the idea for the advantage of making good progress.

His trained eyes told him that he had been preceded by several men, but he could not tell whether they were whites or Indians. He wasn't sure which he wished to avoid more. If he ran into indians other than Cherokees, they would be after his scalp. If they were whites, he would be subject to all kinds of questions about where he was from and where he was going, and whom he knew.

Sure, he could lie to them, but that went against everything he was as an Indian. He had found little of that trait in the villagers. An Indian might exaggerate about a battle or hunt, but to tell outright lies was foreign to the tribe. As he thought about a possible encounter his thinking clarified, perhaps for the first time, as he realized he was more Indian than white. That revelation came upon him like a cloudburst. He toyed with the idea, argued against it, even tried to reject it out-of-hand, but the fact remained. He was Indian in his thoughts and actions, customs and habits. He felt about the Long Hairs in the same way other members of the tribe felt. He felt betrayed by the treaties, the white squatters, and the overwhelming evidence that the tribe would be forced to vacate its lands. They were his lands too, now that he was a part of the Ani- 'yun'wiya!

Everything about him was Indian. He looked like one, except for the cool blue eyes; he hunted and warred like one; lived like one. He recognized these verities as they came together in his mind. He would kill like an Indian, simply and proudly! The Indians were a part of him, and he was joined to them, whatever lay before him.

Nathaniel was so deep in these introspective thoughts that his alertness dulled as he moved forward. Only some sixth sense of danger triggered an impulse to stop suddenly and listen intently to what lay ahead on the trail. Then he saw it, a large coiled timber rattler, poised to strike if he so much as lifted his foot to make another step. The snake was agitated, its rattles shaking furiously. He knew his buckskin leggings and moccasins could not stop the deadly fangs if the snake attacked. There was but one thing to do.

His rifle, cradled in his arms across his chest, was his only chance. As the thought raced to his brain he thrust the weapon from him and jumped backwards. The rifle landed hard on the snake as it lashed out, but the reptile's head was diverted. In the same moment, Nathaniel grabbed his knife and hurled it downward. It sliced into the moving target directly behind the creature's head, and the rattler was pinned to the ground writhing in its death throes.

As it quieted and died, Nathaniel cut off its head and swiftly skinned the snake. He cut several pieces from the carcass to cook later and removed the rattles for Little Eagle. Picking up the remains, he tossed them into the brush off the path. Then he moved on.

His alertness was heightened by the incident. The snake had brought him out of his reverie and he strode along, adrenaline coursing through his body. It was a fortunate occurrence, he thought later, for as he rounded a turn in the trail he saw the white men. He stopped short!

Two of them were rolling on the ground, legs thrashing, while one sat on a log by the path, his attention riveted on the scene before him. Nathaniel heard only some groaning coming from the pair, and his first inclination was to slip off the path and by-pass the trio. Something in the tableau before him, however, suggested that all was not right, and he decided that he would see what was happening. He started forward.

The man sitting on the log turned and saw him, and yelled at the two men on the ground as he reached for his rifle. Nathaniel came closer.

"Don't do it!" he commanded.

Nathaniel's voice reached the two figures, and the first one untangled himself and stood. Then as he buckled his pants, Nathaniel realized what was going on. The second man on the ground was a woman. She had been gagged but not bound, and it was clear the man was trying to force himself on her. The girl sat up. She was in men's clothes—long, black pants and a white muslin shirt. Her top had been ripped open and Nathaniel saw her rounded breasts as she tried to pull the two sides together to cover her nudity.

He was reminded at once of the scene at the outpost village and the Awkerman brothers, and his anger focused on the men standing before him.

"What's going on here?" he yelled. "You there," pointing with his rifle at the older man, "Who is this woman, and why is she gagged? Cut her loose!"

The man reached for his knife and as he withdrew it, twisted his body and threw it at Nathaniel. The blade whistled past him and imbedded in a tree. At that same instant Nathaniel fired, and the man's face changed as he saw the blood flowing from his chest. He glared at Nathaniel, shocked at the pain, and clutched his wound. Then, he coughed a rasping cry, and fell beside the girl.

The second man did not move. He croaked, "Why? Why did you have to kill him?"

"Did you see the knife? Don't ask! Perhaps the girl can tell me what this is about."

Nathaniel moved over and cut the gag from her mouth. His first sight as her hair tumbled loose was devastating. He stared at her. Jenny Howard! This girl and the image of one many years before—one and the same! Same age, same face, same hair, lips and eyes! He had left her in England, but here she sat, as the memories came crowding back. He shook his head to clear it. He judged the girl before him to be about twenty years old. How many years had it been! He was thirty-six and had left Jenny at twenty-one. Fifteen years since they had said goodbye, and now her double was before him, even wearing the same colors Jenny wore at that first meeting.

She looked up at him, catching his expression. "What is it, Sir?"

Nathaniel said, "It is nothing. Tell me, why are you here with these men?"

The stranger interrupted. "We were taking her home. Now you have killed him!" His voice became hysterical. "He was my friend, and you killed him. Why are you here? You did not have to do that."

"I am asking her." Turning to her again, he smiled, "Is what he says true?"

"Some of it is, Sir." She spoke haltingly, as if unsure of her words. "My name is Marie Emmanuelle Lucas. I lived at Cavett's Station on the Holston before it was destroyed. I am French, Sir! A band of Indians took some of us that night, and I have been a prisoner for over a year as a slave to the chief."

"What tribe were you with?"

"Cherokee."

"So how did you come to be with him?" he asked, as he waved his hand toward the man.

"The men came to the village and talked to the chief. They said they were Moravians. They said they wanted to set up a school for the children."

"Yes, go on."

"The chief called for me to come out and talk to them. When they saw that I was white, they offered him gold for me. I do not believe they are Moravians."

"And what happened after the chief let you go?"

"They told me they would take me home."

"When was that?"

"Three days ago."

"Was this the first time they tried to hurt you?"

"Yes."

"Do you know what direction you were taking?"

"Yes. East."

"But your home is west of here."

"I know, but when I pointed this out to them, they laughed and said they had another home for me."

"Meaning what?"

"I don't know, Sir."

Nathaniel had come to one conclusion as he questioned the girl. It was that the men had purchased her freedom from the Indians only to sell her into white slavery. First, they would have their fun with her. He was surprised they had waited this long before taking their pleasure.

He turned to the man. "What say you now? If this girl has told the truth, and I have no doubt about her story, you have much to explain."

"I will explain nothing to you! The girl lies. We bought her from the Indians. She belongs to us! You killed my partner; it is you who needs to explain." Then in a whining voice he added, "You did not have to do that. Why did you kill him? He was a good man."

"You know the answer to that. Your friend should have learned to use a knife. You are no better than he. You sat and watched and enjoyed what he was doing to the girl, waiting for your chance, I suspect."

Nathaniel retrieved the dead man's knife, and handed it to the other. "Start digging, O Pious One. Bury your friend and be quick about it, or you may lie in a common grave together. I have little sympathy for you."

The man grudgingly took the knife and moved to the side of the trail. Nathaniel had just turned to speak to the girl when the man screamed loud and pitifully and raised his arm. The rattler's fangs were imbedded deeply in the flesh as the jaws continued to masticate, injecting the poison into the arm.

Nathaniel's knife was out, and he quickly slashed the snake in half. Then he grabbed the head and squeezed it hard and removed the jaws from the man's arm. Casting it aside, Nathaniel took the man back to the path and laid him down. His eyes were starting to glaze over, and his breathing was faltering as the poison pumped throughout his system. Grabbing a leather thong, Nathaniel applied a tourniquet to the upper arm and sliced open the fang marks to get the blood flowing strong. But he was too late; the venom too deadly. The man started to convulse and gasped for air, laboring for each breath, and Nathaniel knew the end would come soon. He was helpless, unable to comfort him, and for a moment he felt sympathy for the Moravian who lay before him.

During the verbal exchange between the two men, and while Nathaniel was treating the snake bite, the girl said nothing. He had paid little attention to her and she had not offered to assist him.

He turned to her then and said quietly, "I'm afraid you are about to be released from your sentence. I think the man will die."

"I feel sorry for him."

"Yes, he bought your freedom. That is something."

"What can I do now?"

Nathaniel thought for a moment before replying. As he looked at her, he realized how much she reminded him of the Jenny of long ago. How she had complicated his life! This girl was lovely too. He did not need that again. At the same time, he could not leave her to fend for herself! She would be at a complete loss, with only God to care for her. He made his decision.

"I am going east. Perhaps, we will meet some settlers along the way who will be happy to take you farther."

"And then, where will you go?"

He wasn't sure how to explain his journey or whether he should tell her at all. She was white, but the fact she had been held by the Cherokees and knew how they lived cast a different light on the situation.

"We will talk about that later. Now, let us bury the gold seekers and be on our way. That is, if you wish to get home again."

## 17

# MARIE EMMANUELLE

They covered only a few miles that day. They had gotten off to a late start, and were emotionally exhausted after the earlier events. First, they buried the two men. When they had dug a shallow grave, he dragged the bodies over to the site and rolled them in. He fashioned a crude cross and scratched one word, "Moravians," on the crosspiece. He wondered if anyone would ever find the men or care whether they were Moravians or not.

Nathaniel went through their belongings and collected packs of food and ammunition and the one rifle they had with them. There was no point in leaving anything of value behind. The girl watched him as he selected and stored the food and other items.

"I'll take the rifle," she told him. "I know how to use it, but I don't want his knife. Leave it for marking this place where he died."

"Good, Marie, and carry the light pack here." He pronounced it "Mary," but when she did not object, he decided to call her that.

"Marie, if we are to travel together, tell me about yourself."

"I'm twenty-two years old. I came here six years ago with my family. We are French Huguenots. I had a brother killed at Cavett's and one who escaped that night, I believe."

"How about your parents? What happened to them?"

"They are dead," She replied with finality. "They were killed during an earlier raid by the Indians. As for your next question, I do not have any other relatives here. Our whole life revolved around the station, but that is gone now."

They continued walking in silence after the exchange. Nathaniel tried to comprehend the implications of taking her along. He hoped desperately they would catch up with a wagon train moving west so that he could turn her over and be done with her. She was already getting to him a bit too much, he thought, with her ready smile and her physical beauty. Better to get rid of her quickly! His thoughts were suddenly interrupted.

"I asked you, Sir, where you were going? You did not answer me. Now, I ask you again. Where will you go when you get rid of me?"

Her frank question bothered him. That she was so perceptive about what he intended to do also disturbed him.

"I did not answer you because I don't really know. Look, I don't mean to sound evasive, but it is a rather long story, and I doubt you would understand. You don't know me except as a man who shot someone."

"Yes, but that was unavoidable. Who are you; what are you? I don't even know your name."

"I am Nathaniel Tennyson. I came from Sussex, England to Virginia in 1779. I was twenty when I came here. I wanted to see this great country for myself." His thoughts briefly returned to that time long ago. "Remember when I removed your gag? I was shocked to see you. I knew a girl about your age then, and to make a long story short, she could have been your sister— you resemble her so."

"Is that so bad then?"

"No, of course not. But after all these years I had forgotten her, I thought."

"Where do you live, Nathaniel?"

"With the Cherokees in a village, a long way from here. Before you ask, I married into the tribe, and I am accepted as one of them. I have a son, Little Eagle, a fine boy."

"I suspected as much when I first saw you. You are more Indian than white. Everything about you is Cherokee, except your eyes. Remember, I too lived with them for a year."

"So now you know," he said.

"Yes, thank you for telling me. Why are you traveling east, so far from your village?"

Nathaniel hesitated before continuing. "That is the part you will not understand. I am looking for a new place where some of us can live. We plan to move if I find it."

"Why?"

"Simply because we want to continue living as Indians. The whites are growing in number steadily, and we are losing our lands, more every day. Many of our village chiefs are willing to give up land for money. Our chief is not. Believe me, I understand what is happening now, and I am not pleased. I left the settlements in the east because I wanted to be a part of the Ani-'yun'wiya,' but I think the Cherokee Nation is doomed."

She reached out and touched his arm, and he stopped and looked at her. She looked hard into his eyes, knowing at once this man meant something good, and her touch sent a wave of desire through her. She shook her head, wanting to rid herself of the feeling she had experienced.

"I think I know how you feel, and I thank you again for sharing your story with me. I'm sorry for your tribe. I promise you this: I will be no trouble." Then in a lighter tone of voice, she smiled and said, "Maybe we will find the place together, before you have to get rid of me."

Nathaniel stopped for the night at the edge of a small, rushing stream. He felt emotionally drained and was tired and hungry. He had killed a man, watched another die, and had discovered in the woman something that caused him great concern. One day, and his life had changed because of her! He could not say what it was, except for an image she had resurrected from a distant past.

He did not feel like talking, but Marie Emmanuelle regained her strength as soon as they started eating. Her release from the Moravians, and her new-found interest in Nathaniel, triggered an outburst. She told Nathaniel about her family and the move from France, and described the raid on the station and her capture in detail. There seemed to be no bitterness or remorse in the telling, but he wished she would finish eating and go to off to sleep. He tried to be polite, but he found himself answering her in monosyllables and grunts as he fought off exhaustion. He fell asleep as she talked on.

When she noticed he was asleep, she took her pack and curled up beside the man. Marie Emmanuelle had little experience with men, but she instinctively trusted Nathaniel. He had given her another chance, and she felt gratitude for that act of kindness. Besides that, she liked him very much. There was gentleness and warmth in him. She recalled his face when he told her the man would die; it had been a kind face. But more than anything, she remembered those piercing blue eyes as he looked at her on the trail, and she knew desire for him again. She had not long to think about these things, however, for she was asleep in a matter of minutes.

They were underway very early. The Moravians had delayed his progress the previous day, and Nathaniel was determined to regain some of the lost time. He told the girl he planned to move fast, and she was so happy to be with him, she readily agreed.

Then she offered him a suggestion. She asked if they could stop earlier in the day if they made good progress, and to this he acquiesced. He did not know the girl was planning his seduction. The path they continued to follow made traveling easy, and when they came to a broad river, Nathaniel exited the path and went downstream.

"I think it is better if we get off the path, Marie. There is too much opportunity for others to come along. This will give us some privacy."

He found a suitable spot for the night and dropped the pack. "You did well today, Marie. Go down along the stream, and find a place to wash."

She teased him. "Why don't you try the water first?"

He did not catch the subtle question. "I will, later, but first I want to see about supper. Are you hungry?"

Yes, I'm starved. While you sort things out, I'll try the water. Is there an extra shirt in the bundle?"

"No, just a large piece of cloth. Will that help?"

He appealed immensely to Marie Emmanuelle. He was a little older, but that gave him experience and made him much more interesting. As she bathed, she was aware of his sexuality and her own desire for him. While she had been with the Indians, none of the men looked at her with desire or interest. Perhaps it was because of her status as a slave to the chief, she thought, but it was more likely that they found her to be ugly or unappealing in their eyes. Why this was so she could not understand. Many white men had taken Cherokee women as wives, for the Cherokee women were considered to be lovely, and the half-breed population was growing. She was not surprised when he told her he was married.

What was bothering her the most, she realized, was that Nathaniel was not the kind of man who would push himself on her. She knew that he had been affected by recognition of some previous menage' a deux, in the person of Marie Emmanuelle, and she determined to play her role to his satisfaction. She would do everything possible to make him like her; much would depend on how long they were together.

She washed the clothes that had been given to her by her captors. As she bathed, she sang softly in French. The bath itself was a catharsis, for it represented the end of an ordeal with the men and a new beginning with Nathaniel. She threw the clothes over some low branches near the water, and when her body dried, wrapped herself in the long, white cloth before starting back upstream. She decided she wanted this man, and she would have him before the night was over.

She smelled supper cooking as she returned to the campsite. Nathaniel was fussing at the fire and did not look up immediately. She stood there, waiting for him to see her. When he turned to her, he couldn't have moved had he wanted. He was rooted to the spot! The vision of loveliness before him was a metamorphosis, transformed from slave to goddess, and he knew at that moment that Jenny had resurrected from those days long ago. His heart raced, and he wanted to reach out and tear the whole cloth from her. She caught his look of desire before he turned away.

Marie Emmanuelle was smiling. "Do I look different? Do I pass your inspection, Monsieur?"

"Yes, very much, I'm afraid."

"I decided to wash my clothes. God knows when they were washed before, and after three days on the trail they were starting to smell. It feels good to be clean again, Nathaniel." There was a subtle suggestion in her voice which he ignored.

"After we eat, I think you should fetch them and put them on." It was not a request, but an order, and Marie Emmanuelle caught the meaning as soon as he spoke. He is excited by the way I look, she thought, and well he should be. I will have him soon.

He was certain he would have to remind her, but as soon as she had eaten she got up and left. When she returned she was wearing the oversized clothes but they did nothing to hide her figure, and for the second time that evening Nathaniel felt his juices flowing. He did not expect her to lie close to him, but that is where she placed her blanket and where she fully intended to remain. He sensed her warmth, though he did not actually feel it, and tried to stay away from her, but she was having no part of that.

She moved closer to him, aware that she was sowing the seeds of distress and disappointment when she had to leave him, but she also knew that for however long she stayed with him, she would be happy, happier still, if he put his arms around her. She did not want the hurt of rejection, but she had to know what this man was thinking.

In her quiet voice, she said, "Will you hold me for a little while, Nathaniel?"

"I don't think it is a good idea, Marie," he resisted.

"It probably isn't, but it has been over a year since anyone showed me kindness like you have. Please, will you, Nathaniel?" she pleaded.

He did not want to hurt the girl, but her closeness was already starting to make him want her. "Better lie still, Marie, and get some sleep. We made little progress today."

As she snuggled into the refuge of his arm wrapped around her, she sighed and smiled to herself and whispered, "I don't know about you, Nathaniel, but I made a lot of progress today!"

Nathaniel felt nearly as tired in the morning as when he laid down for the night. He slept fitfully, snatching dreams of Jenny-Marie, as the girl clung to him. Frequently, when he emerged into consciousness, he would find her holding him tightly, and he marveled that she should be so strong while she slept. He liked it; he wasn't sure what would come next, but he liked the feel of her in his arms, the curves of her body pressing against his.

Marie Emmanuelle was refreshed from the deep sleep. She was not content just to get up and start the fire, but had gone to the water and caught several fish. They were cooking on the low coals when Nathaniel awoke.

He went to the river and dived in, wanting to shed the feel of her clinging arms he had experienced most of the night. There were many miles yet to travel and he could not allow this woman to intrude upon his duty to the village. That came first, he thought, and anyway, they would probably meet up with someone today who could take her off his hands.

As he emerged, naked except for his buckskin pants, he shook off the water as best he could before the fire. "Morning, Marie. The fish look to be done." He took one and and bit off a chunk, and handed the second to her. "It is very good. You made the fire and cooked the fish like a Cherokee. Might you have had some lessons?" he smiled.

"Just a few, Nathaniel; just a few!" She had won a small victory. "I filled the water bags. When do you want to get started? We should make good time today."

Now he teased her. "After what you did last night, why are you so anxious to get moving today?"

"What do you mean? What did I do? What are you saying?" She was confused and he knew it.

Nathaniel waved his hand, and shrugged. "Don't you remember? You acted very friendly, as if you really cared for me. And now you can hardly wait to get on the trail. Was I so bad? Did I displease you?"

"Of course not. What I mean is . . . I think you are telling stories."

"Really?" he teased.

"Really."

They made good time during the early morning, but after a few hours Nathaniel left the path they had taken through the gap and headed off in a southeasterly direction. The going got harder, and they were forced to stop several times to rest. He was surprised at her cheerfulness and her willingness to do anything he asked of her. Nathaniel remembered that she had lived with the Cherokees as a slave, and he thought that she was more Indian than white at the moment. That was why she was so self-confident on the trail; she had learned hard and well. He suspected that many of her lessons had been reinforced by a club and other indignities, for slaves were treated as personal property and were quickly taught to heed all commands, whatever the consequences.

Marie Emmanuelle thought the day's travel was wonderful and minded it not a bit. She was no longer a hostage, and she had accepted Nathaniel in the last twenty-four hours as savior and friend, and was becoming totally entranced by the tall, burnished man who strode beside her. "Maybe tonight," she thought, as she glanced up at him. "If not then, in the future, of this I am sure!"

They changed directions again in mid-afternoon, as the mountain range in the far distance beckoned Nathaniel. They continued for several hours until finally Nathaniel called a stop for the night. The girl dropped in place, and Nathaniel knew he had been pushing her hard all day. "Perhaps, she will sleep tonight, and I too will get a good night's rest!" Then he grinned to himself as he realized how little the thought meant. He loved the feel of her in his arms and hoped she would suggest it again. He had not crumbled to her charms, but their situation made it inevitable. The love she promised might be very interesting.

After they had eaten, they gathered their packs and moved under a large fir. The night was a repeat of the one before, except that when Marie Emmanuelle laid down next to Nathaniel she immediately crawled closer to him before he went to sleep.

This time, she leaned over him and whispered, "Nathaniel, you have become very important to me, and I want to thank you." Before he could reply she kissed him, pressing her mouth hard against his lips.

He felt himself becoming aroused. He pushed her away, and in the dim light said, "Marie, you are special to me as well, but I don't think you realize what can happen if we continue this way. I like you very much, but you are playing with me, and I am but human. So think hard about what you do."

"Last night I think you held me because you did not want to hurt my feelings. Hold me tonight because you want to be close."

"I like holding you, Marie, but you must understand what you are doing, what you do to me. I'm just a man and you make it difficult for me. Do you understand what I am trying to say?"

"I understand, Nathaniel, that I could love you very easily. It is not only because you saved my life, but I find you attractive."

"And I you. But I am on a journey that allows me no time for love. What you and I might share has happened because of an incident that brought us together. So you see, Marie, when we separate, I want you to think of me as a friend . . . and a friend only."

She leaned on him again. "Touch me, Nathaniel; tell me that you want me as I want you. Don't you know that? Can't you believe that?"

"I know that we have a long way to travel yet, and that morning comes early, and that we will have time for this later." He reached for her and drew her hard against him as he ran his hands up and down her body and kissed her passionately.

She returned his kiss and held him for a few moments. "Thanks, my love. Now sleep if you can, knowing she who lies beside you waits for you, whenever you are ready for her."


Nathaniel awoke and stretched, his hand reaching the sleeping girl beside him. She raised her head, shook her hair to rid it of pine needles, and leaned over Nathaniel as she had done the night before. She kissed him again.

"You are a strong man, Nathaniel Tennyson. I wished for you to come to me, but you slept instead."

"And you, Marie, are a determined young lady!"

"Determined perhaps, but not very successful. Especially with you."

"I wouldn't say that. Come here! Let me look at you. You are beautiful, you know."

She leaned closer, and he reached for her and kissed her soundly. She clung to him. Then he rolled away from her. "That could become a habit, my Marie, but we must get moving. Do you realize this is the seventh day since I left the village? And I've known you half that time!"

"Come back, Nathaniel. We have all day to find your new home." She lay back, inviting him to come to her. When he turned his back, she leaped to grab him, but he was already gathering things for the packs. "Come on, Marie. It will be warm today, and we should travel before the sun gets too hot."

The first signs he picked up were those of the Shawnees. It bothered Nathaniel that a raiding party should be intruding this far south, and he stopped to examine the trail and to tell Marie. She read the concern in his face as he spoke.

"Marie, these aren't good signs, I'm afraid. The Shawnees are not friends of the Cherokees, and my guess is they know we are here and will wait for us. We'll try to avoid them, but our chances are poor. Let's move in single file and try to find our way out of the forest quickly."

"Let me lead, Nathaniel. That way, if we run into them you will have a chance to break away. Besides that, I'm pretty good with a rifle."

"Maybe you are, Marie, but I don't think you can read the trail as well."

"You don't know that! I can read signs too," she reminded him bluntly.

"Anyway, I'm taking the lead. You will follow. Keep my back covered as you trail me, and stay with me. If I start moving too fast, or if you see any of them, whistle like a bird, you can whistle, can't you? Then I will wait for you. Understand me, girl?"

She leaned closer to him. "Nathaniel, be careful. If anything should happen to you, I would . . . ."

"Don't worry, Little One, just follow me quietly."

Marie Emmanuelle was doing just that when she caught the first glimpse of the Indian in the woods to her right. She whistled once, and saw Nathaniel freeze in place. As she watched, the Indian moved on, slipping furtively from tree to tree. When she caught up to Nathaniel, she told him what she had seen.

"You did fine, but only one? There are at least three others. I can smell them, waiting for us. Keep walking. If we stop now they will attack."

"What can we do?"

"Look for some place to make a stand," he replied. "I do not think they will wait very long." He pointed with his rifle. "Let's head over there; maybe we'll find something. Pretend now that we are just walking together, like lovers. Take my arm."

The area they were passing through was formed of long slopes, interspersed with deep canyons. It was the beginning of the mountainous region. In the far distance, several high, narrow ridges protruded from the earth's surface. He wished he were there. For now, Nathaniel had to settle for some land feature that would provide a defensive position, some place that would force the Shawnees to come to them. He quickly saw what he wanted. Several large boulders lay at right angles to each other directly in their path. They were about waist-high and would provide adequate protection for Marie and him. The ground rose several feet, forming a knoll, and the boulders were perched at the top of the rise.

He led the girl around the mound before sliding behind the rocks, and said, "I think this is the best we will find, Marie. We'll stay here. Look, there is some cleared space. If they come, wait until they are in the open. Don't wait for me to shoot, but make every shot count! Are you with me?"

"Yes, I understand."

"They know where we are, so keep down. No point in letting them see us until the last minute," he said.

They waited expectantly, knowing the Indians would come. It was just a matter of time. "Marie, don't be frightened when they rush us. They will scream and yell and make all kinds of noises, but they are scared too."

"Yes, I know, Nathaniel. Remember, I went through this a year ago at Cavett's Station."

"Sorry. I wish you didn't have to repeat it."

"Nathaniel, I'm glad you're here with me. The last few days have meant a lot to me. You're special to me also."

"Marie, I feel the same way. I hate the thought of turning you over to anyone who comes along. Come back with me. Snow Deer will welcome you as her sister. Live with us. You won't be treated like a slave!"

"Look, Nathaniel, I'm falling in love with you. And you think Snow Deer will welcome me? You are not as wise as I thought!"

"Think about it, Marie. When we get out of this . . . look! There they come. Listen to them howl . . . count them . . . four. Good odds!"

The Shawnees attacked, armed with bows and arrows, arguing against any tactical surprise. They suspected the white men would have guns, but did not think they would fight from behind rocks. Indians always took advantage of natural hiding places, but how could the whites know this? The warrior chief led the charge. Arrows swished through the air toward the defenders. Marie Emmanuelle, ignoring the hideous screams, raised and fired once, and the chief fell. He tried to crawl forward, but the wound was fatal, and he died quickly. The raiders yelled, and more arrows sliced the air around them. The girl cried out once as if in pain, but Nathaniel was now firing at the other Shawnees and could not look to see what was happening to her.

Another warrior fell in front of Nathaniel's position, and with a final effort the remaining Indian raced for the rocks. The girl calmly and deliberately fired again, and the warrior screamed once and was flung to the ground. As the fight ended, Nathaniel surveyed the death scene before him. None of the Shawnees moved. He wanted to make sure that none were alive, so he left the mound and confirmed the killings.

"We did it, Marie," he shouted excitedly as he retraced his steps. "Are you all right? You can come out now."

She was slow to answer, and he glanced down at her then. She was leaning back against the rock, holding her left arm. The shirt was already stained with blood where the arrow had ripped through the flesh above her elbow.

"Why didn't you say something, girl?" He was beside her in an instant. He cut off the sleeve and quickly examined the wound. Then he took the waterpouch and washed the cut before taking a piece of cloth and binding it carefully.

"That should hold it. You were lucky. The arrow just broke the skin, but it will hurt a little," he told her. "We got them all, thanks to you." He leaned closer to her and said, "God, but I am glad you are all right! You didn't tell me you could shoot so well."

Her right arm snaked around his neck. "And you didn't tell me that you cared for me. Nathaniel . . ."

Her lips were on his as a wave of desire consumed them, and they clutched each other on the ground. His lips mashed into hers, seeking and finding, demanding now. He pushed her shirt aside and rained kisses on her, and she moaned low and whispered, "Oh yes, Nathaniel. Please, take me, my love . . ." And then she flowered, and opened wide for him, and they came together, lost in the heat of their love, in the forest of death around them.

# 18

## GRANDFATHER MOUNTAIN

When their uncontrollable need for each other was finally quenched, they lay together whispering, touching, exploring, until they embraced again. Marie Emmanuelle, having tasted the delights of love, wanted Nathaniel to take her again. Not yet satisfied, she clung to him urging him on. This time they settled into an easy rhythm, not hurrying until the last moment when both were caught in the exquisite embrace of consummation as it washed over them. Then they slept, like innocent children, content and happy and unafraid.

It was an hour before sunset when Nathaniel stirred. Marie Emmanuelle was sleeping in the crook of his arm, but he hesitated to wake her, filled with joy at the sight of her. He looked down at her unclothed body and felt passion for her rising again. "She is lovely," he smiled, and then mustered up his courage to reach down and stroke her breasts. She awoke instantly.

"That's not fair, Nathaniel. Come here and kiss me awake properly."

He leaned over and kissed her. "You're right, you know. This is a much better way. But up you go; we have to get a few miles before day's end."

She tried to hold on to him. "Nathaniel, one more time and then I'll be ready to go."

"If we wait any longer it will be dark. Come on, Marie, there will be plenty of time for that later."

"You are right, my love. I can be ready in a few minutes."

They were soon underway. Nathaniel set a forced pace that did not end until they had distanced themselves several miles from the battle site. He felt some relief now. He did not expect another raiding party, but at the same time he was cautious. They stopped and washed together at the first creek, and then loved each other again. Their needs were not fulfilled quickly, and they continued long after the sun went behind the mountains and darkness descended around them.

They slept like the dead until daybreak. At first light, Nathaniel was up and they started for the mountains. By mid-morning they reached and passed through the foothills, and the going became more difficult. The land forms changed, and they were forced to climb several ridges and cross open valleys as they went deeper into the mountains. At a distance, the massif reared from the earth's crust, looking in profile like that of an old man. Nathaniel pointed it out to Marie, and when she saw the likeness she called it "Grandfather Mountain."

All day they traveled toward it. In his mind, Nathaniel visualized it as the place he was searching for. It would have water and good hunting and cleared spaces that could be planted. It would offer sanctuary and protection from the whites, and they would find peace there. Marie, not wanting their trek to end, pictured it as a place of utter desolation, devoid of everything that he wanted it to be. She knew that if Nathaniel found what he was seeking she would be considered a handicap, and her life would change again. And so, they trudged wearily along, each lost in his own thoughts. Neither spoke to the other, as if to speak of their expectations they would destroy this love they had just found.

By late afternoon they reached Grandfather. Long shadows were stealing across the face of the mountain, and it was too late to explore. They were ready to drop and rest and regain their strength. Nathaniel wanted meat for supper and decided to chance shooting an animal if they came across one. When he told Marie, she disagreed. She was hungry too, but thought they should use the sling or blowgun and not reveal their whereabouts by firing a gun. They argued until Nathaniel realized the girl was right and set off to find a smaller animal. He was not gone very long. They ate quietly, before the small fire she had laid, neither wanting to express the thoughts that raced through their minds. By the time they finished, black night had enveloped them.

The mountain loomed above them when Nathaniel awoke. The sun had risen with promises of a beautiful day ahead. He lay there, arms around the girl beside him, exhilerated by the love he felt for her. As the sun rose higher and chased the shadows off Grandfather's face, he knew he had reached the end of his journey. After all that had happened since he left the village, he felt good to be alive and satisfied in mind and body.

Basking in this feeling of well-being he turned to Marie Emmanuelle, and realized how quickly she had become a part of his life. He knew when he first caught sight of her that his life would change, but he could not know to what extent she would change it. Now his memory played tricks on him, and the girl lying in his arms was the Jenny of long ago. She had teased him, but he had wanted her from the beginning, and she was a surrogate for the other girl. He had not resisted the temptation too strongly, he thought.

So what to do! He could not return her to Cavett's Station. It was gone, or even if rebuilt it was unlikely that he would find anyone who would know her or her family. White settlers were on the move, like a tidal wave engulfing the land. As a station or outpost village was established or destroyed, the whites displaced to the west. Her brother, if he had escaped the night she was captured, would most likely have moved on. There would be little reason to remain behind. Nathaniel could not leave her to fend for herself, for while she could hunt and live like an Indian, her chance of being rescued again by whites as they moved through the area was unrealistic. What could he do with her?

He lay there, sorting out the alternatives. There were not many, and none that he considered were good. The first thing to do was to explore the mountain. If it offered what he hoped, a place where the village could resettle, then it would be time enough to deal with the girl.

He woke her gently. "Marie, wake up, and see what lies around us."

"Is it time to go?" she asked. "Why don't we stay here for the day?" She yawned and settled herself in his arms. "There are better things we can do."

"Aye, that is right! But then you will miss the beauty of this place."

"Oh, Nathaniel, what can be more beautiful than our love. We have each other and that should be enough for now."

"Perhaps, but time is not what we have this morning. I want to see what the mountain offers."

"It offers me. Am I not worthy of your time?"

"You know, Marie, you have a wonderful way of twisting what I say into something different. You are so much like . . . anyway, yes, you are worth my time. Believe that!"

"Nathaniel, I love you very much. I guess I am afraid of what you will find. Then you will no longer need me."

"Don't believe that! Before I woke you I thought about what to do with you. No, don't say anything. I have decided that I want you to come home with me. You will share our fire and our lives. Snow Deer will accept you, that I promise."

"Dear, dear Nathaniel. My heart bursts when you tell me these things, but you do not know the ways of women, I'm afraid. Snow Deer will accept me as she would a wolf in her lodge! I do not think I would enjoy a long life. I have a better plan, but let's first see your mountain, and then we will talk about me."

While they ate, Nathaniel studied the face of the mountain. About halfway to the summit he spied a rockslide that had wiped out the trees and bushes as an avalanche might have done. The slope was bare save for the stones, and his first thought was that it could be defended with only a handful of men. At the top of the slide, large boulders lay facing the valley, and on each side the ground dropped off precipitously to the valley floor. It looked like a natural fortification, but he would have to climb the mountain to see what lay behind it.

Leaving most of their supplies hanging from a tree, Nathaniel started to explore the base of the mountain first, in the general area of their camp. It would be ideal, he thought, if he could find some cleared land and adequate water for the tribe. Without that, there would be little reason to climb higher. Shortly after they set out, Marie Emmanuelle found water flowing from the mountain above. It poured off the rocks into a large bowl-shaped depression that acted as a collecting pan. From there the water rushed down the mountain in a series of small waterfalls.

Nathaniel had no doubt but that it ended in a shallow stream below the ridges. There was no point, he decided, in going lower into the valley. They commenced the climb. He chose a circuitous route around the base of the mountain to the far side of the rockslide.

Suddenly they emerged from the forest onto a level field that extended nearly half a mile before them. It looked as if a fire had raged through the area and burned it clean. A few trees remained, charred from the fire storm, and Nathaniel was excited by the find. The girl did not share his excitement. He studied the area carefully, trying to visualize the location of the village that might grow there, but when he attempted to explain this to Marie Emmanuelle, she sat quietly, unable to show enthusiasm for what he was doing.

He walked off the length and the width, and with his knife dug into the earth and carefully examined the soil he had spilled. Then he burst out, "There is water here, Marie, and the earth is good for planting. Maybe this is the place after all."

"Then you have decided on Grandfather Mountain?" she asked.

"Not yet. I want to see what lies above the rockslide. And we have no idea what the hunting is like."

"If you find everything to your satisfaction, then what, Nathaniel?"

"Then we will return to the village."

"I am not so sure. It is lovely here. Perhaps I will stay and wait for settlers to come through."

"Marie, have you forgotten so quickly that I want you to come with me?"

"No, my love, I have not forgotten," she sighed. "It is you who cannot remember what I said about that."

"Let's wait a bit, Marie. We still have climbing ahead of us. Then we will talk."

Nathaniel found a well-worn deer path leading from the clearing. The animals used the path daily as they descended into the valley from the heights above for food and water, and it was an easy track to follow.

They started climbing, Nathaniel leading the way. While the upward slope was relatively steep, the deer had traversed the mountain side in broad sweeps, and by following the trail the climbers ascended easily through the surrounding forest. The trees started thinning after they had climbed for nearly an hour. Nathaniel estimated they had traveled nearly a mile back and forth as the trail went upward; and then it opened wide, and they looked upon a wide plateau spread before them. The boulders lay on the forward edge, strewn recklessly as if by a giant's hand. Several hundred yards to the rear the mountain continued up toward the summit, covered by heavy growth, and he knew instinctively that he had reached his goal.

He stopped at the edge of the clearing, Marie Emmanuelle beside him, surveying the opening before them; and then he threw back his head and yelled excitedly, "This is it, Marie! I know this is the place! We will come here and stay and it will be ours, and no one will take it from us. I could have looked forever and not found it. We did it!"

Taking her hand he led her to the boulders and climbed the first one. The view before them was beautiful, a panorama of ridges and valley and open fields as far as the eye could see. Washed by the morning sun, they were painted with colors like nothing Nathaniel had ever seen before, and in his joy he grabbed Marie Emmanuelle and pulled her close and held her and smothered kisses across her face.

"Marie, Marie. What a beautiful place! It almost overwhelms me. I am happy that we found it together."

"Nathaniel, my heart cries for you in your happiness. But do you know what this means?"

"Yes, it means that we can return to the village after we have looked over the area."

"You still don't understand, Nathaniel. *You* can return to the village, but I have decided to stay here . . . not here, but where we have our camp."

"What are you saying? You can't do that! How would you live?" he yelled. "What makes you think you can survive here alone? What if you are found by Indians? You would become a slave again, or worse yet, they would have their fun with you and then kill you. Marie, Marie, come home with me. I want that very much," he pleaded.

"Nathaniel, listen to me! I would rather be a hawk with my freedom for one day then become a slave again. I know you believe that I would be welcomed in the village, but I do not think that will happen. I will stay here and wait for you. Let's just say that I can be caretaker of Grandfather Mountain. When you come back I will stay with you; that is, if Snow Deer agrees. You can tell your people that I am here. Perhaps, that will make it easier for them to accept me."

Nathaniel took her in his arms again. "Marie, I don't like the idea of you remaining here alone. But since you intend to stay against my wishes, we have some work to do. I will not leave you here living like we have lived on the trail the last few days!"

"How long will you be gone? I mean, when will the villagers move?" she asked.

"Certainly not before they gave gotten the corn and other foods gathered. I don't really know, Marie. Perhaps the tribe will wait until spring. I cannot speak for the villagers."

"I think I can stay that long, at least until fall, but I will miss you and long for you, Nathaniel. It will be hard, but I will wait," she declared.

"I still believe you should come with me. That way, I will not be worrying every day about you. Suppose we are delayed?"

"So be it, my love, but I will not go. If I remain here, it will cause you to hurry more," she smiled. "But truly, I will wish for you every day."

They spent the next few hours exploring the clearing, as Nathaniel attempted to visualize the placement of defensive positions if they had to fight there. He had already decided that the village would be located below in the space which the fire had cleared, but this would provide a last stronghold if necessary to do battle with intruders. Again, as he had discovered below, there was water and material for shelters. He thought it offered everything needed to establish a new home, and he hoped to determine that before leaving. When they were finished and he had drawn a mental picture of the place, they descended to the lower area. He was excited by the discoveries, and was eager to get started back to the village. But first, he had to get Marie Emmanuelle settled.

Few words were spoken on the way down, each realizing their time together would soon end. Nathaniel could not readily accept the girl's decision to remain behind. He reasoned that she could not survive alone on the mountain for very long. At the same time, he believed there was a good possibility that settlers moving through the area would take her farther west. He was ambivalent on this score. If she had decided to leave, then Snow Deer would not have to accept the girl after the move, but that would take her out of his life forever. His emotions swirled about him. It was not unusual for an Indian to have more than one wife, but the second one was usually someone related in the clan who had lost a husband fighting, and Marie Emmanuelle certainly did not fall into this category. What to do!

Marie Emmanuelle's thoughts were quite different. She had guessed at the beginning, when he freed her from the Moravians, that he would leave her along the way, but that was before she had found love with him. The thought of his going was devastating to her. She loved him, her world was fast sinking, and she was adrift once again. He had given her strength and a reason to live, and now she would be alone. Should she change her mind and go with him? Should she wait for him to return? If so, could she share him with Snow Deer, however kind and generous his wife might be? Could she really be this independent and on her own while he was gone. She pondered these questions and more, but could find no answers that satisfied nor any that offered her relief from her dilemma.

Her day-dreaming was suddenly cut short as Nathaniel stopped on the trail ahead of her. He raised his hand, motioning her to halt, and she saw him raise his rifle. She thought, "Oh no! Not the Shawnees," and she was afraid. Then he fired once, and she looked at him and he was smiling.

"We have meat for supper," and he bounded down the slope. She saw the deer laying on the trail, and her fear subsided.

"So we have, Nathaniel, and I am hungry as a wolf," she cried. "Here, let me help you!" They dragged the animal off the path before gutting it. Then Nathaniel tied a rawhide thong around the antlers and they pulled it down the hill toward the campsite.

The sun was high in the sky. They went first to the water bowl, and when they had drunk their fill, returned to the deer.

"I had wanted to leave you with plenty of meat, Marie, so this is the first step in getting the camp in order. In this heat the meat will spoil quickly, so let's get it dried."

"I agree, but aren't you forgetting something?" she said.

"What?"

"You shot the deer. What makes you so sure that no one heard the firing?"

"I'm not, and you are right again. So why don't we pull back into the woods and at least be shaded from the sun? We will be able to see better if anyone approaches."

They set a small fire on the edge of the clearing and set up drying racks in the sun. After they had skinned the deer, Nathaniel placed a large piece of meat on a green spit and started it cooking. All the rest was cut into strips and placed on the racks. Each of them took turns watching for intruders while the other worked, and it was several hours later before the meat was divided and drying in the sun. Digging in the clearing, they found some wild potatoes and placed them on the fire to roast. As they ate, each tried to understand the feelings they had experienced since the initial meeting.

"Ah, Marie, I still want you to go home with me, but I understand better now why you don't want to go."

"Nathaniel, we have discussed it enough. You know that I love you, and want to be with you, but I think this is the better way for us."

"I know, but when I think of you being here alone it makes me wonder if I will ever see you again."

"That depends on you, Nathaniel, and whether you can convince Snow Deer what I mean to you."

"You know that you have given me great joy, but you also know that I promised you nothing. Yet, I feel indebted to you somehow ... for bringing love and understanding into my life ... and God knows how exciting it has been. More than I really needed on this journey."

"Come here, my love, and hold me and tell me what I am to you. At least, I will have that to hold onto when you leave me."

"You are an insatiable wench, and I will miss you terribly."

Before falling asleep, Nathaniel told Marie Emmanuelle they would prepare a place in the morning for her to stay, and try to find more food that could sustain her until he returned. Then they slept, utterly exhausted in their love for each other, knowing that time was slipping inexorably from their grasp. It was their last night together.

At first light, Nathaniel stirred and reached for Marie. She was gone from the pile of pine branches that had served as their couch. As he lay there in the stillness, savoring the moment, he heard her scream. One long dreadful cry, and he knew it was too late. He catapulted from the bed they had shared, grabbed his rifle and raced to the water bowl, and there she lay crumbled and dying, alone in her death. He ran to her, but as he moved the Indian leaped from the bushes beside the water and was beside him, raising his hatchet to deliver the final blow. Nathaniel, reacting to the charge, sidestepped and fell.

The Shawnee was on him, trying to get in position to use the weapon and end the fight, and they rolled together on the ground. In his anger and frustration, Nathaniel reached for the knife strapped to his calf and plunged it deep into the Shawnee's side. The Indian yelled and raised his hatchet and slashed downward, but death had finally found its mark, and he died with a look of hatred on his face. Nathaniel continued to jab the knife and more blood poured over him, but he could not stop himself. He stabbed again and again, and when he finally rolled the dead Indian from his body, he continued to mutilate the corpse.

Then he went to Marie Emmanuelle, and looked down into the dying face. He lifted her and held her to him and cried over her, asking God to keep her, and she smiled once and opened her eyes, and died in his arms. He buried her then, wrapped in the long white cloth that she had worn earlier, and said goodbye to her for the final time. He tied the dead Shawnee to a tree in an upright position for the buzzards to eat; and without turning to look again at her grave, he left Grandfather Mountain.

# *19*

# *T*EARS OF THE *P*ILGRIM

The journey back to the village went without incident. Nathaniel had left the mountain as soon as he buried the girl, and as he struggled along his thoughts kept returning to her and the love they had shared together. If only he had been more careful during the night or had stayed awake, she would be back on the mountain waiting for him. Oh God, she was there waiting, sleeping an endless sleep from which she would never awake. He would never see her again. He was punished more by his conscience, for in sorrow he knew that in his own way and time he had loved the girl. But more than that, he had never told her, and she had died failing to hear him speak the words.

He walked along all day in a dream-like state of mind, beyond caring what was around the next bend in the trail or behind the next tree. He had lost himself in the memories of a few short days, and his heart saddened as he thought of Marie Emmanuelle lying in the white shroud in a shallow grave on the mountain.

He stopped then and screamed aloud, "God! God! Why did You let it happen?" and pounded his head with his fists and collapsed onto the ground, crying as he had not cried since he was a child. Deep sobs racked his body, and he tortured himself more as he thought about the girl. Finally, when he had cried all the tears that surfaced from the innermost depth of his soul, he fell into a troubled sleep where he lay and dreamed of a smiling Marie Emmanuelle as she came to him in the night.

He was drenched when he awoke in the morning. The sky was dark, and it was raining as he gathered his pack and started home. Again, for the second day, he did not care what lay ahead, or for that matter, that he was wet. He was both physically and emotionally exhausted, but he trudged wearily along deep in his own world, oblivious to the difficult path he traveled. His mindset was as gloomy and black as the weather, until the sun suddenly burst through the trees above him and brought a degree of sanity to his mind.

He took some parched corn from his pouch and ate it as he walked. When he found some wild berries growing along his route he stopped long enough to strip handfuls from the bushes, and then continued on his lonely trek. At dusk, when he pulled from his pocket a piece of the cooked venison he and the girl had shared that last night, he could not eat it and hurled it mightily into the woods surrounding him. He had one last thought of Marie Emmanuelle as it dropped from sight, and then he went on into the night through the dark forest until he reached the river.

Two days later he met Indians from his village. His head told him he was home again when they greeted him warmly and welcomed him back, but his heart failed to respond.

"Hai, Na-tan, It is good to see you again," the first man called out. There was no answer from Nathaniel. He appeared to look beyond them, to see something far off.

"Are you alright, Na-tan?" another asked kindly. Still no reply from the man.

They sensed immediately that something had happened to Nathaniel. It was so unlike him. He had been with them for many years, and in these few short days since he left the village he had changed. He did not greet them, and they could not understand his countenance. The smiling face, which they had come to expect and delight in, was dark and brooding and he looked beaten and confused. They backed away from him and let him pass.

One said to another, "There is an evil spirit he carries with him."

"He is not the same person he was when he left us."

"His face is sad. Something has happened to him. There is death in his face," another offered.

They looked after him as he moved unsteadily toward the village. One said, "It was a hard journey, and he is tired, I think."

"He has been tired before. No, there is something more about him that makes me afraid. Na-tan has seen death too much on this journey."

When Nathaniel got within sight of the village he skirted it, and approached his lodge from the woods behind. He did not want to be confronted by friends, who would deluge him with questions and expect answers, and he was not ready to talk. Snow Deer was alone when he slipped into the lodge, and cried out and ran to him. He grabbed her and held her close, but did not speak for long moments, and she too knew something dreadful had happened to him while he was gone.

"What is it, Na-tan?" she whispered. "Do you want to talk about it?"

"Not now, Snow Deer, for it is a long story to tell. Where is Little Eagle?"

"He is with Nantatola for the day. They will not come until late."

"That is good. I need to sleep first, and then we will talk. And I will tell you everything about the journey. There were men outside the village who saw me. If they speak that I am here, many will come to the lodge. I ask you to keep them from me until I awake."

"My dear, Na-tan, I know that your heart aches and is filled with sadness. I will do whatever you want. Now go rest. I will not let anyone know you are here." She kissed him and helped him to the sleeping bench, and sat holding his hand until he fell asleep.

The cooking fires were burning in the village when Nathaniel awoke. Snow Deer was still beside him holding his hand, and he wondered if she had sat patiently while he slept. The rest had renewed his energy, and he was hungry and ready to eat. She looked deep into his eyes, trying to understand the despair that she had seen when he first arrived, but his face had changed remarkably and she was pleased to see him smiling.

"It is good to see you smile, Na-tan."

"I am happy to be home again."

"It is good to have you back. Are you hungry? I have bear stew and corn cakes."

"Yes, I am very hungry. There was not much to eat on the trail."

"Then we will eat. After that, I want to hear about your journey. I know that something happened to you while you were gone."

"Snow Deer, many things happened. We will talk together about them. Now, fetch my food, and I will eat."

They had finished eating when Nantatola arrived with Little Eagle. The reunion of the big man and his son was a joyous one, and Nathaniel was as excited as Little Eagle. The boy ran to him and reached out, and the man lifted him from the ground and held him to his chest. It seemed to him as if the boy in his arms had somehow taken the place of the lost girl, and for what seemed like minutes they held each other, not wanting to separate. Nantatola waited and watched the scene before him, and when Nathaniel finally put the boy down, he reached for Snow Deer and pulled her beside him.

Then Nantatola came to Nathaniel and placed his hands on his shoulders and said, "It is a good thing that you have come, and I welcome you back. You have had a hard journey, I think, and must be tired."

"I have rested now."

"There are others who saw you before. They believe a great evil spirit has come upon you. All wait for you to tell them what you have seen and what you have found."

"My friend, much has happened since I left here. There are both good words and bad words to tell the Council. It has not been an easy journey, but I think the Council will listen to me. Will you call a meeting so that I can say what is in my heart?"

"Yes, it will be good for you to tell us. Your face tells me that you are sad and weary, and talking will be like the black drink. It will clear your thoughts, I think."

"I need to do that. It is not good to keep everything in my heart."

After Nantatola had gone and Little Eagle was asleep, Nathaniel and Snow Deer sat together closely in front of the lodge talking late into the night. He held her hand, and talked openly and frankly about the journey and everything that had occurred. He told her about Marie

Emmanuelle, and how they had fought off the Shawnees, and the girl's pursuit of him. She did not pry into his thoughts or question him, but allowed him to say what he wanted to share with her. When he talked about the girl, she did not ask why, for she understood what had taken place after the battle which had caused her man to take another. If she felt hurt by what he had done, her love for him was so strong that she accepted it as a natural event under the circumstances. She wanted this man, more than any other in the tribe. She worshipped the ground he walked on, and nothing meant more to her than that he was there with her again. Hours later, when the moon was high in the sky, she turned to him and they loved each other. He took her gently, knowing that she was his forever, and when she arched her back and sought release, he held her tight and emptied into her before she sighed and rested in his arms.

The Council House was packed and overflowing, and the sun was at its zenith when Nathaniel arrived, escorted by White Horse and Bear Claw. They had come to the lodge to walk with their friend after hearing of his condition. Since he had started on his trek the excitement and anticipation generated by his return had brought most of the villagers to the clearing. As he passed through the crowd many reached out to touch him, and the people pressed in on him until he was surrounded by a sea of faces. If he had any doubt about their love for him, it was quickly dispelled as he walked by them.

"Na-tan! Na-tan!" A chorus of voices shouted his name.

Then he was being pressed into the Council House by his two close friends. The shouting slowly tapered off and died away, and the Chief came forward and placed his hands on Nathaniel's shoulders.

"I greet you, my Brother, on your return home. The people are happy that you have come back. We have waited to listen to your words for half a moon. Now you are here. We think that you must have much to say to us."

"My heart is glad to be here with you. Many suns have passed since I left you. Fifteen suns! I thought many times about the people who waited for me . . . all of you . . . my family and my friends, and sometimes I did not know if I would come back to you or ever see you again."

When he said these last words, the men and women groaned and started talking to one another. They were listening to every word he said, and this was the first indication that something had happened on the journey. Several Indians, who had met him on the way to the village, had told the story of how he looked and acted, and the word had spread quickly that evil spirits had somehow infected him. Many believed Nathaniel had confirmed that by his statement; others in the Council did not. But all waited to hear his story.

Nanatola raised his hand for quiet, and the murmuring voices subsided. Then he spoke slowly, wanting all in the Council to hear why the meeting had been called.

"As Na-tan has said to us before, many suns have gone since he left the village. There are some who did not meet in Council with us the last time. They may not know what was said then. I want their minds to be more clear now. This is what happened that day.

"All of you know that another treaty has been signed with the whites. The treaty says that we can trade with them and get fair prices for our goods. Many did not believe that would happen, and thought the treaty was not good for us. Only Na-tan said what many believed, that the Long Hairs would want more land . . . and even more land after that . . . and some day we would have no more land to give, no more hunting grounds to hunt. Then we would be like them.

"Hear me, my Brothers. We are fast becoming like them now! The lands of the Ani'yun-wiya' have grown smaller. Many of you did not know that our lands were once great in size! The deer and the bear are going too. Many of you have never seen or killed a bear! The town chiefs fight among themselves, wanting to gain the white man's favor. Many of you may some day be willing to do the same thing! I say this to you so that you know what we decided in Council that day.

"Na-tan believed that in the big mountains, there would be a place where we could go. And live. He thought he could find it. Some of us talked to him before he left on his journey. What he said was in my own mind to say, but I did not see what Na-tan sees. My eyes are not his eyes. This is what we decided in Council: we would wait until he returned. That is all we said. If he has found a new home for us, there are some who will go to it. Anyone who wants to stay in the village can do what he thinks is right.

"Now, I think it is time for Na-tan to speak. My son, we wait to hear your words. We have heard that you came to the village yesterday with a heavy heart. Some said that an evil spirit was on you, and another said that death had been your companion on the journey. Tell us only what you want to say, nothing more or less. Perhaps, in the telling, Na-tan, you can rid yourself of the evil spirit and the shadows of death that followed you."

Nathaniel, who had been sitting between White Horse and Bear Claw, rose to his feet. For a moment he did not speak, but looked slowly around the Council at the assembly. He knew there were those who would choose to remain in the village, and he did not want to criticize them for their decision. Many others would be willing to move on a moment's notice.

He thought about Grandfather Mountain, and the girl buried there under the tree where they had spent the fatal night together. When she said she would wait for him he expected to convince the tribe, or some of the tribe, to move within a matter of months. Now, he was not so sure. Perhaps, it was better to remain where they were now living.

He had their attention, and he spoke in a strong voice in order that those outside the Council House could hear. "I want you to know that I carry no evil spirit with me, but death was on my shoulders several times. When I returned I was weary and my heart was not happy. I did not greet my Brothers with joy. Now that I am here, my heart is glad again.

"My Chief has told you that I went on a journey to find another land where the people could live. I did not think of it first. Snow Deer thought there might be a place in the mountains. She was wise to think of that. I believe I found it on Grandfather Mountain."

The Council erupted again. It was common to speak in Council indirectly about a matter of importance, and after a necessary buildup the member would then address what was in his heart. Nathaniel's simple declaration caught them by surprise. The debate about moving the tribe would come later, but for now his announcement was momentous and they could not let it pass unnoticed. He held up his hand before continuing.

"Hear me! I said I believe I found a place. That is for the Council to decide later. It is a beautiful land, and it is far from the white man's trails that lead west. It has water and fields for growing. There are many signs of animals. I killed two while we were there. It has a natural fort on the side of the mountain which we can defend. It would be difficult for the whites to get to us there. It can be made stronger with a little work, and we can put supplies up there easily. It would take a strong army to drive us out!

"It is a land that can be defended with a few men. I tell you this because there are some who will not want to move, and you should not believe that if you decide to remain behind, you might cause the rest of us to perish. I have never seen a better place to live. It is where the winds blow free and where I am prepared to live and die as a Cherokee!"

He had finished what he wanted to say, but before he could sit several Indians jumped to their feet and started speaking, but Nanatola raised his hand for quiet.

"Na-tan, we thank you for going on the long journey, and for telling us of it. There are those here who would like to hear more. I ask you now, before we discuss this, when do you think we should move the village?"

"This must be a matter for the Council to decide. I think that we must not give up the lands that we now have. How long we may be able to stay here depends upon the white movement into our lands. I have always believed they will come. It is a question of when they will try and force us to move. Every treaty that we sign gives them more power, and they are not followed. Some day we will no longer be strong enough to fight them. When that day comes, then I think we should go to the new place."

"How far is it, Na-tan?" the old chief asked.

"Six or seven suns from here. I traveled ten suns to find it, but as the crow flies, it is not too far."

The Chief now opened the meeting for discussion. "I want to say again that I asked Na-tan to tell us only what he wants to say. If any of you wish to understand better, you may speak now."

"You were gone a long time, Na-tan. Why did it take so long to find the mountain? Where did you travel?"

"When I left here, I did not know where I would go. I went along the Long Man for most of the first day until I heard whites moving about, but then the passage got much harder. I went east and north for three more before I found a pass which led to the mountains. The fifth day was not good. I found two white men who had a young woman they had bought from one of our chiefs. One of them tried to kill me, but I shot him first. The second one died shortly after a rattlesnake finished him off."

"What happened to the woman?" another asked.

"Remember the raid on Cavett's Station. She was captured at that time and was taken as a slave to a chief. I took her along with me after we buried the Moravians. I hoped to run into white settlers who would take her with them, but we did not see any."

"She was white then? What did you do with her?"

"Yes, she was white," he said quietly. "We traveled together. We ran into a band of Shawnees several days after she found her freedom. Four of them attacked us. We killed them all. She killed two herself. After that we continued looking. When we got to Grandfather Mountain, she helped me explore it. I wanted her to come back with me, but she had decided to stay on Grandfather and wait for us to move. She died there. Another Shawnee killed her before I killed him. That is why I appeared to have an evil spirit when I returned. I buried her there on the mountain."

As he finished the tale of the journey, silence descended upon the Council. The Indians respected this man and did not want to intrude upon him further. Nanatola realized how hard it had been for Nathaniel to tell the story, especially the last part. His love for Nathaniel, the man who had become more Indian than white, had grown in the telling of the story, and he did not want him to suffer further.

He stood up, straight as an arrow, and looked at Nathaniel. "It is a good thing you have done for us, Na-tan. We thank you for finding this place for us. The Council is closed. We will speak more about the move to the mountain again."

# 20

# ASSIMILATION AND WAR

At the next Council meeting the decision was made to remain in the village and to do whatever necessary to work with the whites under the terms of the latest treaty. Nathaniel did not believe this would end the intrusions, and suspected the whites would continue their land grab.

As he was leaving, Bear Claw caught up to him and said, "Na-tan, what you said was not good. You could have the village moving now, but I did not hear excitement in your voice."

"As always, you are wise, Uncle. I did not speak for the move because of what happened on the mountain. I am not sure I can go there so soon."

"Yes, my friend, I heard pain in your words. I am sorry that you did not come to me when you returned. Perhaps, I could have helped you." Bear Claw put his arm around Nathaniel. "Sometimes, we must bear our pain alone. At other times, it is better to share our loads. White Horse and I have good ears to hear what you tell us, and we will help carry your load."

"I told Snow Deer everything that happened on Grandfather Mountain. She shared my load . . . my sadness at losing the woman. She understands me . . . and what I did . . . and she holds no bitterness. She loves me, Uncle, as I love her." Nathaniel stopped walking, trying to find the right words for Bear Claw. "Thank you for listening, my friend. Someday, I will tell you the story of my journey and what happened on the mountain. Then I think you will understand."

"Na-tan, I remember many things in my life. Maybe they were the same as yours. I see now why you did not argue during the meeting, and why you were willing accept the Council's decision to stay here. I believe you knew what the whites would do. It is not good for you to go to Grandfather Mountain at this time."

In 1798, the Treaty of Southwest Point was signed. Known also as the Treaty of Tellico, it brought the loss of more land. Now the Cherokee Nation faced an even greater insidious enemy: the unraveling of the political and social fabric that held the nation together.

The changes, which Nathaniel and others had predicted, commenced almost immediately. The net effect was an intensified civilization process directed toward assimilating the Cherokees into the white man's culture. By this time, three general divisions of the Nation had developed separately. There was no longer a strong unanimity of purpose in the affairs of the Nation. The lower, middle, and upper towns had become autonomous units led by local chiefs who governed largely by example and persuasion. As they gained political and economic strength, they often placed their town's welfare over that of the tribe.

Farms began springing up in the western region of the Cherokee homeland. To encourage cultivation of the lands, farm implements were provided by the government. Individual farms flourished and prospered, but land ownership resided in the tribe. New churches, grain mills and timber operations, all of which gave substance to the process, soon followed. Although the woven fabric of the new civilization program appeared to be strong, it started to wear thin very quickly and dissension among the Indians soon erupted.

The Cherokees became disillusioned and discontented. The same year, two major issues captured their attention and contributed to further unhappiness. The first was their recognition that giving up land under the treaties resulted in few benefits to them. They felt betrayed by the government that had promised them much and had given so little in exchange. In debt to the new government, they felt shame and disgust over the land cessions and their effect upon tribal integrity and harmony. The second was more visible. It manifested itself in the inferiority of goods that were pushed on them by the factors of the government stores where they traded. The fair prices promised did not exist, or if they did, the traders were not honoring the agreement as they exchanged goods with the Indians.

For a people who had always known, or at least sought, harmony in their lives, the combination of these two critical happenings was threatening and divisive. Their anger grew and intensified. However much they tried to understand the events taking place around them, they could not reconcile in their minds what they believed were betrayals on the part of the government. The Cherokees again chose to go on the warpath.

The general tranquility that had reigned between the whites and the Indians for two years came to an end. There were tribal members in the towns who held the belief the two races could no longer live together, and they ignited the spark that grew into a firestorm of hatred for the whites. They believed, right or wrong, that fighting to maintain their land and way of life was the only hope for survival.

The season of the New-born-Leaf returned to the lands of the Cherokee. Throughout the preceding fall and winter, raiding parties of Indians and whites roamed freely. Pitched battles between both sides became an almost daily occurrence. Casualties mounted, and the people wondered how long the fighting would continue. Fear and apprehension came upon them like a plague, permeated their very lives, and the harmony they had known for several years started to slip inexorably from the tribe. Day and night, through the season of Cold-in-the-Ground, all talk centered around what would happen with winter's end.

Something was terribly wrong. Nathaniel had not been able to sleep well and kept twisting and turning from side to side. It was not the wind swirling leaves, or even the sound of intermittent rain that dashed against the lodge. It was something that intruded on the soul of the man who lay on the sleeping bench. Snow Deer was awake also. She had sensed the same thing, and was uneasy as she lay beside him. Strange and frightening shadows flitted across her mind, reminding her of other times when there was something amiss. Some Indians could see what lay ahead for them; they possessed what was called the "seeing mind." Not all had this psychic power, perhaps borne of the closeness of the Indian to the land around him, but those who had the gift accepted it and took heed whenever it beckoned.

"What is it, Na-tan?"

"There is something on the wind that tells me to listen, and to listen carefully."

"I know." She sat up, pulling the fur robe around her. "I do not like the sound. I think there is death around us, and I am afraid that if we do not soon leave this place it will be on us and we will not escape."

"Aye, you are right, my love." Nathaniel left the bench and moved to the still warm fire. There has been too much fighting already. I think we should leave for Grandfather Mountain now. Today, before the sun sets, perhaps we will be on our way."

"We can do it, Na-tan, but you must tell the people what you are hearing on the wind. It is not easy for them to move from this place. We have stayed here for many snows. You know that all will not go. But they will understand if you speak how you feel."

"It has been spoken of in Council. Two suns ago we met, after the last raid on the settlement. It should be no surprise. All agreed that now was the time."

"That is true. What was not decided was when the move would be made." Snow Deer was becoming impatient with him. "Sometimes, you men are like old women. You sit in Council and talk about what the tribe should do, and then agree that it should be done, and nothing happens. It is nearly light. Get dressed, Na-tan, and go tell the others what we have decided!"

"Be quiet, woman, and let me think hard about what we are doing. I will go soon." Motioning to Little Eagle, he said, "Let the boy sleep. I can think better if he is not taking sides with you."

When he opened the flap and stepped outside, the foreboding weather pulled him up short. The heavens were filled with dark, angry clouds heavy with wet, scudding around the sky in a crazy pattern. Nathaniel looked around the clearing, hoping to see someone standing outside, but all he saw were village dogs seeking shelter under the branches of the lower trees, or cowering from the cold wind beside of the lodges. Even as he stood, the skies opened and the drizzle of the night turned into a deluge. He ducked back into the lodge. Little Eagle was still asleep.

"I do not think we will leave today," he said simply, as the heavy rain pounded against the lodge roof.

"Perhaps, it will end quickly," she replied.

"It does not matter. It will give us time to pack for the journey. And when the village stirs, the men will go to the Council House. Then I will speak to them about our move."

"Na-tan, are you ready to go? I mean, will it be hard for you to return to the mountain?" Snow Deer asked.

Nathaniel knew she was thinking of the woman on the mountain. "I do not think so. It has been several snows now. Our lives did not change much because of the woman. You came to me without anger when I returned. I will remember that a long time."

"We have shared much, Na-tan, more than most. My heart has always been happy that you found me in the river." She laughed quietly, "Would you jump in the river for a girl again, Na-tan? Or would you let her drown?"

"You ask silly questions, woman." Then he smiled at her as he pulled her toward the sleeping bench, "I think it would depend on whether the girl was good to me. Is she ready to show me how she would thank me?"

"Na-tan, you are good to me. This is what the girl would do for him." She crawled upward on his body, showering him with thanks.

By midday the rain had stopped falling. The sun broke through the scattered clouds, bringing a bit of warmth to the village.

When the Council met late in the afternoon, Nathaniel spoke of his uneasiness. "I am happy to see the sun again. Last night, in the storm, I had a bad dream . . . there was death all around us.

"It made me want to leave this place. The evil spirits have come to us, and it is not good. Snow Deer and I talked about it when the winds were strong and the water beat down. We plan to go to the mountain when the sun rises. Some may want to leave too, but it is not for me to say. I will not be happy until we find a new home."

There was much discussion. Nanatola was convinced that Nathaniel's "seeing mind" had seen death ahead; and while he was not quite ready to go, he deferred to his brother in the matter.

The men listened carefully as the Chief said what was in his heart. "Na-tan has spoken well. He sees death around us and has told us what he intends to do. I think it is the right thing for us to listen to his words.

"Our raiding parties have all returned but one. Red Arrow is still missing. I will not move until he comes. It is not easy for me to go. Our people have lived in this village for many snows. From this place we have hunted and fought, and it has brought harmony to our lives. Our children have been born here, and they know no other place.

"Death has come to us many times, as it will come again. Our war parties have fought for our lands, but more and more our lands get smaller and the whites grow stronger. They have come against us now because we have hurt them. They have destroyed many of our villages. I believe they will come again.

"When Na-tan returned from his journey and told us he had found a place where we could live, some of us decided to stay here. Others thought that we should go. That is the way it should be. Every man must choose what he wants to do. I have decided to go soon and make a new home. I do not ask any of my people to do the same thing."

"Listen to what I say now!" he commanded. "A new chief must be found among you. Those of you who remain here must have a new leader. Think about it!"

As soon as he had uttered the words, White Horse leaped to feet, shouting "No! No! We want no other chief!"

"There is no one else to lead us," a second voice echoed.

Another said, "You cannot leave us here then."

"No one will stay behind," a voice chimed in. "All will go to Grandfather Mountain."

The Chief raised his hand. "It is better for the tribe. Surely you are wise enough to see this!"

Again, a loud murmur went through the lodge. "I want to say more. It is also a good time for a new chief to take you to the mountain. I am tired. You must choose someone from among you to lead you there."

Nathaniel could not believe what he was hearing. Nanatola had told him before he left on the journey that he wanted to step down, but if he understood correctly, the Chief was saying that he would lead neither those left behind nor those who moved. Two chiefs must be selected.

He had to know for sure. "My Brothers, I think I understand what Nanatola is saying. He is asking us to choose two chiefs: one to lead the people who remain here, and the other on the mountain. I believe it is wise to have a new leader here, but since the Chief will go with us, I think he must lead his people there. That is the way I see it."

Other Council members threw out suggestions. Some thought that the Chief should stay with those who remained behind. Others knew that he would not accept that and agreed with Nathaniel that since Nanatola was going anyway, he should continue as chief. There were some who believed that the Chief was right to step down. Nathaniel reminded them of what he had said minutes before. The vote was taken. It was agreed that Red Arrow would be elected chief of those who stayed in the village, and Nanatola should continue to serve the group that was moving until they were established on the mountain.

The Chief sat silently for some time, looking around the Council at each man. "My heart is tired, my Brothers, but it is filled with joy when I listen to you. I will accept your wishes . . . but only until we have built a new village on the mountain. Then it will be time for a new chief. As for the journey there, Na-tan will be in charge of the move. Only he knows the way to the mountain! I have spoken all that I want to say."

When the Council ended, agreement had been reached that the group making the move would leave in three days. Certainly Red Arrow would have returned by then, and could assume his newly-elected position as chief of the village. As word of the decision spread throughout the villagers, the people set about getting ready to make the journey. It was agreed that those who wished to stay behind would be welcomed on the mountain if they chose to move later, and there was much excitement as the villagers sorted out and packed their belongings.

The day following the Council, Red Arrow and the raiding party returned. He brought home several raiders with minor wounds, but none had been killed. Nanatola called him to his lodge and told him of the Council's deliberations and decisions, and turned over the village control to him.

"My Brother, Red Arrow, you have been a strong and willing warrior. The Council has met and spoken. I am no longer your chief. You will be the leader. I am leaving with Na-tan and the people who want to move to Grandfather Mountain. It is not easy for us to leave this place. I think in my heart that this is the best thing to do.

"There is something more I want to say to you. If the whites come strong and push you from the village as I believe they will, and you cannot stop them, come to the mountain with the rest of the people. There will be a place for you. Choose one of your men and send him with us. That way, he will know the trail and be able to bring you there."

The two men looked into the other's eyes. "Goodbye, my Brother. I ask the Great Spirit to help you."

"And I ask the same for you," Red Arrow replied.

Nathaniel called those who were going together the night before leaving and explained the order of march and other details. He wanted to ensure that they knew what was expected before they got on the trail. He designated the scouts who would precede and travel on the flanks of the main group. He explained very carefully how they would defend themselves and what each person would do in the event of an attack. He did not want to be caught by surprise by a white raiding party during the trek, nor did he want the pack animals to be driven off. Their control and protection was vital to the success of the move.

After an early morning meal, the villagers assembled. There were nearly one hundred twenty men, women and children. Among them was White Horse and Bear Claw. They were among the oldest ones making the journey, and Nathaniel appointed each to be responsible for certain groups of travelers on the trail.

They had selected younger braves to form a fighting force if they were attacked on the way. Two of Red Arrow's raiders would also make the trek, and they were placed in command of the younger men who comprised the defenders. The baggage, most of which was being carried on their backs, held everything the tribe would need in their new home, and even the children were assigned loads to carry. A few horses and some dogs were used to pack the grain and other dried food and hides and equipment that had been allocated to the group leaving the village.

When all were ready, Nathaniel was asked to speak to the villagers making the journey. Wise in the ways of his people, Nanatola knew the importance of communicating verbally before some important happening. The previous night he had suggested this to Nathaniel. It would help make their leaving easier, the Chief declared, and would be important to those who were remaining behind to hear what he said. As their leader on the trail, Nathaniel was selected.

"Listen, my friends, before we start for the mountains. We are leaving a homeland, perhaps for the last time, to begin a new life in a new place. We will not say farewell to the friends who stay here, for if they are forced off this land, they will come to us. I will lead you there. If we have no trouble, we will be in our new home in about six suns. New lodges must be built and fields planted, but we will be safe there. Now, prayers should be made to the Great Spirit, to give us safe passage to the new land."

When he had spoken, families and friends formed into small bands as though there was safety in traveling together on the trail. Scouts were sent off to form the protective shields on each flank. Nathaniel, surrounded by his family and Chief, led the march from the village. As they departed, those remaining behind gave a great roar, wishing Nathaniel and the travelers a good journey. Some cried as they saw old friends leaving, while others made light of the exodus, but there was a palpable sadness as both groups separated.

As he had gone before, Nathaniel led the party southeast along the Long Man. When they left the watercourse, the going became more difficult and Nathaniel was forced to slow the march to keep the people moving in a tight group. The first day was the slowest, but by the fourth day they had reached the foothills and Nathaniel stopped at midday by a small stream to give the people time to rest their weary bodies. He sent hunters out to kill game, and when they returned a feast was prepared, and the journeyers recovered quickly as they gorged themselves on the fresh meat.

By the time the meal was finished it was too late in the day to move farther, and they stayed where they were. Again, Nathaniel posted guards for the night; he did not want any surprises.

After they got settled, Nanatola sought him out. "My Brother, when you returned from the mountain, there was much sadness in your heart."

"Yes, that is true. You are wondering why I did not choose to discuss it with you then?"

"Na-tan, when I spoke in Council, I asked you to say only what you wanted to say. It is the same now. I knew the death of the girl had made you that way. You loved her, that I know."

Nathaniel did not answer immediately. He thought about the girl he had buried there. Now, the Chief was resurrecting a few days of his life he had mentally placed behind him. "Yes, I guess I did, but that was many moons ago and what happened on the mountain is not important now. When I first returned your sister and I made peace together. She understood then, perhaps better than I understood, what caused the happening. I truly love Snow Deer . . . and have from that first day. It was not the same with the girl."

"You have made my heart glad, Na-tan, You know that I love Snow Deer above everything in this land, and if she were not happy because of something you had done, it would cause me great pain. Thank you for telling me this." He paused, looking into the fire at his feet, and then spoke again.

"Will it be bad for you, Na-tan, to be in the same place where she lies?"

"I do not know, but I think not. It was long ago."

"Na-tan, when we get to the mountain, if you want to talk to me about it, or if you find that coming back is not good for your soul, then I am willing to listen."

"I thank you, Brother. I will remember what we said here tonight."

# 21

# *WHERE THE WIND BLOWS FREE*

The travelers had made good time, and the villagers sat around the fires talking about reaching the mountain. A sense of expectancy and confidence permeated the gathering, and many were reluctant to bed down for the night. Nathaniel had not expected to make such rapid progress and was as happy as the others. While he enjoyed the people's excitement, he also knew that hard climbing lay ahead of them before they reached Grandfather Mountain. He moved through the camp talking to one group after another, encouraging them to rest for the coming day, but his pleas fell for the most part on deaf ears. Everyone was excited, and they took pleasure in the security of family and the tribe. "Oh well," he thought, "tomorrow they will feel the effect, and there is little I can do. Let them stay awake."

He made his way to Nanatola's fire, wanting to talk about the new village to be built on the mountain. The Chief greeted him warmly and complimented Nathaniel on the progress made. "You have done well and we have traveled far without incident. It was a good journey."

Seating himself by the fire, Nathaniel replied wearily. "That is true but the hardest part will come tomorrow. I have tried to tell the people this, but they are too excited to sleep."

The Chief said nothing. Nathaniel continued, "If all goes well we should be on Grandfather by nightfall. I came here to ask for your help. There are two things that must be done. First, we must lay out the new village. Secondly, I want to set up the position on the mountain from which we can fight. I believe the whites will follow us here, and I want to be ready if that happens."

"Tell me what you want. If I can help you, I will."

"That is easy. The people will want to get settled quickly, and that means building lodges and a Council House. But I think that should wait until we get the land prepared and the seeds in the ground. It would be foolish to delay."

Nanatola looked at Nathaniel. "That is good. I think you are wise to do that. You must tell the people. They will want to build shelters, take care of their families, try to bring harmony back into their lives."

"They will not find harmony if they have nothing to eat later. This is what I want from you . . . to speak to them when we get there and tell them. I am not the chief; I am only leading the people to the mountain."

"That is true but they will still want you to tell them what must be done. They consider you their leader; I am a chief in name only. Now get yourself some rest. As you said, tomorrow will be a long day."

As Nathaniel got up to leave, he turned to the Chief and said, "A leader can only be as good as the people he leads. I am proud of them, and I want them to re-capture a peace here which has been taken from them. I do this because I love them. I can do nothing less."

Early the next morning the long line of Indians assembled and started moving. Now that the mountain was within sight, an urgency caught up the travelers and hurried them on the way. They were excited about reaching their goal before sundown and few wished to stop during the day. They kept plodding along. As Nathaniel had predicted, the going became more difficult as they climbed.

They crossed another stream that he remembered from the earlier journey, but they tarried on its banks only long enough to replenish the bags with cold mountain water before moving on. After catching their breaths, they redoubled their efforts to reach Grandfather. By mid-afternoon, when they stopped for a longer rest, Nathaniel called them together again. Only a few miles remained before they would reach the camp.

In a strong voice he announced, "My friends, we are nearly there. We have only a few miles farther to travel. If we keep moving, we will get there before dark. My intent is to set up a temporary camp to use until we build the village. There is water near the camp, and I have sent several hunters ahead of us to find food. There will be much work for each of us. I am telling you this so that everyone knows what is expected after the long journey. Now stay together as much as possible. I want all the scouts to be alert and to stay within shouting distance of the main body. Maintain the pace. I know we are tired, but we have come too far to be stopped by a war party. Now, let us get on the trail again."

As he had told them, they reached the broad field located at the base of the mountain within the hour. The men, remembering the description that Nathaniel had given them earlier, could scarce contain their joy when they arrived and confirmed for themselves what he had said. The women, tired from the trail, shook off the exhaustion and walked through the area hardly believing their good fortune. The children, no longer confined to the discipline of the trail, scampered about exploring the rocks and trees, shouting their discoveries for all to hear. Off to the side was the bowl-shaped depression that Marie Emmanuelle had discovered when they first arrived. Water was flowing steadily over the lip of the collecting pan. The people gathered around and offered thanks to the Great Spirit for bringing them safely to Nathaniel's mountain.

After prayers, he quickly pointed out the campsite in a small wooded area near the water source. He had decided when he first came to the mountain that it offered the villagers the perfect place to settle. It was near water and the planting fields, and there was another level area that he thought could serve as the playing field. He was pleased with it.

Nathaniel looked upward, focusing on the rockslide, and his thoughts returned to the first time he and the girl had seen it together. He wondered what Marie Emmanuelle would have said had she been there to greet the Indians as they arrived. He shook his head to clear it, wanting to rid it of the ghosts of the woman intruding upon his return. It was not good to dwell on what lay behind. He looked then to the villagers, faces aglow with happiness and excitement, as they stood waiting for him to speak.

Snow Deer came over to him, as if aware that old memories were returning to her beloved Nathaniel, and quietly asked, "Are you right, Na-tan?"

"Aye, my Love," and reached for her and put his arm around her. "Are you happy that we have come home?"

She smiled up at him. "You know I am happy with you. I can hardly wait to go exploring with you . . . to get you away alone with me . . . I will show you instead of talking," she added.

"We will do that as soon as I speak to the people," he said. "They need to know everthing." He squeezed her hand. "I am ready for you, more ready than you believe. Just give me a little more time."

Grandfather loomed above them as he turned back to the waiting men and women. He wanted them to know that he had chosen a good place to defend the village if the whites came. They could easily see the rocks above, but had no way of knowing what lay behind them. They gathered in a tight circle except for the scouts he had not called in. The Chief, visibly excited by the location, now stood waiting as Nathaniel commenced speaking.

"Look above you. Up there . . . to the rocks," he pointed. "When I spoke in Council, I told my brothers that I had found a place which we could defend easily. From here, all you can see is the rockslide at the edge."

"That is true, but what more is there, Na-tan?"

"Much more than meets the eye. I will show you tomorrow. There is a clearing behind the rocks. It is large enough to provide for all our needs. There are many places hidden among the rocks where we will store food. The water runs strong also. You will look from those heights and see as the eagle sees, across the hills and valleys . . . such sights as you have never seen before."

"When can we go?" one of the Indians grunted.

"Soon, very soon, but there are other things that must be taken care of first." He turned to the Chief. "I have asked my brother to tell you what we need to do."

Nanatola stepped forward and stood beside Nathaniel. "Na-tan selected the camp where we will live. I think it is a good place, and I will be happy to build my lodge there. All of you want to get settled as I do.

But we will not be able to build until other work is done. Na-tan believes that we should first plant our fields and establish a base on the mountain. That is what we will do.

"Tomorrow, some of us will climb to the new base. I want to see it myself. We may have some work to get it ready. We do not know when the whites will come, but we want to be prepared to fight them if they follow. We will build and store our supplies in two places. Our fields will be planted here; and when we have gathered food, we will carry some to the mountain and store it up there. If we have to defend ourselves we will be able to stay for a long time.

"Only when our fields are planted will our lodges and the Council House be built. Then we will have a big hunt and bring meat for the winter. If we work together, the village will be a good place for us."

When he finished speaking, Nathaniel again looked over the assembly. "The Chief has spoken well. We must work hard for the next several moons. Now that we have arrived on the mountain, I want to say what is on my heart. I am proud to be one of you, and I am more proud of how you made the journey. We are home at last! I will not be chased from it until I die. Enjoy it, for it is yours as long as one of us lives."

The following morning, with little direction, the villagers commenced the task of digging the soil and planting the seeds. At the Chief's bidding, Nathaniel laid out the communal fields. The soil was rich and soft from the spring rains, and the men and women and children cleared off the brush and grass and started planting. Fences were constructed around the enclosure to protect the fields from roaming animals.

Some men were given the job of finding young saplings in the campsite to use for the fence, and as they cut and trimmed and brought the branches to the fields, the older women and children wove grass ropes and tied the poles together. By the end of the first day, several of the smaller fields had been planted and fenced, and the villagers returned to the campfires to cook and rest from their labor. As Nathaniel had told them, it was hard work, but the people were pleased with their effort and celebrated far into the night.

At the same time a group of warriors, led by Nathaniel, climbed the mountain to the defensive site that overlooked the camp. They followed the same trail that Nathaniel and the girl had used before, and when they came to the leveled field they found it exactly as Nathaniel had described it. Its commanding view held them in awe for a few moments.

One of the warriors ran over to the edge where the boulders lay. "Come!" he shouted excitedly to the others, "Na-tan was right. You can see the fields down below and the people too. They look like ants from here."

As the others rushed toward the rocks, Nathaniel cautioned them. "Be careful! There may be snakes around. They like the warm sun."

The men slowed immediately, looking at the ground now as they approached the rocks. Then one climbed onto a boulder and looked out across the scene spread before him. "It is the right place for fighting if that is what we must do. We can see for miles from here. Like the eagle sees, as Na-tan told us."

Nanatola had remained with Nathaniel, basking in the fresh breeze, savoring what he saw around him. "Don't you want to see it?" Nathaniel asked.

"Yes, but I know you were right about this place. What you found down below and here is far more than I expected. When the fields are planted and the corn is green, we will have much to be thankful for."

"While the men are enjoying themselves, I would like to show you more. Come along. Then I would ask that you decide how we can improve our fort. I have some ideas about how to make it stronger but your thoughts are probably better."

"Na-tan, my thoughts are no better than yours. You have had much time since you first came here to think what should be done. Besides, my days as chief are about over. When next we meet in Council, I will ask you to take my place."

As Nathaniel opened his mouth to speak, Nanatola stopped him. "No! Hear me. There is no one better to lead us. You found this place, you guided us here, you set out the campsite. The people have started digging and planting the fields because they believe in you. How can you say that you will not lead us more?"

"You say too much. There are others in the tribe who should be chief."

"No, I have not said enough. If you had not been able to see what the tribe could not see or understand, we would be in the old village still waiting until we were driven out like wild animals. No one went on a journey to look for another place. We sat on our backsides doing nothing. No one believed the same as you believed. I have spoken, Na-tan, to White Horse and Bear Claw about this.

"My sister also has listened. Everyone is in agreement. You must be our new leader! Remember when I spoke in Council? I said I would be chief only until we moved here. I am not the leader that I once was. I ask you to do this for me."

"I will think about it." Nathaniel answered. "It is not good to make a quick decision. Right now there are other needs to take care of." Changing the subject abruptly, Nathaniel asked, "What do you think we should do here . . . to improve it, I mean?" Then before the Chief replied, Nathaniel sketched out his plan. "First, I believe we should move some of the smaller stones to give our warriors better cover. We should be able to roll them easily.

"I think we should also build permanent storage sites for our supplies, and several large lodges for protection. If we are forced to leave the village below, we must have shelters already prepared for the people. We must build a catch basin to hold water for many suns. And we need some way to make signals so the villagers will know when the white soldiers are approaching. We can use the old people to watch and give warning. We must think about this quickly and get ready."

"Is that all, Na-tan? We have never fought this way. You will show us how?" he added.

He was caught up in Nathaniel's display of knowledge about preparing the fortress for war. He realized that Nathaniel was taking a chapter from the whites and intended to use it against them if needed. Nanatola had gone into battle many times, hitting and running, never staying in a fixed position as the whites did, but he understood the wisdom of getting the fort ready. "Surely, this man is a great leader," he thought. "There is no one in the tribe who could have envisioned these things."

"No," Nathaniel replied. "You must instruct several men to get started on the work here. They can begin now. We will return to the camp and send up whatever is needed. There is no time to wait until a Council is formed. It is better to do it first, and then debate its wisdom."

"Then, Na-tan, you must do this. Select the men you want, and put them to work. You know what has to be done. The rest will descend with me. If I choose them, they will want to meet in Council and talk about this plan or another. As you say, we do not have time for that." The Chief grinned. "Besides, my heart tells me this is good training for a chief. Not one of us could have planned this, or have the second sight to see it finished."

Calling the men together, Nathaniel chose four men and quickly explained what had to be done and laid out their tasks. He told them food and supplies would be sent up the mountain, and that they would be relieved every other day by another group of men. No one questioned his directions or authority, and the remainder of the group left the position and descended to the camp.

Arriving at the camp, Nathaniel was pleased to see the planting well underway. Whole fields had been stripped of brush and already the fencing was being positioned. Everyone was busy and seemingly happy as they dug and planted and worked together. He dispatched several men to go hunting, and the rest he assigned to the fields to assist the others. Then he assembled the tools that would be taken to the men working above.

Both at the base camp, and what he now called the Upper Camp, the Indians labored as they had not done for many moons. Nathaniel pushed them hard, wanting to get both camps ready as quickly as possible. In seven suns the fields were prepared and seeded, and the villagers who were not working above on the mountain commenced to lay out the permanent village.

Nathaniel had seen a number of villages strewn along rivers and streams, most of which had been placed in a random fashion. While the layouts had provided the Indians with freedom of expression, they had not served the inhabitants well during a raid. In fact, he had observed that mass confusion reigned whenever an attack occurred, and he believed that at least some of it could be attributed to the way the villages were constructed. In his mind, he felt that order took priority over randomness, and so he patiently called the people around him to explain what they should do.

He had prepared a rough sketch on the ground laying out the village surrounding the Council House and the playing field. The cleared areas throughout the camp were prominently displayed. As they clustered around, Nathaniel pointed out the significant features of his plan.

"If it is agreed, I would like to build a more permanent village here that will provide for our needs better. Here is where the lodges should be placed . . . and here is the location of the Council House. There are two entrances into the village—one from the growing fields, and the other here—the way we came in the first day." With a stick he traced each area for the villagers. "The water supply is located close to the lodges and the clearing where it can be used more easily.

"It will be colder here than what we have known before. I think the lodges should be built so that we will be warm when the the snows come. Cut strong wood for the lodges so they will stand strong.

"Look now at the exit to the mountain. If the whites come, we will leave by the back way, past these rocks and go up here to the mountain." He carved the route with the stick. "No one but ourselves will know where we have gone until it is too late. The path to the Upper Camp is concealed summer and winter. As some of you know we have already started to build shelters on the mountain. There are storage places for more provisions. That camp will be our second village. Now I think we should start to build here."

The villagers set to work in earnest. Nathaniel rotated the men on the mountain as he had promised and soon both camps were well underway. The seeds sprouted from the fertile ground, and soon gave way to corn and other fruits of the soil. By the second moon the village was complete, the Council House built, and the Upper Camp completed on the mountain. The hunting had been good, and the people were settling into their new home. There was much laughter and excitement, games were being played, new babies born into the tribe, and the people were commencing to regain the freedom they had almost lost.

As harmony returned to the tribe, Snow Deer remembered the girl whom Nathaniel had left there on the mountain. In some inexplicable way she believed the girl's spirit had helped the tribe recapture its happiness. Perhaps Nathaniel would not have found the mountain if she had not been traveling with him. Long ago, Snow Deer had forgiven him—it was something she accepted as happening after the heat of battle—and she loved Nathaniel too deeply to end the marriage because of the girl.

She had thought about it ever since their return to the mountain, but had never questioned him. She felt the time had come—that if he had any remaining thoughts about the girl, they should be purged from his mind.

Coming to him one day, Snow Deer said. "Na-tan, I would like to see where you buried the girl."

"Is it important to you?" he asked.

"I think so. The tribe has found peace and harmony in this place. You might not have discovered the mountain if you had been alone. Perhaps, it was because of her."

"I do not believe that. She was with me because I could not leave her on the trail."

"Have you gone back since coming here?" she probed.

"No."

"Then, we shall visit her together."


It was a time to enjoy the results of their labor. Summer passed into fall and through the cold winter months. But the people were happy and grateful for the bounty they had received. Food and water was plentiful; the harvest had been good. The hunting too.

Then came the season of the New-born-Leaf. The people greeted the warm days and prepared the ground again as they had when they arrived on Grandfather many moons before. Hunting parties went again on the mountain to bring in fresh game. The people basked in their work and pleasures and found themselves at peace with the Great Spirit who had brought harmony and happiness into their lives in the place they called "Where the Winds Blow Free." Little did they know that a white army was on its way to find and destroy them once again.

## 22

# THE LAST LINE

In the season of Sun-high-in-the-Sky a year earlier, Nathaniel had met in Council with the villagers and was voted in as chief. Nanatola had raised the issue soon after the village had been built and the fortification on the mountain completed. Never before had a white man become a chief of the Cherokees. But there was no opposition by the villagers. His leadership in bringing the people to Grandfather Mountain, and his understanding of the tribal customs and traditions, made him the unanimous choice.

He had become a respected leader, one who governed with love and justice. All that he had promised as they left their village many moons before had come to fruition under his guidance. Without his vision the people would have lost the very heart of their culture, and they loved this man for the gifts he had brought to them.

Now, the very essence of his leadership ability was being tested. The white raiders lay before him, with their cannon and superior weapons, and the people waited for him to overcome the enemy below. It was not an easy task to accomplish.

The enemy force had been sighted while it was still several miles distant from the village. The attackers, made up of foot soldiers supported by horse-drawn cannons, were moving slowly along the trail the villagers had traveled a year earlier. The group was large, but it did not appear to be slowed by the heavier weapons that brought up the rear of the column.

The warrior chief manning the Upper Camp alerted the village at first full light. On watch since midnight, he saw small fires in the distance during the dark night, but had waited until the sun rose and the mists lifted before raising the alarm flag. During the night, he dispatched a runner to alert Nathaniel.

When the observation post was established, Nathaniel had a tall post planted in the ground at the front of the slide near several large boulders. It was to be used to run up a white flag as a signal to the village below that something was amiss. The people had been instructed to report any sign of the flag. Throughout the day, whenever Nathaniel was in the village, he glanced upward to check out the post. This time, many of the villagers awoke to see the signal and knew that something was wrong on the mountain.

Night signaling was accomplished by a runner, one of the younger members who stayed on the mountain for several days. Only once before had the runner's service been used. That time, the lookout observed burning torches carried by a raiding party as it traveled through the night in preparation for a dawn attack on the village. The message, passed to Nathaniel, enabled him to get a force together that set up an ambush which destroyed the Shawnee raiders about a mile from the village.

The runner arrived nearly out of breath at Nathaniel's lodge. "Chief Na-tan! Chief Na-tan!" he called.

"Yes, what is it, my young friend?" Nathaniel asked as he was awakened by the outburst, and came to the lodge opening.

"Grey Wolf sent me," the boy gasped. "He said to tell you he sees many fires at a great distance."

"Did he say small or big fires, Boy?"

The runner was breathing easier now. "He said many small fires . . . and they are not moving."

"Anything else, my friend?"

"He said maybe they were two or three suns away as the crow flies. He was not certain in the darkness."

"That is good. Now go to Grey Wolf. Tell him as soon as it is light to tell me what he sees. Do you understand?"

"Yes, my Chief. I will say that when it is light to tell you what it is he sees." Then he turned to leave.

"You have done well, Boy. And tell him that he has eyes like an owl, and I thank him too."

Nathaniel went back into the lodge. Snow Deer was sitting on the edge of the sleeping bench. The small fire in the center cast dancing shadows on the wall behind her.

"I heard the boy, Na-tan. Does it mean we must fight?" she asked.

"I do not know," he answered quietly. "Perhaps, it is one of our own war parties."

"You do not believe that! It is the white army, isn't it?" she probed.

"I cannot say, Snow Deer, but do not fear. They are several suns from us, and we have time to prepare ourselves . . . to fight, if we must."

"I am afraid, Na-tan. I am very much afraid for you."

Nathaniel went to her then. "Let us wait for the morning, my Love. Then we will know what army it is, and whether we fight. Now, go back to sleep. I must walk and think about things. I will be back before the sun rises."

He needed the solitude of the night. As soon as he left the lodge, his steps led him down the trail to Marie Emmanuelle's grave. He had visited it only once, and that was nearly a year before when they returned to the mountain. Snow Deer had gone with him then. He remembered now what she had said as he stood beside the tree where he and the girl had lain together.

Perhaps it was because of her that he had been led to Grandfather. It was true the tribe had found peace here. The people were happy and secure in their old ways. They lacked for nothing. Now a new threat was upon them. Would the fortress above be their salvation or their grave? When he first had seen the rocks above and while it was being strengthened for battle, he hoped it would never come to this. But it had come, and as chief he must win this battle, regardless of the odds against him or the strength of the enemy.

He looked at the gravesite, and sensed the Great Spirit's presence, and he cried out, "Help us now, O Great Hianequo! Let the men fight with the courage this young girl showed when she fought the Shawnees.

Let us be worthy of her death." Then he turned and went back up the trail to his lodge.


Nathaniel called the War Council to convene at first light. He trusted the observer at the Upper Camp, and knew that he would not have sent the runner had he not foreseen trouble brewing.

When the warriors assembled, he told them what he knew about the warning, but had little information to pass on to them.

"Last night, Grey Wolf sent a runner to tell me that he had seen many fires several suns away. I think they were made by the white army, but until he can see more clearly, we must wait. It is possible they will not come here. We do not want to give away our position on Grandfather. Listen to me! There will be no cooking fires today until we are certain they are coming against us."

One of the younger warriors spoke up. "Should we move to the fort?"

"I do not think so. We should wait and see what direction the enemy is moving. If they come, they will find empty lodges, cold ashes, and no sign of us. Perhaps, they will then move on."

"They are good at tracking, Na-tan. What if they find the trail leading to the mountain?"

"It is well-hidden, but we will do something to confuse the enemy. Today, all the people will leave the village by way of the growing fields. Then we will make a wide circle and double back on the trail we used when we first arrived here. That will make it appear that we have abandoned the village.

"Several men should climb the mountain at once and make sure everything is ready. Check the arrows at each position and the catapults. We want plenty of stones at each one. Also, fill and store water bags along the forward edge. It may be a long fight."

The catapults had been another idea he had come up with. None of the Indians had used them previously and were excited when he explained to them how they would function. He found several young saplings growing among the boulders and had them trimmed and a pocket fitted at the top to hold the stones. When pulled back by a leather thong attached to the tree near the pouch and tied to a stake, they could be loaded and released on command. Both women and men had trained with several of them and had become quite proficient in judging distances as they practiced hurling stones against an imaginary enemy below. Nathaniel was pleased that they now were part of his arsenal at the Upper Camp.

Bear Claw spoke. "Na-tan, I want to say something."

"Yes, what is it, Bear Claw?"

"I think the older men and women should go up the mountain now. Some are not as light on their feet as they once were or have as much strength, but if they go now they can help get the fort ready."

Nathaniel said, "There is much wisdom in what you say. I think you are right. You may select the people to climb."

"Does anyone want to speak more? I will listen to good thoughts."

"Na-tan, you know this way of fighting is not what we know. If the whites come against us, it may not be easy to stay on the mountain and fight."

"Do you remember the back trail down the mountain—the one we discovered when we worked there?"

"Yes, but what good will that do?"

"Let me explain it to you." He picked up a stick and scraped ground at his feet to clear a small square. Then he used the stick as a pointer. "These are the great stones and the camp. At this side the trail leads from the clearing and goes down. Is that right?"

The Council members clustered around the drawing grunted their understanding. "How many have come down to the playing field this way?" He did not expect that many of the tribe had descended the trail, for he found no signs they had followed it a month before. "I have walked that way. About half-way down the trail splits." Here he divided the trail with the pointer. "This one leads to the valley behind Grandfather Mountain, and the second trail comes out at the playing field.

"If we are forced to leave the mountain, we will follow the trail into the valley. I do not think that will happen. Go tell the people what we know. They will need to pack for the move."

* * *

The white army had not been diverted from its purpose of destroying the Indians. Picking up the trail that showed a large, recent passage, the army followed the track to the village, only to find it deserted. They set up camp near the water basin.

The soldiers, discovering the Indians had fled, were happy and spent hours relaxing and rummaging through the lodges. They found little to use there before turning to the growing fields. They stripped these of the fresh, ripe corn before burning one of the fields to the ground.

Their commander was furious when he found the abandoned village and the cold cooking fires and no sign of the Indians that he had been intent upon destroying. Now, he was certain they had been alerted to the army's movement, and had crossed over the mountain to wait him out. He reasoned, and his orders made it quite clear if that were so, he would keep them on the run and attack as soon as he found them.

Looking down from the mountain, Nathaniel could see the smoke billowing from the burning field and felt great sorrow for the people he led. Soldiers could clearly be seen moving in and out of the camp area, and he felt violated as he realized what would happen to the village when they left. Surely, they would burn it, along with everything they found, and the thought made him angry. He turned away to try to come up with a plan to prevent such an occurrence.

Mulling it over in his mind, Nathaniel knew what he would do. First, he called the War Council together.

He spoke sharply and angrily to the assembled warriors. "The white army has come to our village. The soldiers walk in and out of our lodges, and I fear they will burn everything before they leave.

"We have built a strong fort here. Never before have we been able to control a battle as we can now. The white commander will not expect us to fight like he does; and when he comes against us, he will suffer many losses.

"They have not found our path to the mountain; but if they do not, they will continue to hunt us. Wherever we go the whites follow. This is my home, and this is where I have decided to stay."

White Horse rose. "I speak for many here, Na-tan. This is our home too, and I am prepared to die here if the Great Spirit wills it. I will not run any more. Besides, I am getting too old to travel far."

"I think we should fight also," another added. "I am tired of being hunted like an animal."

"You are right, Na-tan. We have a strong place here, better than any before. I say we should not leave our mountain."

Nathaniel asked for a vote, and when all had been heard, he said, "Then it is agreed. We will stay. Little Eagle will be my runner. If he brings a message to the warrior chiefs, listen to him! Now, I want a small raiding party to go down the trail when the moon is dark." He quickly selected a few men and issued instructions. "Slip into the camp quietly. The soldiers will have guards posted. Watch for them. Kill as many as you can quickly. Do not take hair tonight. One last thing, throw one of the dead soldiers in the water; the army will get very thirsty when they find him swimming there.

"One final thing: I do not want to give away our position early. War leaders will tell their men not to show themselves on the mountain. Keep away from the edge! And no fires . . . not even small ones. Is that clear?

"Now get what rest you can. We must be ready for the battle when the sun rises."

Like a general preparing for battle, Nathaniel had evacuated the entire village several times during the past year. Even the old and feeble had been helped or carried to the mountain. Once there, he had assigned work for each of them, including the children, and everyone knew what was expected to be done and why.

Log and earthen barricades had been erected at the entrance from the trail to the plateau, and a second barrier erected at the site of the gate that could be moved into position when everyone had reached the fortified haven. On top of the barricades he had positioned heavy logs. They could be released to roll down the mountain on top of an enemy trying to assault the fort. The catapults were loaded and ready; extra arrows had been placed in the scattered firing positions; water bags were filled. His force was poorly equipped with rifles—perhaps only 12 warriors or one-third of his men possessed them, and ammunition was in short supply. He decided ammunition would be used only as a last resort. Let the white soldiers think he had bows only. There was nothing more to do but wait for the sun to rise.

The Indian raiding party dispatched by Nathaniel returned before sun-up. They had killed six enemy soldiers quietly and as instructed by Nathaniel, dragged one of the bodies to the catch basin and dumped him in. They reported that no guards had been posted, but could not tell him the number of enemy soldiers in the camp. No matter, Nathaniel had told them, in the morning they would see the soldiers swarming like hornets. The battle would be joined, he said, because the commander would know Indians were lurking nearby and ready to fight. His announcement, made so calmly, was fulfilled at first light.

Looking down on the soldier army, Nathaniel guessed they numbered more than a hundred soldiers. His own force was less than a third of that, but he knew he could count on another thirty-five women ready to fight, and to support the men whenever necessary. He was not concerned about the difference.

For a brief minute or so, Nathaniel thought the commander would leave the village and move on. He could clearly see him gesturing wildly and walking back and forth as the soldiers on awakening started to collect their comrades and report them to the army chief. Several men gathered around him. Nathaniel suspected they were his staff, attempting to reach some decision after discovering the events of the night.

They kept looking upward and pointing, the sun back-lighting their movements, and he guessed they must realize where the threat lay. Damn! One of the villagers must have been spotted. He saw the commander send out runners toward the cannons and soon the booming of the guns and the burning black smoke left little doubt about what the commander was going to do.

The first volleys hit the rocks below the crest, and then started their ascent to the top as the gunners adjusted their guns. Nathaniel quickly passed word to the warriors to expect the bombardment to get heavier, but to withhold firing. He still had a small hope that the soldiers would pass on, assuming that no one was on the ridge above them.

"Do not show yourselves, but get your men in position. Cover the north entrance. If the white soldiers have discovered the trail, they will be coming there."

The firing continued as the cannon soldiers sent the cannon balls hurtling across the clearing behind him. The first one hit a shelter, and two women and children caught the blast and died. The screaming commenced, and Nathaniel could not stop the frightened cries. Another ball exploded, and still another part of the shelter was torn and tossed into the air, and several more Indians died. Nathaniel had not prepared for cannon fire, but he knew how deadly the explosions could be. These had been lucky hits. No one below could guess at the damage or whether they were killing anyone unless they heard the screaming from above.

Then to his horror, he heard yelling at the north end where the barriers had been placed. He ran there quickly and his fear was confirmed. The soldiers were attacking the fort. How they had stumbled onto the trail leading to the summit he did not know, but they were below the gate firing wildly toward the defenders. None of the warriors returned the fire, but they were ready to use the bows and arrows that had been stockpiled beside them.

"Keep down!" Nathaniel shouted. No longer was it necessary to maintain silence. "Use the bow! Let the soldiers come closer. "Now, shoot fast!" he encouraged them.

Bullets were ripping into the log barricades. As soon as the firing lulled, the Indians raised up and unleashed their arrows at the soldiers. They whipped through the air like angry bees and fell in the midst of a large group of soldiers. As Nathaniel watched the arrows impact, the men screamed and seven soldiers fell. The others retreated under the deadly hail of arrows.

The women manned the catapults. Turning to them now, Nathaniel ordered the first three to be released. They were loaded with small round stones.

"Strike the short catapults!" They were deadly. They struck the advancing attackers and knocked down another half a dozen men. This caused the others to scurry off the trail into the woods.

"Reload and stand-by," he shouted. His idea had paid off. The training he had given the women had now been proven.

"Hold your fire," he yelled. "Now strike the long catapults! Aim for the camp below."

The heavier catapults released their missiles. Nathaniel had left the north barrier and returned to the observation post. He could see the large stones hurtling through the air and striking below. He saw the first one hit close to one of the cannons where it shattered on impact. Stone fragments whipped among the gunners and they dropped in place.

"At least one group of cannon soldiers are out of commission," he thought. "May we be so lucky to hit another."

Again, the attackers surged up the mountain, encouraged by a young officer who had rallied the charge. Nantatola was directing the defense at the barricades. The soldiers were struck again from above by the short catapults and arrows hurling down. This time they retreated down the trail, licking their wounds and dragging the wounded. The officer kept yelling at his men to return, but they had been badly beaten and refused to mount another charge!

Nathaniel sent Little Eagle to find Grey Wolf.

"Give him my words to stand down," he instructed the boy. "But tell him to remain alert."

"I will tell him, Father."

"Tell him I do not think the whites will attack again today. It is getting too hot for them. They may wait until dark."

"Also, tell him, as soon as the sun sets, to send a party after the dead soldiers' rifles. Have him take the bullets off their bodies, and anything else we can use. But the rifles are the most important. Can you remember that?"

"Of course, I can."

"Then go, but be careful, Son."


The army commander had indeed been forced to call off the attack on the fort. He was surprised and frustrated by the events of the day. His casualties had mounted quickly. Of the assault force, thirteen had been killed and another six wounded. In the lower camp two had been killed and three wounded. The toll now was twenty-one dead and nine wounded in less than four hours.

His frustration and anger in not being able to dislodge the defenders gave way to unsound judgments. He gathered his officers around him in his tent. He sat while they stood before him.

"We will rest for the night and attack at first light! Captain, I want you to personally lead the assault."

The old captain, who had weathered many an Indian fight, stood watching the glaring eyes of the colonel. He thought it was a stupid order.

"My Colonel, I will follow your command, but you must realize we are not chasing Indians as we normally do."

"What? What do you mean?" the colonel shouted.

"Just what I said, Sir. This band has built a fort on the mountain. They are disciplined. They fight like white men fight. And they are using home-made weapons unlike anything we've seen before."

"So," the colonel screamed, "that is why you have the best equipment, so you can kill those heathens all the faster!"

"I don't think you understand, Sir. They have a commanding position. It is nearly impregnable."

The colonel was on his feet now, arms swinging around his body, eyes glaring madly, spittle running from his mouth. "How dare you question my judgement, Captain? I am in command here. You will follow orders. Do you understand?"

The captain, resigned to the colonel's foolish decision, stared at him, but said nothing.

"You have not answered me, Sir. Do you understand what I have ordered?"

"Yes, Colonel," he finally answered, "but you know our casualties will be high, and you must take full responsibility for ordering the men to their deaths."

"Out! All of you. You are nothing to me. Get out!" Then he reached behind him and started drinking from the brown jug.

At dawn, the guns commenced firing. The captain attempted to show the cannon soldiers where the barricades lay, but they were not able to adjust the cannon tubes properly, and the balls soared harmlessly over the fortifications. The assault group, led by the officers, again started up the trail. The bodies of the dead soldiers lay scattered where they died, but their rifles and other personal items had been stripped clean. None had been scalped or mutilated by the defenders. The captain ordered them removed before starting a new attack. The recovery process was met with little enthusiasm as the soldiers picked up their dead and thought about their own mortality, as they carried the bodies down the mountain.

It was mid-morning before the soldiers came against the barricades, but as before the Indians forced them back down the trail. This time only two were wounded as the soldiers grew wary and moved carefully in the assault. The captain, conscious of the strong position above, refused to order his men to attack again and for the reminder of the day they rested in the woods below the fort, only occasionally showing themselves to the Indians who waited above. Sporadically, the cannon fired toward the summit, and just as infrequently Nathaniel ordered the catapults to be released on the soldiers dug in below. That served to infuriate the colonel even more, and he ordered the cannon soldiers to resume their frantic firing at an enemy he could neither see nor kill, perched in the rocks above.

As he sat in his tent issuing insane orders to his officers, he reached for the jug and started drinking the harsh whisky to calm his nerves. Soon, he had put himself into a catatonic state. His eyes glazed over as a sweet lethargy permeated his body, and he closed his eyes and slept, immune to what was happening around him. It was the second day of the battle.

While he lay unconscious on his mat, the other officers met and tried to make sense of the fight and what they should do. The captain led the discussion. "I went to his tent, but he is sleeping off the whiskey. At least, he does us no harm when he is like this."

"What can we do?" a lieutenant asked.

"I think we should try and make peace with the Indians. This group appears to be peaceful. They tried to make us believe they had abandoned their village. They did not want to fight; they did not start the battle. Our illustrious colonel did that!" the captain said.

"I do not think we will be able to beat them," another lieutenant said. "They are well dug in. We keep losing men, and I see no sign of them letting us on the mountain. I say, let them live in peace."

"Then we must tell the colonel when he awakes."

"He will order another raid tomorrow," the lieutenant said.

The battle waged on. By the end of the second day it became apparent that both sides had suffered greatly. The white army had taken casualties far in excess of the Cherokees, but nearly a quarter of the villagers had been lost, either wounded or killed.

Nathaniel wished for the fighting to end. The cannon balls had taken their toll. Without calling a Council, he decide to launch a counterattack on the white army at the base of the mountain. He sent for Grey Wolf. When the warrior arrived, Nathaniel sketched out his plan. They would descend by the back trail and surprise the soldiers as they came upon the camp from the playing field. Twenty warriors would make the attack. With twelve rifles taken from the whites, all were now armed and ready for battle. A light rain had started to fall, a good omen for the attack about to get underway.

He found Nanatola standing under a shelter. "We can wait no longer, Brother. I am tired of the fighting and the killing. I plan to attack the soldiers tonight."

"I was certain that you would do that, Na-tan. How will you go down the mountain?"

"By way of the playing field. The whites do not know that trail."

"Can you not send Grey Wolf to make the attack? I believe you should stay with those left behind."

"Grey Wolf will go with me, but the warriors expect me to lead them. We should be in and out of the camp quickly. Perhaps then, the army will know we will not give up our land."

"I would go with you Na-tan, if I could. I think it will be a great battle." Growing serious, he said, "What you do is right. We must choose the right path to follow. And you have chosen well. Take care. May the Great Spirit be with you."

"Thank you, Brother. I do this for my people. I want them to have peace in this place."

The attack on the whites was devastating. Nathaniel and Grey Wolf led a two-pronged assault into the camp. The colonel, still in his drunken stupor, made a vain attempt to rally his men, but few were guided by what he said. Mass confusion reigned as the soldiers, awakened by the firing, lashed out at Indian and white alike, indiscriminantly killing as many of their own as did the raiders. The soldiers feared for their lives as the Indians moved among them, firing into their midst, and used the war hatchets brutally to win the battle. The colonel died screaming as Nathaniel sank his blade into the soldier chief's head, and he fell at Nathaniel's feet. In that instant, the commander's dream of glory vanished. He was not to know the Indian leader who ended his life was as white as he.

The whites were disoriented but tried to make sense of the battle. They fought valiantly against the night marauders, shooting and slashing as the Indians surged around them. Nathaniel was caught between two of the soldiers. As he raised his hatchet to bury it, one soldier fired and Nathaniel fell, the bullet tearing a great hole in his leg. A second shot entered his arm, smashing the upper bone. With his remaining strength, he pushed forward and sank the hatchet blade deep. It was his last conscious effort, and then he fell as the third bullet struck him hard in the chest and he collapsed on the ground.

The battle raged on and around the man lying still. Grey Wolf, remembering Nathaniel's words to hit hard and withdraw, now ordered the warriors away from the camp. As he passed the large rocks at the edge of the playing field, he sensed rather than saw movement in the shadow cast by the stones. He raised his axe to strike again, and with great horror and fear recognized the still, huddled figure of his Chief. Bending low over the unconscious body, he screamed to the Great Spirit to save his friend.

Then he called out to his men, and they lifted the broken body and carried the badly wounded man up the treacherous trail to the summit. Of the twenty-one attackers, two were dead and several wounded, but the tide of battle had changed forever. The next morning, when the rain clouds lifted, the saddened people watched the remnants of the army leaving the lower camp under a white flag of truce. It was a tragic end to the battle for a few brave Cherokees left behind.

# EPILOGUE

Nathaniel was terribly tired. The mortal wounds he had suffered in the final battle were draining strength slowly from him. Every part of his body screamed at him to give up and let the Great Spirit come to him. He closed his eyes for the last time and felt Snow Deer's hand grasping his tightly, willing him to stay with her. But the Great Spirit was not to be denied. It was just as well.

He was not to see the dissolution of the five civilized tribes of the Old Southeast. Friends and enemies alike would be pushed from the lands they held, and forced westward across the Tennessee and Mississippi Rivers and eventually take up their shattered lives in Indian Territory. The process of removal would start with his own people. Almost immediately, in 1801, tribal dissension rose again over the issue of land cessions.

Then in 1802, Cherokees met with whites after Sevier raided towns on the Hiwassee River, and the Treaty of Echota was signed. Cherokee lands north of the Tennessee River from Muscle Shoals to Hiwassee were sold to pacify the whites. The best hunting grounds the tribe had known vanished, and with them another strike against Cherokee independence fell. Jefferson, the great statesman, yielding to the pressure of his countrymen, continued his trading policies and resorted to bribing and corrupting the various chiefs.

Using a friendly Indian agent, Jonathan Meigs, the government gained cessions in 1804, 1805 and 1806. The Chickamauguas, led by the brutal and dishonest Doublehead, a chief of one of the lower towns, willingly gave up the Great Island of the Holston in exchange for pieces of silver. As a result of Doublehead's treasonable act, the tribal council established a new law in 1805. It decreed the death sentence for anyone selling tribal lands, and Doublehead was executed for treason in accordance with the law in 1807. The following year, the blood law, that had been set aside years earlier, was resurrected and clan revenge for the death of one's kin was reinstituted.

By 1819, the Cherokees land cessions with the government numbered twenty-six. During the War of 1812, the Cherokees had gone to war against the Creeks. When the Creeks were defeated at Horseshoe bend, large land cessions were forced on them and their days were numbered. Just a few years earlier, the Chickamauguas, the outlaw branch of the Cherokee Nation, left the great lands of the east and emigrated to their new home.

The United States still was not satisfied, and tracts of native lands in Alabama, Georgia, and Tennessee were exchanged for land further west in Arkansas. This great land, measuring 200 miles east to west, and 120 miles north to south, was soon to be lost forever. Despite the promises of the government that future migration cessions would stop, and that Cherokee independence and permanent residency would be granted, nothing of the sort happened.

Realizing the weakness of a loose confederation, and intent upon the protection and preservation of their remaining lands, the Cherokees painfully and reluctantly accepted religion and adopted educational programs with the aim of becoming assimilated in the white culture that surrounded them. It could not have been an easy task to replace their ancient culture by urgent assimilation, but they set out to do just that. It would not be enough.

As for the other Southeastern tribes, Nathaniel would never know that the Chickasaws and Choctaws went the way of the Creeks, uprooted from the lands their ancestors had established hundreds of years before. Nor would he know that Osceola, the Red Fox, Great Chief of the 'isti sim-a-no-le', the wild man, would put together an army of 5000 warriors, some of whom were Creeks from lands north of the Seminole Nation, and continue to fight eviction from the swamps of his homeland. With dogged determination, the Indians waged war with the whites in the Florida Everglades, not willing to give up their lands and go west. Then the old chief surrendered under a flag of truce and was thrown into prison. Suffering from malaria, he would die there in 1838, locked in a cell, dreaming of his beloved swamps.

In 1830, under the presidency of Andrew Jackson, "Pointed Arrow" or "Sharp Knife" the man whom the Cherokees respected and fought for in the Indian Wars, a man whom they had helped to defeat the Creeks at Horseshoe Bend, Alabama—this man, now called "Chicken Snake"— signed the Indian Removal Act providing for general re-settlement of all Southeastern tribes to lands west of the Mississippi.

After a successful legal battle, the Supreme Court, headed by Chief Justice John Marshall, ruled in 1832 that the Cherokee Nation had every right to remain on their homeland. Not to be foiled in his plan to move the Indians, Jackson arrogantly proclaimed: "John Marshall has made his decision. Now let him enforce it." It was good that Nathaniel would not know or see the anguish and the pain that followed.

In 1838, the Ani'-yun'wiya, the Principal People, a civilized tribe with its own society and culture assimilated into the white man's way, were dragged from their farms and homesteads and driven into stockades by government troops to wait for passage to Indian Territory. The resettlement, heartbreaking as it was for the Cherokees to leave their homes and many of their possessions, was obscene in the extreme. The lack of supplies, coupled with the hastiness of the westward move, was filled with heartache and despair and cold and disease. Four thousand Cherokees died in the roundup, the stockades, along the way, and within months after they reached their "Promised Land." The journey was called the 'Trail of Tears'.

A horrifying wilderness lay before them, one which they faced with fear and trepidation, a land of hostile tribal enemies and unscrupulous white pioneers. Few of the Southeastern tribes would ever know the winds that blow free as they had known it in their homelands. The air would no longer carry the fragrance of the forests or swamps or water, the gentle breezes that gave life and sustenance to the tribes and made them whole. Now they would suffer dust and feel the hot sun on their heads, and pray for rain. Many cried out to the Great Spirit to give them peace. They no longer wanted life; it was too bleak and foreboding in the new land.

So the wind blows softly now, across the great open spaces of Indian Territory, while in the mountains of Cherokee country the Eastern Band of Cherokee Indians rests. Here, a few strong descendants of those intrepid Principal People, the Ani'-yun'wiya, seek the promises of Nathaniel's vision made two hundred years before.